SINS OF THE FATHERS

When DCI Michael Thackeray enters the kitchen he finds the bodies of a mother and her young daughter, and outside a trail of crimson in the snow leads him to another girl, still alive. With Scott, another young child, missing and his father gone, the police conclude this is a domestic row turned violent. As Thackeray searches for the father, Gordon Christie, journalist Laura Ackroyd wonders just *who* the missing man is, for he left no personal items and there are no traceable records of him. Thackeray is driven to the brink of resignation before the full tragedy is uncovered.

SINS OF THE FATHERS

SINS OF THE FATHERS

by

Patricia Hall

Magna Large Print Books
Long Preston, North Yorkshire,
BD23 4ND, England.

British Library Cataloguing in Publication Data.

Hall, Patricia
    Sins of the fathers.

    A catalogue record of this book is
    available from the British Library

    ISBN   0-7505-2542-8

First published in Great Britain in 2005 by Allison & Busby Ltd.

Copyright © 2005 by Patricia Hall

Cover illustration © The Old Tin Dog

The moral right of the author has been asserted

Published in Large Print 2006 by arrangement with
Allison & Busby Ltd.

Magna Large Print is an imprint of Library Magna Books Ltd.

Printed and bound in Great Britain by
T.J. (International) Ltd., Cornwall, PL28 8RW

Chapter One

The boy could not understand why it had all turned out so badly. But he was old and wise enough to have known immediately that the appearance of a gun on a morning's outing over the moors was a threat, not a joke, although his father still seemed to be smiling, a fierce, rigid sort of smile that was in no way reassuring. That sort of gun anyway was never a joke, never just a bit of fun, as his dad might say when things got a bit out of hand; that sort of gun was not for shooting rabbits. No way. And that was not the first thing which had gone wrong and filled him with dread since he had been picked up as he had dawdled down the road to school, more than usually reluctant to go because his sister had been allowed to stay at home with what she claimed was a bad cold, more likely a test today, really, he'd thought.

The snow had come on suddenly soon after they had set off, rattling icy flurries against the windows at first, rolling and bouncing across the road in front of them even as the sky turned from grey to almost black. Within ten minutes it was nearly impossible to see out of the windows, the wipers struggling to keep even a narrow triangle of the screen clear. They slowed down as the demarcation between the edge of the road and the edge of the moor became blurred and then disappeared completely. He had pressed his face against the cold glass, misting it up with his breath and then wiping the mist off with a red woollen glove, and he had realised that there were striped poles at intervals along the edge of the road, marking out the way, but they were swinging wildly by then as the tyres struggled to keep their grip.

The boy's panic grew as eventually they slid to a halt, wheels whining, nose down close to one of the poles where the front had found an ice filled ditch rather than solid ground and, for a moment, he thought they would tip right over and he clung to the seat in front, trying not to scream. Outside he could see nothing but the whirling white flakes, a dancing blanket which seemed to suffocate the vehicle, allowing little light into the interior. Inside he felt sick and his breath seemed to come in small pants as he concentrated on the outside world, trying not to look over the seats into the front of the car where he knew there was nothing but danger and some sort of madness. He could feel it like a vice around his chest.

Cautiously, making no sound, he took hold of the door handle and pulled. There was a shout from behind him and then the stunning reverberation of a shot in a confined space but he had already fallen headfirst into the soft wet snow as soon as the door swung open and he felt nothing as he staggered to his feet, his boots scrabbling and sliding for a purchase in the ditch and up the other side. He heard more shots behind him but nothing hit him and he realised that he must have become almost invisible as soon as he moved a couple of feet into the whirling storm. He glanced down at his anorak and saw that he was already white from head to foot, like a snowman, he thought, momentarily delighted at the thought, before the terror overtook him again.

Behind him he could still hear a voice shouting. Terrified, he ignored it, plodding on through the deepening snow and still visible tussocks of grass until finally he could hear nothing at all except the wind which was already whipping up small drifts. I'm like one of those explorers in the arctic, he thought, but not optimistically. The snow had already worked its way into his wellington boots and his feet were beginning to feel very cold. His anorak hood was little protection from the gusty squalls and his ears tingled at first, and then began to stab him intensely. He knew that he needed somewhere to shelter, and he knew that shelter would be difficult to find up here, and he began to cry.

9

He never knew how long he struggled across the moor, shivering and sobbing, his tears turning to ice which clung to his cheeks. He had no watch, and after what seemed like hours he stumbled and came to rest in the lee of a half-demolished drystone wall where the snow provided a soft enough resting place for him to begin to relax as numbness succeeded the fierce pain in his feet and hands and ears. He no longer had the strength to get back to his feet. Someone would find him there, he thought. Someone would come.

Half asleep, curled up with his arms round his knees in search of warmth he couldn't find, his mind wandered. Funny to be lying here in so much snow, he thought. It was almost like the sand at Guincho, deep and soft and slippery, but cold and wet while the sand had been too hot to walk across to the sea. His father had been good then, enjoying the sunshine and taking him into the waves and jumping him over them in strong arms, the spray catching him harmlessly and making him scream in a frenzied mixture of fear and delight. Dad had been different then. Dad had been fun. None of this would have happened then.

He closed his eyes and felt the snowflakes settle on the lids, but he could no longer find the energy to brush them off. He could not find the energy for anything any more. In spite of everything, he hoped his dad would come and fetch him soon. Perhaps then everything would be all right and they could go back to the hot sun and the thundering, shimmering sea and the burning sand. That's what he would like to happen, he thought, as he drifted into sleep beneath the deepening blanket of snow. He would like to see the sun, and the foaming waves and the golden sand again...

DCI Michael Thackeray pulled on the regulation plastic overalls he was required to wear before venturing into a crime scene with an expression of distaste. He knew he should not admit it, even to himself, but he found himself increasingly reluctant to become a voyeur of death. You didn't become more inured to it. In fact, he had found the reverse to be true, although he had undoubtedly become more expert at hiding his feelings when he faced the constant reminders of mortality, often bloody and frequently stomach-churning, which his career provided. Flurries of snow whipped around his legs and shoulders, sliding off the white plastic but clinging to dark hair and eyebrows and beginning to settle quickly on the frozen ground. Behind them the hills had disappeared beneath heavy clouds, rolling in fast from the north. It would not be long, he thought, before they were enveloped in the blizzard which seemed already to be raging

11

across most of the Pennine hills.

Thackeray glanced at Sergeant Kevin Mower, who was tying plastic overshoes over his smart city loafers. From what they had been told before they had driven from police headquarters to this cottage at the very farthest edge of Bradfield, he knew that this particular catastrophe would test his stomach and his ability to disguise his feelings to the limit. Even as he pulled up his hood, two anxious looking paramedics appeared from round the side of the cottage carrying a stretcher and the inert form which lay on it, already attached to a drip, was painfully small. Children had been hurt here, or worse, and he found that the hardest thing of all to bear.

'Right?' he asked Mower brusquely, and together they moved through the cluster of parked police cars, past the ambulance and into the narrow doorway of the cottage to be met by the grim-looking scene-of-crime officer.

'How many?' Thackeray asked, his mouth dry.

'Three,' the SOCO said. 'Woman and a child dead, another child as near as dammit. All shot.'

Kevin Mower whistled faintly between his teeth.

'Weapon?' Thackeray asked, but the SOCO shook his head, his eyes shadowed and unreadable beneath the plastic hood. Everyone, Thackeray thought, was put through the wringer by this sort of case, and he knew his own vulnerability only too well.

'No sign,' the SOCO said. 'But it's a pistol job, not a shotgun as you might have expected out here. An automatic – we've found cartridge cases. It's slightly less messy than a shotgun, but not much.' He smiled mirthlessly.

'No sign of the perpetrator, then? Not hanging up in the garage, by any chance?' Mower asked, his voice deceptively casual though his eyes were as bleak as Thackeray's. 'That's the usual scenario.'

'Uniform have done a thorough search of the property,' the SOCO said, not smiling. 'It looks as if the bloke worked here as a mechanic of some sort. There are work-shops at the back, but no one there, no car, no gun, certainly no suicide. Zilch. Who-ever's responsible for this has scarpered, and probably a while ago. The pathologist hasn't arrived yet but the bodies are pretty cool already.'

'Not surprised, in this bloody weather,' Mower said, glancing at the leaden sky out-side the front door with a city man's deep mistrust.

'They've been forecasting heavy snow for days,' the SOCO said.

'We'll take a look now,' Thackeray said,

knowing his voice was unusually strained and conscious of Mower's eyes quickly flicking in his direction. 'Let's get it over with.'

They followed the SOCO into the main hallway, past the open door of what was obviously the living room, scantily furnished and scattered with toys, and into a kitchen which appeared to be an extension at the rear of the original stone structure of the cottage. But what had been a comfortable family room, the table still covered by a buttercup yellow cloth and a clutter of used dishes, had been turned into a charnel house. A woman who might once have been pretty lay sprawled on her back on the tiled floor, with a gaping wound where her left eye should have been and a pool of blood around her head and clotted in her untidy blonde hair. Closer to the door was the sight Thackeray had been dreading and which caused Mower too to take a sharp breath. A small child of perhaps three or four lay face down near the open door, as if she had been running not towards her mother, whose protection had probably already been beyond reach by then, but in a desperate attempt to escape the other way on still babyishly chubby legs from the fate threatening her from behind. One small hand reached beyond the threshold, its fingers splayed on the doorstep, the other still clutched a small brown teddy bear drenched in blood. She had been shot more than once the observers guessed, her back reduced to a mass of bloodily clotted fabric, her blood spattered over the tiles and onto the kitchen cupboards closest to her remains.

'Jesus wept,' Mower muttered under his breath while Thackeray simply stood transfixed, his face ashen and his breath shallow as he swallowed down the nausea which threatened to overwhelm him and tried to banish the image of his own son, still as clear as the day when he had found him dead, back into the dark recesses of his mind.

'What's the betting it was her own fucking father,' the SOCO said, his voice far too loud in the crowded space.

'Where was the other child found?' Thackeray asked sharply. 'The one who survived?'

'Outside,' the scene of crime officer said. 'She was hit in the back too, and another shot creased her head, from what I could see, but she seems to have dragged herself into one of the barns out there. The bastard seems to have gone completely berserk with the gun. I've counted six or seven bullets without even trying. Shall I show you?'

Thackeray nodded and the three men stepped over the small child's body, all of them taking deep breaths of the bitterly cold air as if their lives depended on it as soon as they stepped outside. In one corner of the yard there was more blood in a viscous, half-frozen pool from which a smeared trail led into what was little more than a shed half-filled with workbenches and tools. The swirling snow was already beginning to soften the outlines of the yard, covering frozen mud and, quite possibly, vital evidence.

'She was lucky to be found in time.' The SOCO's voice was dispassionate. 'Apparently she was semi-conscious when she was discovered by this bloke who came round looking for the father, Gordon Christie he's called – the father that is. All this is from the first uniform on the scene. Christie had been doing some work on this bloke's lawn-mower and he turned up to fetch it about eleven this morning. Says he found the front door open and he went inside, poor sod. Found the kitchen the way you just saw it and staggered out here to be sick. Heard some moaning and found the surviving kid just over here. Had enough sense to dial 999 on his mobile. Lucky to get a connection, apparently.' The SOCO glanced down at another rusty stain where blood had soaked into the dusty wooden floor of the shed.

'Will she survive?' Thackeray asked. 'What did the ambulance crew say?' He hoped neither of his colleagues would guess from the question just how fiercely he wanted the answer to be optimistic.

'She was lucky not to have bled to death, they said. They weren't holding their breath

16

they'd even get her to hospital alive.'

Thackeray wearily ran a hand through his unruly dark hair. He felt cold and suddenly immensely tired as if the sheer weight of this outrage against an innocent family was crushing him from above. He closed his eyes briefly as he tried to steady his heart rate and re-order his disjointed thoughts.

'So we've got a double murder, an attempted murder and a hundred to one a man who's blown his own brains out somewhere not far away. Wonderful,' he said. He turned away from the two younger men and walked slowly around the yard with his hood pushed back and the snow clinging to his dark hair, glancing into the various sheds and outbuildings where Gordon Christie evidently pursued his trade. Then he made his way to the side gate and the narrow lane beyond where his car was parked close against the hedge. Mower followed quickly, catching up with his boss where he was leaning against the door of the car, apparently oblivious to the bitter cold and the thickening snowfall. Mower said nothing but his eyes were full of anxiety. He had lost a lover, and survived, just, but was still able to admit that to lose a child must be the worst death of all. And to lose a child and blame yourself for the death, as he knew Thackeray did, must be a hell he could barely imagine.

'Set it all up, Kevin, will you?' Thackeray

asked, his voice weary and his expression unreadable. 'You know what needs to be done – a statement from the man who found the bodies, a trawl of the neighbours to find out what you can about the family – and get a search under way. He won't have gone far. They never do. But if we don't find him before this weather closes right in it might be weeks before he turns up. Get the chopper out if you need to. You could lose an army of gunmen up here in a blizzard.'

'Right, guv,' Mower said. He glanced around at the square stone cottage behind them, sheltered from the prevailing wind by a spur of dark millstone grit topped by heather and rough grass, and at the rutted lane and scrubby fields and patches of faded grassland between the Christie home and the rest of the village of Staveley. He shrugged. 'Not many neighbours up here.'

'Chat up the village. I was brought up in a place like this, remember? They'll know everything there is to know about the Christies, and then some. The suburbs are creeping out here but they haven't quite taken over yet. There'll still be plenty of folk who've spent their whole lives in a village like this and whose eyes are sharper than they ought to be. You'll see. The wife must have done her shopping somewhere, the kids must have gone to school, he's obviously got customers he's been doing work for. They may have some idea where he could have gone. And when the scene of crime people have finished and you can get in there again, give me a call. I'm going back to HQ for now. I'll report to the super and organise an incident room. This looks like one of those where we don't need to work on the who, we just need to know the why for the coroner.'

'Right, guv,' Mower said again, wondering if it was ever possible to pin down anything as rational as a motive for such an unfathomable outburst of rage as this must have been.

'What I've never understood in these cases is the arrogance of the fathers,' Thackeray said slowly. 'I can understand a man rowing with his wife, perhaps using violence, even killing her, but the kids as well? Why the hell does he need to kill the kids?'

It was a cry of pain and he turned away abruptly and got into the car, where Mower watched him briefly rest his head on the steering wheel, his shoulders hunched, before he started the engine. He let the wipers clear the snow off the screen, then eased the car forward and down the lane.

'Jesus wept,' Mower said to himself again, guessing how much of that story might have been Thackeray's own, though never to the extent of violence turned against a child. He needs this case like he needs a hole in the head, he thought, and his sense of deep foreboding only grew as he turned back towards the cottage and steeled himself to face the slaughter inside again.

The snowfall accelerated its whirling descent almost as soon as Thackeray had driven away, and Mower realised that the forensics team would have difficulty amassing any evidence from the murder scene that was not under cover in the cottage or its outbuildings. He gingerly picked his way back towards the front door, astonished at how quickly the soft heavy flakes had begun to settle on the narrow paved pathway and the lawn in front of the house, but before he could go back inside he became aware of a flurry of activity behind him. He turned and found himself face to face with a small red-cheeked woman, her face barely visible beneath an enveloping hooded duffel coat and scarf, with snow clinging to her head and shoulders.

'Whatever's happened?' she asked, breathlessly. 'I knew there was summat wrong when I saw the ambulance come back down the lane with its lights flashing. Is someone hurt? Has there been an accident? Are Linda and the children all right?'

'And you are?' Mower asked.

'Dawn Brough,' the woman said, her agitation barely under control. 'Linda's a friend of mine. The kids are all at school together.' She glanced at the cluster of police vehicles behind them. 'Are you with the police? What on earth's been going on?'

'DS Kevin Mower, Bradfield CID,' Mower said briefly. He brushed the snow off his hair irritably. 'You'd better come and sit in one of the cars out of this stuff. We can't go inside just now.'

The woman followed him obediently, her face pale and set, as if she had already guessed the truth, although Mower knew that what he had to tell her would far exceed her worst imaginings. As they huddled on the front seats of one of the patrol cars she listened to what Mower had to say with her eyes full of tears, which eventually brimmed over and poured down her weather reddened cheeks.

'I'm sorry,' she said. 'I don't think I've got a hankie.' Mower reached awkwardly into one of his pockets and pulled out a packet of paper tissues which she used to dab her eyes dry.

'It's all right, Dawn,' Mower said. 'It must be a shock. Have you known the family long?'

'Well, not the family, not really. It was just Linda and the kids. Gordon was an odd man, not friendly at all, you never got much more than a good morning or a good afternoon out of him if he was around. But I met Linda at the school gate, as you do, you know?'

That was a parental pleasure Mower was in no hurry to explore. If he had ever had any ambitions in that direction they had been brutally snuffed out some years before by a single bullet. But he contained his irritation and let the woman talk at her own pace, allowing her to come at least partly to terms with the unthinkable.

'We both had one in a buggie at the time, when the Christies first arrived. My Jenny's at school now. And little Louise is due to start next term.' She hesitated, realising what she had said and the tears began to flow again. 'Was due to start. Oh God, I can't believe this...'

'Let's take this another way, Dawn,' Mower said. 'It'll be easier for you. Tell me where you live, and when you first got to know the Christies. How about that? Have they lived up here long?'

'No, not long. A couple of years, that's all, two and a half, maybe a bit longer. My house is the first of the new ones at the end of the lane. We're their closest neighbours, really, though it's not that close, must be half a mile. I always thought this cottage was a bit isolated but Linda never complained. It was on the market for ages before the Christies bought it. But when Linda and I discovered we both lived at this end of the village she started to bring Louise down for the afternoon sometimes, to let her and

Jenny play together.'

'And did you bring Jenny up here?'

'Not really. Not nearly so much anyway. As I say, Gordon was a strange man. Unfriendly really, and he worked up here a lot, in his workshop at the back. I don't think he liked visitors. I came up once or twice but I think she only invited me when she knew he'd be out. I never saw him much at all.'

'You say they'd been here a couple of years. Do you know where they came from before they moved here?'

'They lived abroad, I think. Spain, Portugal, somewhere hot. I don't think Linda ever said where exactly, but she talked about how nice it was to live in a hot climate. Especially in the winter. I think this place got her down a bit. She didn't seem like a country woman, to me, and as I say this cottage is a bit isolated, a bit remote.' She glanced out of the window where the snow was now coming down hard and covering the windscreen. 'Give this weather another couple of hours and you won't be able to get up the lane without a four wheel drive. You can get really snowed in up here.'

Wonderful, Mower thought. Finding Gordon Christie looked like becoming more difficult by the minute. He started the engine and put the fan on hard.

'What did Gordon drive then?' he asked.

'Oh, an old Land Rover thing. Not one of

these smart new all-singing, all-dancing tanks with central heating. More the sort of muddy old thing the farmers use up on the moors. I don't know how good it would be in the snow. It looks clapped out, my husband always says.'

'I don't suppose you know the registration number, do you?'

'No.' Dawn Brough looked ready to cry again as she worked out the implication of the question. 'He's disappeared, hasn't he? He's not here?'

Mower shook his head briefly.

'Did you have any idea he had a gun?' he asked.

'A gun? You mean a shotgun? A lot of the lads around here have shotguns. Shooting rabbits is a local sport. And lamping foxes at night.'

'Not a shotgun. More likely a handgun, a pistol of some sort. Did Linda ever mention that he was interested in guns?'

Dawn shook head and swallowed hard before she answered.

'I know he used to hit her,' she said, her voice choked with emotion. 'Linda never said owt. They don't, do they, battered wives? But I saw the bruises. She couldn't always hide them. I think he was a violent man and he beat her up. But what really upset me was that I once saw Scott with a bruise down the side of his face. He said he fell in the yard but

I didn't believe him and I didn't know what to do about it...'

'Scott? Who's Scott?' Mower interrupted her sharply.

'Scott's the son. There's three children: Louise, Emma and Scott. He's eight, I think, maybe nine now. Adored his dad, though I could never understand why.' She glanced at her watch. 'Scott and Emma should be at school now, but they come home for lunch...' She looked at Mower with wide horrified eyes.

'Emma's not at school, she's in hospital,' Mower said, all the sympathy gone from his tone now as he was seized with a terrible sense of urgency. He revved the engine hard. 'Show me where the school is,' he said, letting in the clutch gently and skidding slightly across the fresh snow as he set off down the rutted lane. 'We need to find Scott.' But less than ten minutes later he found himself standing in frustration in the porch of the village school calling Michael Thackeray on his mobile and getting a less than perfect signal.

'Guv,' he said urgently. 'Can you hear me? There's a Christie son, called Scott, eight years old. He should be at school but the headmaster says he's not. And he's not one of the victims. Not that we've found so far, anyway. I think the father must have taken him with him. He drives an old Land Rover,

25

apparently, so we need that chopper right now. The boy might just possibly still be alive.'

Chapter Two

Laura Ackroyd sat with her legs tucked underneath her toying with a vodka and tonic and waiting for Michael Thackeray to come home. She had left the curtains open at the high sitting room window and could see the snow weighing down the trees in the garden outside. The fall had lasted the best part of the day but now the clouds had cleared, a crescent moon and Venus hung in the navy blue sky like jewels, apparently almost close enough to reach out and touch, and the world outside the warm flat was silvered and shimmering in the frost. But the wintry scene did not fill her with the exhilaration it might have done. She had spent a tense afternoon in the newsroom of the *Bradfield Gazette* trying to concentrate on her own work while nervously aware of the horrific story that was unfolding on the crime reporter's computer screen nearby, knowing that the murders at Moor Edge cottage in Staveley would be the last thing Michael Thackeray needed after the traumatic death of his wife, Aileen, a couple of months earlier.

She had heard nothing from him all day and assumed that he still intended to come home for the meal she had prepared, which was now filling the flat with a savoury aroma that told her that it was ready. But she did not feel like banking on his arriving in time to eat it. She had almost ceased banking on anything with Michael these days. Since she had sat beside him through Aileen's requiem mass at her parents' church in Northumberland, he had not, as far as she knew, had another drink. But his hand had clutched hers so fiercely throughout the service that she had lost all feeling in it by the time the coffin was carried out and they fell into line behind Aileen's parents to move on to the burial at a bleak and windy hillside cemetery on the edge of the town. Back home, the iron control with which he usually conducted his life appeared to have returned, to the extent that she barely knew what he was feeling or thinking from one day to the next. They were speaking little and communicating anything of significance even less. The loss of Aileen, which should have been a relief after all the years she had spent in hospital, instead seemed to have cast a pall over their relationship which Laura had so far found no means of lifting.

She sighed and gazed at the bubbles in her glass, alert for the sound of a car on the road outside. But the surface had already been covered with compacted snow when she had parked her own Golf outside, and it would now be turning, she guessed, to ice. The blanket of snow muffled the normal sounds of the town going about its business and the silence seemed heavy and oppressive. She wondered if the police could still be searching for the murdered family's father in the dark. She could not imagine that the fugitive was still alive. She was as convinced, as she guessed Thackeray would be, that cases like this did not usually have any sort of happy ending and she knew how that would crush him, though if past experience were anything to go by he would not tell her so. He would, as usual, say nothing at all.

'Damn and blast,' she said explosively as she got up to turn the oven down in the kitchen and refill her glass. 'How can men turn on their own children like that? It's monstrous.'

On any other night she would have called her friend Vicky Mendelson to help unburden herself, but she knew that Vicky was away visiting her sick mother and there would be no opportunity to share confidences there. Even Vicky's mobile phone was unreliable in the pocket of the Cumbrian valley where her mother's cottage was. And as she sat on alone, sipping her third V and T and watching the moon slip slowly across the sky, her anger grew so that when she heard Thackeray's key in the lock and he came into the room looking grey with fatigue, all she could think of to say was 'Have you got him yet?'

Thackeray shrugged himself out of his coat and scarf.

'No,' he said. 'You can't put men on foot out there in conditions like this. The drifts on the moors are four foot deep. We've got the chopper up, looking for unusual signs of movement now the snow's eased off. But I think he's long gone. Judging by the state of the cottage the family were shot around breakfast time and not found until almost midday. He could have been out of the country by then.'

'Or long dead,' Laura said, vodka on an empty stomach making her bolder than she would normally have been in stepping into Thackeray's domain.

'And buried under the snow. It could be a week before we find them up there,' he said.

'Them?' Laura said.

'He seems to have taken his eight-year-old son with him,' Thackeray said grimly. 'I don't really expect to find either of them alive, to be honest.'

'I didn't know about the son,' Laura said, appalled.

'We didn't realise he was missing straight away,' Thackeray said.

'How can they do that?' she asked. 'Why do they imagine that if they die everyone else has to die with them? Arrogant bastards.' Laura could not contain her anger, although she knew it would do neither of them any good.

'Oh yes, they're all of that,' Thackeray said, turning away from Laura so that she could not see his face.

'Can we eat?' he asked, obviously as unwilling as she had expected to discuss his own reaction to the case.

Laura got to her feet somewhat unsteadily and crossed the room to put her arms round Thackeray's neck.

'We can eat,' she said. 'Or we can just go straight to bed. If you're interested in that, at all?'

Thackeray disentangled himself from her embrace and flung himself down in a chair, not answering directly.

'Sometimes I wonder if I can go on with this job any more,' he said, and the words jolted Laura back into some sort of sobriety.

'You don't mean that,' she said quietly. 'The job's part of you. You're good at it. You know you can make a difference.'

'How can I make a difference to a four-year-old child with not one but four bullet wounds in her back? What can I actually do about that, whether her killer is still alive or already dead? What bloody difference can I possibly make?'

'Oh, Michael,' Laura said, with tears in her eyes. 'I'm sorry.'

Laura sat in the *Gazette*'s editorial conference the next morning doodling idly on her notepad as the chief reporter ran through the agenda of that afternoon's council meeting with mind-bending slowness. There must be, she thought, some connection between a reporter's character and the specialism they chose to follow. She could easily imagine the paper's crime reporter, Bob Baker, commonly to be seen, even in the office, in designer shades and a sharp suit, hustling for Mr Big in some sleazy scam, while sweet-faced Jane Archer, who liked nothing better than to write a feature about nursery schools or the downside of testing young children to destruction, looked as though she could run a Montessori establishment with her own eyes tight shut.

It was just the same with Steve Edwards, who was now boring the meeting rigid with an agenda even more tedious than the one which would occupy the town council's cabinet for most of the day. She could remember a time when Steve had displayed some sparkle, even inviting her out once to a club in Leeds where an ecstasy-fuelled throng had danced until well after dawn. But the town hall job seemed to have sucked him in and spat him out altogether smaller and greyer and with all the life choked out of him. She must, she concluded, get herself out of the *Gazette* before some similar fate overtook her.

She was startled out of her daydream by the editor, Ted Grant, bellowing her name from the far end of the table.

'Are you with us, then, Miz Ackroyd?' Ted wanted to know, with a dangerous glint in his blue eyes, obviously having failed to gain any response to earlier inquiries. 'Do we get owt on our feature pages today, or do I hand 'em to sport for an extended inquest on United's slim chance of escaping relegation to the Vauxhall bloody Conference?'

Laura grinned, and pushed a stray strand of copper hair out of her eyes, although she knew no charm offensive on her part would mollify Ted. The dislike, personal and professional, was too long entrenched now for either to budge an inch and there had been more times than Laura could count when she had concluded that she had better jump ship before she was pushed. But this morning, at least she thought she had something which might mollify her boss.

'For today we've got the stuff Jane did about the new technology academy they're opening officially tomorrow,' she said. 'Loads of loot and a mission statement direct from God, apparently. But I thought for later in the week we ought to do a spin-off from these murders out at Staveley. It looks like another case where a father's gone ape and wiped out his entire family. We've had a couple of these cases in the last twelve months. I looked up the cuttings. I thought some sort of background piece on the stresses that drive men to those lengths, why they get so desperate they want to take the kids with them, all that stuff, might make a good page. Obviously we can't talk about this case in particular until they find the bloke and his son, but...'

'Did you say his son?' Grant asked suspiciously. 'Do I know about a son?' He hauled his substantial bulk upright and went to the door of his office. 'Bob!' he shouted across the busy newsroom. 'Get in here, now.'

Bob Baker, looking flustered for once, did as he was told and stood awkwardly in the doorway under the concentrated gaze of the paper's senior staff.

'These murders out at Staveley. Laura here says there's a kid missing as well as the father. Why don't we know owt about that?'

Baker flashed Laura a look of unadulterated dislike.

'My contacts are bloody good,' he said. 'But they'll never be as close as hers, will they? Stands to reason, I can't compete with pillow talk. Officially no one's said anything about a kid being missing, as far as I know.'

'The eight-year-old son,' Laura said, knowing that she had no choice although she realised with a sinking feeling in her stomach that she seemed to be breaking a confidence which she had not imagined existed. 'So I'm told, off the record, of course.'

'You'd better check it out,' Grant said to Baker. 'If they're hunting for a kid on the moors in this weather that's the front page lead, and it's bloody late to be standing it up. Let's get on with it, shall we? Chop chop! Soon as you like!'

The meeting broke up in disarray and Laura assumed she had gained permission by default to pursue some research into violent families. As she settled back into her desk she caught Bob Baker's eye across the room.

'Bitch,' he mouthed at her, and she stuck out her tongue in response. She could not imagine why the police had failed to reveal to the *Gazette* that they were looking for Gordon Christie's son as well as the man himself, but she had no sympathy to spare for Bob Baker. She knew he had made himself so unpopular at police headquarters that the Press office could conceivably have left him out of the loop deliberately. Baker had picked up his phone and now seemed to be shouting unintelligibly into it. Laura smiled to herself. Embarrassing Bob Baker was the least of her worries. In fact it constituted one of life's little pleasures.

DCI Thackeray had arrived at the Christies' isolated cottage by eight that morning, parking his car in the icy ruts that had been left by the dozen or more vehicles which had been up the snowy lane the day before. Not even a lowly panda car remained now, and the cottage faced the world with blank, dark windows in the early morning light. With Kevin Mower on his heels, Thackeray had been waved through the front door by the uniformed constable stationed morosely in the porch. He was in a more steely frame of mind than he had achieved the previous day, determined not to let his own demons cloud his objectivity. The forensic examiners had completed their meticulous work by now, packed up their samples of blood and hair and fibre; fingerprints and footprints and traces and smears of unidentifiable materials had been found and collated; the pathetic bodies of the two victims discovered in the kitchen had been removed to the mortuary. The house had been left overnight, empty and forlorn, the detritus of everyday life all that remained of the family of five who had lived there until yesterday, the dirty breakfast dishes on the table the starkest indication of how normal service had been so catastrophically interrupted.

Thackeray came to a halt in the still blood-stained kitchen and took stock, aware that Mower was watching him while seeming not to. The place smelt of death and he swallowed hard to control his revulsion.

'So let's think what can this place tell us?' he said, with unusual uncertainty. 'Let's assume, for now, it's Christie we're looking for, shall we?'

'No one's come up with any evidence that there was anyone else here, guv,' Mower said mildly. 'Forensics may say different, of course. But there's no sign of a break-in.'

'Right, so if it's Christie we want, he evidently had a gun. Where did he keep it? He had a pretty ancient Land Rover. Where are the documents? He had a business. Was it in trouble? Did he have other financial worries? Did he have a dodgy past which caught up with him? Was he being treated by a doctor for anything, mental problems maybe? In other words, what the hell motivated this massacre?'

'There's not always an obvious reason,' Mower said. 'These things sometimes come right out of the blue.'

'I don't believe that,' Thackeray said. 'There has to be some underlying cause, and it's usually pretty obvious: marital trouble, financial trouble, depression. See if you can find his doctor. There can't be more than one practice out this way.'

Mower nodded. 'And his bank manager,

his customers, and whatever family he has left,' the sergeant enumerated. 'So far everyone we've talked to in the village says they appeared here a couple of years ago, she was pleasant enough, he was the strong silent type, the kids were well behaved and well-turned out, and they never talked about where they came from.'

'No visitors?' Thackeray asked.

'Not that anyone could recall, guv. Only customers. He was a good mechanic, by all accounts, and didn't overcharge, so people were soon bringing him odd jobs. But Mrs Christie's friend Dawn did say one thing which seemed a bit odd when I eventually got back to her. She said they didn't seem short of money.'

Thackeray looked at Mower for a moment.

'What's she suggesting? Lottery winners hiding from their family or what?'

'She just seemed puzzled, that's all. She didn't seem to think that Gordon Christie could be earning enough from his business to keep five of them in the style they seemed to be living in. Good quality clothes for the kids, a long holiday in Spain last summer ... people notice these things, don't they?'

'And this is quite a substantial house, as it goes,' Thackeray said thoughtfully. 'A bit run down but what – four bedrooms? A big yard and garden behind. The way house prices are going it must have cost a bit.'

'Dawn said it was on the market for £250,000.'

'Right,' Thackeray said. 'You stay up here, Kevin, and go through the place for anything that fills in the gaps. I've got Val Ridley at the infirmary with the surviving child in case she regains consciousness.'

'And the chances of that are...?'

'Remote, apparently,' Thackeray said, his face perfectly impassive. 'In the meantime we've got the chopper quartering the moors again in case the Land Rover's up there somewhere in the snow. What I need as top priority is the registration number of that vehicle. The DVLA can't trace anything in Christie's name, or Linda Christie's, which is very odd. See if you can find the registration document and let me know. I'll send Sharif up to help you as soon as he gets back from court.'

'Right, guv,' Mower said. 'And you'll be...?'

'I'll go to the post-mortem, for my sins, and then I've got a meeting with the super, who's planning a Press conference this afternoon when he wants to expand on the fact that the son's missing as well. That should get us some coverage in the national papers and TV. If Gordon Christie's responsible for this mess I'll not be too bothered if we find him dead in a ditch. It's the boy I'm concerned about.'

There's a surprise, Mower thought. Thackeray might think he was concealing his emotional involvement in this case, but to anyone who knew him as well as the sergeant did, Thackeray's painful accommodation to the case was as clear as day.

Mower glanced around the room.

'No photographs,' he said. 'Hang on a minute. I think there's something in the other room.' But he returned holding only a single cardboard frame.

'Just this. A school photo of the two older kids,' he said. Thackeray took it off him and gazed at the two children, both blonde and blue eyed, the girl, shyly smiling at the camera, who was now lying fighting for her life in the infirmary and the boy, a couple of years younger and with a mischievous glint in his eyes, the son who had vanished with his father. He felt suddenly suffocated.

'Let me know if you find any others. I'll keep this for the Press conference,' he muttered, striding quickly to the front door and brushing past the uniformed constable who was stamping his feet to keep them warm.

Mower watched him go. He had no children himself but he knew only too well what strong emotions they aroused in others. He hoped for Thackeray's sake that this case would be resolved quickly before it shattered the iron resolve with which he normally led his life. But the cracks, he thought, were already beginning to show.

Chapter Three

By lunch time Sergeant Mower and Detective Constable Mohammed Sharif – generally, and apparently happily, known as Omar – were sitting in the sitting room at Moor Edge surrounded by the meagre results of the morning's close search of the Christie family's lives. And nothing, they had concluded gloomily, gave them much inkling why Gordon Christie might have turned a powerful handgun on three members of his family and subsequently vanished with his son.

Mower shrugged and glanced down a checklist he had made in his notebook. Amongst the documents on the floor in neat piles was a log book for a Land Rover, which had apparently been registered in 1989, but of which the DVLA in Swansea could find no trace – not for Christie or any previous owner. As far as officialdom was concerned the Land Rover with the registration number on the document simply did not exist. There was also a series of unexceptionable bank statements dating back just under three years which revealed a steady but modest income stream, presumably from Christie's repair business, but also with occasional and totally unexplained injections of large sums of cash.

'Whoever he was, he was up to something dodgy,' Mower said. 'I thought the banks were supposed to be watching out for un-explained cash payments but no one seems to have noticed this.'

'I think it's only sums over £10,000, sarge,' Sharif said.

'So maybe that's why he's been paid £9,000 a time, for whatever it is he was paid so generously for,' Mower said.

'Or maybe he's only put that much into the bank at any one time,' Sharif suggested. After all, there is the money we found in the wardrobe.' He glanced at a blue leather sportsbag stuffed with notes which they had found hidden behind Christie's meagre selection of neatly stored clothes upstairs. The whole house, Mower had thought as they worked their way around it, had been preternaturally tidy, with a place for every-thing and everything in its place, even in the children's bedrooms, where the toys and books and even the teddy bears were neatly marshalled into their allotted places. Some-one, he concluded, had had this home in an iron grip.

'You'd better count that lot before we go any further,' Mower said, glancing at the bag. 'We don't want any allegations that a few hundred went walkabout.' Sharif glanced at Mower with dark, unreadable eyes, as if unsure whether or not to be insulted by this remark, but he pulled a bundle of notes out of the bag anyway, and began to count.

'I'll call the boss and give him this registration number,' Mower said, without much enthusiasm. 'Though if the plates are false, Christie may have changed them for another set by now. If you can lay hands on one false set you can no doubt lay hands on another if you need them. And I'll bring the DCI up to date on the rest of what we've found before we tackle the garage and the workshop. There's no papers at all here for his business so I guess they must be out there somewhere. He's obviously a meticulous bastard, so he'll have them filed away safely for sure.'

'The other odd thing is that there's no passports for any of them,' Sharif said. 'I thought you said they'd lived abroad.'

'So the neighbour said,' Mower said. 'Damnation, we should have looked for a passport sooner. If he's taken it with him we need to alert the ports. I'll pass that on, too.'

Sharif glanced around the sitting room where they had displayed some meticulousness themselves in working through every drawer and cupboard but had left the place very obviously less tidy than it had been before they began, and he wondered, like most of his colleagues, at the mental explosion which must have led to the carnage of the previous day. He came from a community where fathers were known occasionally to turn their wrath on their children, on their daughters in particular, and he understood, though he did not condone, the motives for that. But this father's terrible rage, this madness turned against small children, he did not understand at all. He hoped Gordon Christie was dead while hoping equally fervently that his son was out there somewhere and still alive. While Mower continued his phone discussion with headquarters he pulled the sportsbag towards him again and tipped the bundles of notes onto the floor and began to count again. They were used and dirty and he felt defiled.

Half an hour later they had moved out of the house and into Christie's workshop at the back of the house, where the pool of blood in which his older daughter Emma had been found had been sprinkled with sand and the door closed. But when Mower opened it, he did not find what he expected. The previous day, when precedence had of necessity been given to the forensic examiners, he had glanced briefly through the door and immediately taken on board the carefully ordered layout of the skilled craftsman: tools in racks, nuts and bolts and screws in their individual small cabinets, the workbenches tidy, the floor swept clear of debris, the rubbish binned and the small desk and filing cabinet in one corner clear of any sort of junk.

Mower took a deep breath as he surveyed what was inside and held an arm across the doorway to prevent Sharif from following him inside.

'Go and get that woodentop off the front door,' he said angrily. 'Someone's been in here before us.' The workshop was no longer tidy. Paperwork was strewn on the floor around the desk, the drawers had been pulled out and turned upside down and several of the cupboards along the back wall also appeared to have been ransacked. What, if anything, had been taken would be almost impossible to know, Mower thought, and he knew that his fury at the carelessness which had allowed this to happen overnight would be nothing to Michael Thackeray's.

Behind him he heard Sharif return and spun round to face the uniformed constable who followed him.

'Were you on duty here overnight?' he asked, his voice harsh. But the constable, his face boyish under the helmet, shook his head dumbly, his eyes anxious.

'I came on at eight,' he said. 'I don't think

anyone was up here overnight, sarge. There was no one here when I was dropped off. The place was locked up, they told me. They just gave me the keys to the house.' He dug into his trouser pocket and pulled out the bunch of keys which he had used earlier to open the front door for them.

'Is there one for this door?' Mower asked, gesturing at the workshop, but when they examined the keys carefully it was evident that there was not.

'So this place was probably left unlocked all night?' Mower curbed his anger, knowing it should be directed elsewhere. 'Bloody marvellous. Why didn't they put up a sign inviting the local burglars in? Did you check round here at all?'

The constable nodded.

'I had a walk right round when I arrived,' he said. 'It all looked in order to me.'

'You didn't think to try the doors?'

The constable shook his head uncomfortably.

'I didn't think of that, sarge,' he mumbled.

Mower glanced around the still snowy yard which was just beginning to thaw, the tracks left by the previous day's invasion beginning to darken and fill with water.

'If they've left any signs out here they'll be gone in half an hour,' he said bitterly. 'The same with car tracks in the lane. How did you say you got up here?' He turned again to the

45

uncomfortable constable who was stamping his feet to keep out the insidious cold.

'The panda car dropped me off,' he said.

'Are you the community bobby for the village?' Mower asked.

'No, that's Gav Hewitt. He brought me up, but he's on the front desk at the nick this morning. It's a bit of a laugh, this community stuff, when we're so short staffed, to be honest. I don't reckon they get round their patch more than once a week.'

'How far away's the nick,' Mower asked, still caught out occasionally by Bradfield's complicated and hilly geography. 'Thornton Lane, is it?'

'Aye, that's right, three miles or so. Technically we're still in Bradfield here, but in fact we're out in the sticks. You can see that.' He gestured with ill-concealed contempt at the open moorland which loomed darkly above them beyond the end of the track which led to the cottage. 'Nowt out there but sheep and the odd tumbledown barn. Not for miles. They reckon you can walk to Scotland without getting to another bloody village from here if you just keep going north. Nowt but heather and sheep and grouse and the odd road to cross. So Gav Hewitt says.' The constable was obviously not impressed by this piece of local folklore.

'I'll have a chat with your PC Hewitt later. For now we'd better see if our nocturnal visitor has left anything we might be interested in. Come on Omar, let's see if we can find anything useful. Hopefully the intruders were more interested in the odd Black and Decker than the paperwork. Let's see shall we?'

At police headquarters DCI Thackeray was standing in the main control room listening to the conversation between the police helicopter pilot and his controller, his face taut with suppressed anger. It was clear that the pilot and his observer were drawing a complete blank as they worked their way at low level in increasingly wide circles over the open countryside around Staveley. Many of the remote moorland roads were still impassable to vehicles and so far they had found no sign of the missing Land Rover holed up anywhere within a ten mile radius of the Christie's cottage. This was the second sweep they had made above the barren hilltops and moors and Thackeray knew that the enterprise was beginning to look like a waste of time and resources.

He knew the sort of countryside they were searching: the miles of unfenced moor and bog on the high fells, with small fields squeezed into the valleys divided by tumbledown stone walls and dotted with often derelict barns; the boggy surface frozen at this time of year but still terrain where even the most robust four wheel drive would have difficulty manoeuvring, and certainly not without leaving a clear track through the snow. Thackeray was increasingly convinced that if there was no sign of Christie and his son trapped up there in the freezing wilderness then he had probably made his escape much further afield, and he worried, in the light of what Mower had told him about the absence of passports in the house, that he might not only still be alive but be attempting to flee abroad with his son.

'Tell them they might as well pack it in,' he said gloomily to the control room manager. 'They're wasting their time up there. I think he's long gone. Have you put out the registration number to the ports and airports?'

'We put out a general call last night for the two of them,' the manager said. 'We've added more details this morning.'

'But no response?'

'No sightings at all so far, sir.'

Thackeray spun on his heel and pounded up the stairs to his own office, thankful to be moving vigorously, if only briefly. What had seemed like an open and shut domestic tragedy was showing disturbing signs of turning into something more complex and it was time, he thought, to do something about that possibility. When he opened his office door he was only mildly surprised to find Superintendent Jack Longley standing by his window, evidently waiting for him to arrive.

'Sir?' he asked.

'Have you found him?' Longley asked, and his usually cheerful countenance darkened when Thackeray shook his head.

'It doesn't look as simple as we thought,' Thackeray said. 'I'm organising a full house-to-house around the village this afternoon to see if we can pick up anything else about the family that might help. And I want every copper in the country looking for that Land Rover. I think if he'd shot himself – and probably the boy as well – we'd have found them by now in spite of the weather. He wouldn't go far to blow his brains out. Why should he? If the tragedy happened after the lad had set off to school that would explain why he took the vehicle and maybe picked him up before he got there. Or maybe the boy ran, and he chased after him in the Land Rover...' He swallowed hard to control the turbulent feeling in his stomach which had dogged him ever since he had stepped into the murdered family's kitchen the previous day.

'The girl who survived, Emma, seems to have run out of the house and it looked as if even the little girl tried to as well, but couldn't quite make it. That would make sense if he shot his wife first.'

He stopped talking, knowing that if he pictured the probable shooting scenario too clearly in his mind's eye he would not be able to go on. Longley looked at him sharply, and the question in his eyes was obvious.

'It's all right,' Thackeray said quietly. 'I can cope. It's a lot to ask of the whole team, especially those who went to the house. These things are always difficult to handle if children are involved. You never really get inured to it. But we'll deal with it, one way or another.'

'Sure?' Longley asked.

'Sure,' Thackeray said firmly.

'You'll be at the Press conference at two?' Longley asked.

Thackeray nodded. 'I want to concentrate on the Land Rover,' he said. 'Mower's come up with some odd things about Christie's lifestyle, and the vehicle itself looks dodgy, but the urgent task is to find Christie and the boy – dead or alive. I can't see why he should decide to drive miles to finish the thing off in the way we expected, quite honestly. So if he's not been discovered in the immediate vicinity by now it's possible he's run with the boy for reasons of his own. And Kevin can't find any passports in the house, either, even though they're supposed to have lived abroad, so maybe he's got a long trip in mind, perhaps back to wherever they came from. And just maybe we're looking for someone else with a gun. Perhaps it's not a domestic at all.'

'You haven't found the weapon, I take it,

50

so we're assuming he's taken it with him?'

'Whoever used it has taken it,' Thackeray said. 'The house and workshops have been searched and the area round the house seems to be clear, though the snow's not making it easy. But what's not helping is that Christie's workshop was ransacked last night and there are some lockers that are empty. Kevin says there's oil and grease around, but that could just be from tools rather than firearms. I've told Thornton Lane nick that I'm less than happy with the level of security they provided overnight, and sent forensics up there again to look at the workshop for prints and anything else they can find, but there's no way of knowing what's missing. Mower's brought all Christie's paperwork back here and he's going through it now. It was scattered around his workshop, so even that's not simple.'

'So if we locate the Land Rover, we have to assume Christie's armed? I need to tell county that,' Longley said.

'We have to assume that,' Thackeray agreed. 'Kevin found a shotgun securely locked up inside the house, carefully cleaned and put away. But as I say, there's no sign of the murder weapon, which seems to have been an automatic pistol, according to the cartridges forensics found. Until we find Christie and the boy we just don't know. So we'll leave everything else under wraps with the Press, and concentrate on the missing boy. We've got a photograph of him and the sister who's in hospital, so we can use that. Nothing of the parents so far.'

'A photograph of Christie himself would be useful,' Longley said.

'He seems to have been a retiring sort of man, does Gordon Christie,' Thackeray said. 'No pictures so far, sir.'

'They're often the ones who explode in the end,' Longley said. 'Bottle everything up for years...' He stopped, realising he was treading on dangerous ground.

Thackeray allowed himself a wry smile.

'Tell me about it,' he said softly, as Longley opened the door and eased his bulk through it. He hoped he might be the only one to recognise aspects of himself in the portrait of Gordon Christie he was beginning to glimpse through the fog. But he would not, he thought, be so lucky.

Chapter Four

The road to Staveley village swung into a hairpin bend at a gradient that Laura Ackroyd found slightly alarming in the grey slushy snow that still narrowed the carriage-way at each side. At the top of the hill she found herself in a narrow square with a car park off to one side where she found a space facing up the main street, which twisted through stone cottages to end in a narrow single-track lane across the moors. To the left, the squat village church sat in its tiny overcrowded graveyard, the stone tombstones at random angles and black against the lingering drifts. To the right a red and gold post office sign hung outside a small shop right next door to the Fox and Hounds, another low stone building whose walls and gables seemed to have sunk and tilted over the years to offer a slightly drunken face to the world.

The shop or the pub? she asked herself as she crossed the road. The lights were on at the pub but inside the bar appeared deserted and she opted for the shop, where she could see the silhouettes of customers through the steamy windows. But if there had been, as she suspected, animated chatter before she arrived, there was total silence when she opened the door and stepped inside. Three women well muffled against the cold clustered by the checkout counter where a dark-haired young Asian woman fingered her electronic keyboard nervously. Laura smiled and pulled her own scarf more loosely round her neck.

'Chilly out,' she said. The oldest of the shop's customers offered a thin smile.

'A bit parky,' she conceded and Laura guessed that curiosity would overcome reticence in the end.

'I'll be off then, Doreen,' one of the other women announced, picking up her shopping bag and opening the door. 'I'll see you next week.' She closed the door quickly behind her, letting in a draught of icy air as she went, and the second woman in the check-out queue began to unload her basket onto the counter next to the till. The older woman, last in line, looked Laura up and down carefully with sharp blue eyes in a lined face but said nothing.

'Dreadful business, this shooting,' Laura said to nobody in particular. 'It must be up-setting to have something like that happen out of the blue in a small village.' Her best hope pursed her lips, which creased the peach coloured powder with which she had dusted her face liberally.

'Sightseeing, are you?' she asked, her voice as icy as the weather. 'One of them ghouls they talk about in t'papers?'

'Not exactly,' Laura said. 'I'm from the *Gazette*. I'm going to write something about crimes like this, whole families getting murdered. It's a dreadful thing...' Suddenly the second customer turned away from her shopping just as she was about to pay her bill, and Laura was startled to see tears in her eyes.

'D'you know how Emma is?' she asked. 'She were one of our Samantha's best friends at school and I don't know what to tell her. She wouldn't go this morning. I couldn't persuade her. She thought someone would come after her with a gun.'

Laura took a deep breath, knowing she was treading on ground so delicate it could open and swallow her up.

'She's as well as can be expected, I think. You know how hospitals put it. That's what I heard in the office this morning before I came out again.'

'Poor little lamb,' the older woman said. 'It's a dreadful thing to say, but she might as well be dead wi' all t'rest o't'family gone. How's she going to get over that? How can anyone get over that, never mind a little lass like that? And the little lad? Is he still missing then?'

'I'm afraid so,' Laura said carefully. 'Did you know the family, then?'

'By sight, that's all,' the older woman said. 'Kept themselves to themselves by all accounts. But that Gordon, he looked a right surly beggar to me. Though I did hear he were a good car mechanic. I don't suppose that Weldon up at t'Old Hall would have employed him else, would he? He'd not put up wi' owt shoddy, the brass he's lavished on that place since he bought it. More money than sense if you ask me, but that's the way it is these days. More money than sense, most folk. They change their curtains almost as often as they change their knickers, some of these youngsters. Never crosses their minds to wash 'em instead.'

'Mrs Christie was a nice lady,' the girl on the till said suddenly, causing three pairs of eyes to swivel in her direction. 'She was always a pleasant lady. And her children were well behaved in the shop.'

The unspoken comparison with other children hung in the air for a moment before Samantha's mother snapped her purse and her expression shut before picking up her shopping bag.

'You can never tell with men, can you?' she flung over her shoulder as she pushed her way out of the door. 'You just never know.'

The second woman put her purchases on the counter to be paid for.

'D'you want a cup of tea, love?' she asked Laura unexpectedly. 'You look fair starved. Warm you up a bit?'

Laura snuggled into her scarf again and tried not to smile too enthusiastically.

'That'd be very kind,' she said. 'Thanks.'

The woman, who introduced herself as Dorothy Emmett, pulled her coat hood up over her tightly permed grey hair and led Laura across the slushy village street to one of the stone cottages on the other side. Even the handle on the sturdy wooden door gleamed with much polishing and, inside the chintzy living room, a myriad knick-knacks and ornaments sparkled – and covered every inch of horizontal space in the room and much of the walls as well in a kaleidoscope of shape and colour.

'Sit yourself down, love,' Dorothy said, taking off her coat and hanging it on one of the hooks provided by the front door. She bustled into the kitchen and Laura heard her put the kettle on and the chink of cups being arranged. When her hostess came back with a loaded tea tray she felt duty bound to accept a piece of the heavy fruit cake which was passed in her direction.

'You look as if you need building up,' Dorothy announced, helping herself to an equally generous hunk. 'You're much too thin, you modern girls. I can't see the attraction of looking like a clothes prop, myself.' She was not a woman to spare herself the duty of offering helpful advice, Laura thought wryly as she bit tentatively into the cake and found it delicious, though she hoped it would not push her far towards Dorothy's ample proportions. She settled back in her soft and capacious chair.

'So don't you think anyone had any idea the Christie family was in trouble?' she asked.

'Staveley's a close village,' Dorothy said, after a long pause for consideration. 'You could say we don't take to strangers right quickly. Mebbe we're at fault there, but I can't say as I know anyone who'd got to know the Christies well. You used to see her wi't'pushchair on the mornings the playgroup were running in t'church hall. She'd bring the little one down at t'same time as the other two came to school. The other mornings she let them walk down thisselves. It's safe enough down that lane, I dare say. There's no traffic to speak of between the cottage and the school and Emma looked like a sensible little lass.'

'Did Mrs Christie not have any women friends then? I thought they'd lived here two or three years.'

'I saw her talking to Doreen, that's little Samantha's mother who were in t'shop just now. But I'd not say they were right close. And I think she knew Dawn Brough from t'new houses up at t'top there. But as I say, they seemed to keep themselves to themselves mostly. You'd see t'whole lot of 'em going off to t'supermarket on t'Bradfield Ring Road on a Friday after school finished. She didn't use t'village shop much. I don't think I had more than a couple of words with her all t'time they were living here. She were very quiet, and he were an evil-tempered looking fellow, though I don't like to speak ill o' t'dead. You'd bid him good morning and get nowt but a grunt back. He looked the type to go doolally with a gun, if you ask me. A nasty bit o' work, by t'look o' him. Ruled those kiddies wi' a rod of iron an' all, so I'm told, though that's no bad thing these days, wi' most of 'em running wild before they're out of nappies.'

'You must have lived here a long time,' Laura said.

'All my life,' Dorothy said with satisfaction. 'There's not a lot of us left now, though. Most o' t'village is newcomers. Live out here and rush off to work in Bradfield or Milford, or even Leeds, some of 'em. Can't do 'em any good, all that rushing about, but it's all change these days, isn't it? Change for changes sake half t'time, if you ask me.' She passed the plate of cake towards Laura who shook her head.

'Where did the Christies come from?' Laura asked. 'Does anyone know?'

'Someone said they'd been abroad, but I don't know where. Came back because she didn't like it, apparently. I don't know why folk are so set on living in hot places myself. All them snakes and insects.' Dorothy shuddered. 'Any road, they came back with enough brass to buy that place. It's a good solid house, is Moor Edge – belonged to the Fawthrops for years. They had sheep up there until young Jim Fawthrop went off wi' some bit o' stuff from Leeds. Wi' all them outbuildings at t'back it were ideal for Christie.

He set himself up there with a repair business and seemed to be making out well enough, by all accounts.'

'And Mrs Christie didn't work?'

'No. T'little one were only a babby when they blew in. There's not much work for women out here unless you've got your own car. Buses only come up every hour and sometimes not even that if t'mood takes 'em. Some of them go down to that call centre place in Thornton, but Linda Christie never did, as far as I know. He must have been doing all right with his repair work. They never seemed to go short, those kiddies.'

Dorothy shuddered and her face creased with genuine pain.

'How could anyone do that?' she asked and Laura shook her head helplessly. She could offer no answer at all.

Ten minutes later she lifted the latch on the wooden door of the Fox and Hounds and found herself in a dimly lit bar entirely empty of customers. Oak tables and stools clustered around the huge open fireplace, which was still filled with the ash from what she assumed had been the previous night's roaring fire. She glanced around the bar curiously. It was decorated to overflowing with slightly tarnished horse brasses and pewter tankards, notices about village events and photographs of long-superannuated cricket teams. TV advice on décor and the fashion for turning country pubs into trendy restaurants didn't seem to have penetrated as far as Staveley, yet, she thought wryly. This was an old English pub, unexpurgated in its scruffiness and no doubt the haunt of unreconstructed countrymen for miles around.

Eventually, the thick red curtain at the back of the bar was pushed aside and a heavy set dark-haired man with a full beard and appraising blue eyes, came towards her. She assumed from his proprietorial air that he must be the landlord, the Gerald Foster whose name was on the license board over the door.

'What can I get you, love?' he asked, without much enthusiasm and certainly with no hint of a welcoming smile. She ordered a vodka and tonic and perched herself on one of the tall stools next to the bar and introduced herself.

'I'm covering this shooting at Moor Edge Cottage,' she said, taking on board the landlord's frozen expression at the mention of the *Gazette*. 'Not the police investigation so much,' she said hurriedly. 'I'm not a crime reporter. I'm much more interested in some background about the family. How something so dreadful can happen to a perfectly ordinary family, which the Christies seem to have been. Did you know them at all, Mr Foster?'

'Not for quoting in the newspapers, I didn't,' the landlord said, not disputing his status. 'I'd not want anything I said about my customers repeated in any rag, would I? Stands to reason.'

'Off the record, then?' Laura said. 'It's only for background. I want to write about how quite ordinary families suddenly explode like this. Not just the Christies – there's been quite a few cases like this in Yorkshire recently. Apparently quite normal fathers, in most cases, suddenly losing it. Don't you think it's a frightening thing?'

'Frightening?' Foster asked grudgingly, as if the thought had never occurred to him. 'You never know what's going on in anyone's head, do you? That's a fact, if nowt else is.'

'Was Gordon Christie a customer of yours? Was he a regular?'

'I told the police all I know about Gordon Christie when they came round yesterday,' Foster said. 'And that's not much. I doubt if any beggar got the chance to find out what went on in his head, any road. He came in, ordered a pint of Tetleys and a whisky chaser and sat in that corner over there and drank them. Sometimes he'd have two, but not often. Many customers like him and I'd be out of business.'

'He didn't come in to see friends then?'

'I don't think he had any friends, and

that's a fact. He were a right loner.'

'But he must have talked to someone,' Laura said, getting desperate.

'No,' Foster said, vehemently. 'I don't think I ever heard him say owt to anyone, certainly nowt pleasant. He was a loner, was Christie, I told you. And surly with it. If he'd just blown his own head off he'd not be missed. Doing it the way he did it, I reckon most folk in the village will wish him in hell.'

Laura drained her glass thoughtfully as she digested this vehement denunciation, but she did not get the chance to follow it up as the door opened, wafting cold air into the bar. She half turned as two burly men in green Barbours and heavy boots made their presence known with much huffing and puffing and blowing on hands.

'Morning,' the landlord greeted the newcomers, with only slightly more enthusiasm than he had offered Laura. He might, Laura thought, usefully turn his complaints about taciturn and surly customers in his own direction. A beaming benevolent host he was not.

'Morning Gerry, a bit parky out,' one of the newcomers said. 'Who's this you're sending to perdition today, then?' He picked up on Foster's last words which he had evidently overheard. He nodded at the empty fireplace. 'A few flames in here wouldn't come amiss on a day like this.'

'My missus has gone down to t'cash and carry. She generally sees to all that,' Foster said huffily.

'Right, well we'll have two double malts to warm us up a bit,' the newcomer said. He glanced at Laura with an interrogative smile. 'Can I fill yours up, love?' he asked. The face was broad and looked recently shaved and there was a whiff of expensive aftershave about the man which surprised Laura slightly, but the eyes beneath the close-cropped hair were pale and chilly in spite of the generosity of his offer.

Laura shook her head. She did not feel encouraged to continue her inquiries with this pair.

'Thanks but I'm just off,' she said. But she was not to be allowed to withdraw so easily.

'This lady's a reporter asking about Gordon Christie,' the landlord said over his shoulder as he held the glasses under the optic behind him. 'From the *Gazette.*' The two newcomers looked Laura up and down for a second before the man who was obviously the senior partner of the duo smiled again, though without warmth, and offered his hand.

'Bruce Weldon,' he said. 'I've just had a policeman knocking on the door because I made the mistake of employing Gordon now and again.'

'Half the village employed him, Mr

64

Weldon,' the landlord said. 'He was a miserable beggar but he was damn good at what he did and he didn't charge over the odds. He serviced my lawn mower last year. How was anyone to know it'd end up like this?'

'No, well, that's what I told the copper who came calling this morning. They'd found my name amongst his records, believe it or not. I don't think I've spoken to the man for six months, but he did some work on my cars for me last summer. I thought I'd paid him in cash, no questions asked about VAT and all that rubbish, but he must have made a note. Daft, that. Asking for trouble if the VAT officers come calling.'

The two men took their drinks and turned away from the bar to take one of the tables close to the empty fireplace and Laura guessed, looking at their broad dismissive shoulders, that she would get no further with them. It was as if they and the landlord had staged that little conversation to pre-empt any further questions she might feel like asking. She shivered and fastened her coat more firmly and pulled her scarf around her neck. She felt oppressed by Staveley and the village life which had obviously had no inkling of the impending tragedy in its midst. The hurly-burly of the *Gazette* newsroom suddenly seemed much more inviting than it usually did.

An armed man, a boy and a Land Rover can't just disappear off the face of the earth,' DCI Michael Thackeray said angrily as he and his team reviewed the progress – or lack of it – of the Staveley murder investigation at the end of a long and frustrating day. 'The top priority in this investigation now is to find an eight-year-old boy who, as far as we can tell, is in the company of an armed man who has already killed twice. As I told the Press conference earlier, finding Scott Christie alive is what this is about. What's the latest on the search, Omar?'

DC Mohammed Sharif glanced down at his notes.

'All the roads over Staveley moor are open now, sir, and the snow's melting fast,' he said. 'But the chopper's still not sighted anything significant. Mobile units are up there now scouring the ground at least until it gets dark. If they've gone any further, we've had the registration number out there for the best part of the day and there's not been a single sighting so far. Nothing from CCTV anywhere has been reported. Nothing from motorway or street cameras. A blank, in fact.'

'Start working on garages. If they've gone far they must have stopped for petrol,' Thackeray said.

'I reckon the vehicle must be under cover somewhere,' Sergeant Kevin Mower offered.

'Either that or at the bottom of one of the reservoirs up there in the hills. You could sink a tank in one of those lakes and no one would be any the wiser till the next drought brought the water level down.'

'We'll have a long wait for that after this winter,' a voice from the back of the room muttered.

'I've asked for the search teams to keep looking until they can't see a hand in front of their faces,' Thackeray said, trying to fight off the immense weariness which kept threatening to overwhelm him. He was aware of Kevin Mower's sharp eyes watching him, for signs of weakness no doubt, and was determined to give neither him nor anyone else cause to question his ability to handle this case. His own doubts, he reckoned, were his own affair.

'There are barns up there that don't see anyone for months on end at this time of the year,' he went on, confident that if nothing else he knew the terrain around Staveley. 'But if he doesn't turn up locally soon I think we have to rethink the suicide theory and assume he's made a run for it, taking the boy with him, for whatever reason. And with a powerful handgun involved that's a serious problem. We need to alert serious crimes, other forces, whoever.'

'And in that case the absence of passports in the house has to be significant,' Mower added. 'He's probably taken them with him.'

'The picture of the boy on TV tonight may help,' Thackeray said, trying to inject some optimism into the proceedings to boost the team's obviously flagging morale. 'There's no doubt people take more notice of a case if children are involved.' He ignored the tightening of his own stomach as he contemplated the recurring image of Gordon Christie's dead wife and daughter and the likelihood that his son had already met a similar fate.

'Val,' he said. 'Anything on next-of-kin?'

'Nothing, guv,' DC Val Ridley said. 'Kevin found nothing to indicate any relations at the house – no address book, no mobile phone, though that's not necessarily significant because reception in Staveley's notoriously poor. We've turned nothing up on any of the computer bases we've got access to. No one questioned in the village has recalled any mention of grandparents or aunts and uncles. They really do seem to have been a completely isolated family and the father seems to have done everything he could to keep them that way. And he's been self-employed, running his own business, so there's no old employment records. Apart from odd references to living abroad, possibly in Spain, they might have dropped into Staveley from another planet for all we've been able to find out about them. I'm waiting for the itemised bills for the fixed phone as we speak. That may give us some clues.'

'No one can be that invisible,' Thackeray said.

'Unless...' Kevin Mower paused, as if reluctant to finish the sentence. Thackeray looked at him, waiting.

'Unless he's hiding from someone or something. Or being hidden. It might be worth checking with our own people. He could be on a witness protection scheme of some sort.'

'With a wife and three children?' Thackeray's tone was sceptical, verging on the dismissive. 'That's not normal procedure. It's too dangerous for the family. You can't keep kids locked up in safe houses.'

'So maybe he was trying to protect his wife and three children on his own account,' Mower suggested. 'We've never strayed far from the assumption that Christie himself was the gunman up till now. But what if he wasn't? What if he was the target?'

The meeting fell silent as they took this idea on board.

'What have we got from forensics on the bullets?' Thackeray asked eventually.

'Nothing yet, except the calibre,' Mower said.

'Well, give them a kick up the backside and say we need to know everything there is to know about that gun,' Thackeray said. 'If it's on record anywhere I want to know about it first thing in the morning. I never like the assumption that any crime is "just a domestic". A domestic victim is just as dead as any other and just as deserving of justice if we can provide it. And this domestic is beginning to look distinctly odd in any case. I don't like the smell of it one little bit. I think it's time to redouble our efforts, don't you?'

Chapter Five

DC Val Ridley took a detour into the intensive care ward at Bradfield Infirmary on her way into work the next morning, as she had ever since Emma Christie had been brought in two days earlier. One of the nurses on duty at the desk smiled at her vaguely as she came in.

'Any change?' Val asked. The nurse shrugged, glancing at the small form in a large bed, wires and tubes attached to more machinery than any lay person could comprehend.

'She was a bit restless in the night,' the nurse said. 'I was just writing up her notes for the day shift. It could be a good sign, or it could be nothing.' Val nodded her thanks and approached the bed. As far as she could see the pale face on a delicate stalk of a neck, eyes closed, chest barely moving with each assisted breath, looked no different from the way it had looked the day before. What hair was left after the doctors had cut it away was limp and lifeless, so blonde it was almost colourless, the rest of her head heavily bandaged. An inch to the left and the bullet which had creased her skull would probably have killed her, the nurse had told her the day before. Emma had been lucky, but perhaps not lucky enough. The bullet wound in her back had required major surgery and her life still hung on a thread. Val guessed that the gunman supposed her dead when he left her bleeding on the floor. Judging by the way he had pumped her sister's body full of bullets, there seemed little doubt as to his intention to kill the whole family. Emma's survival was some sort of miracle, although Val doubted that she would see it that way if she ever regained consciousness.

She took the chair by the bed and gazed sightlessly at the floor. The child hovering between life and death had only deepened the pall which the original shooting had caused throughout CID and although she had perfected a stoic face for the rest of the world, she was not immune. The usual motives for murder – lust, greed, revenge,

sudden anger – she could at least comprehend. Parents who turned their rage on
their children she could not. Emma's
mother and father should be sitting here,
holding her hand and willing her to live, she
thought angrily, not a police officer she
would not recognise if she ever did open her
eyes again. It was the ultimate betrayal.

She glanced at her watch. She was late for
the start of her shift at police HQ but she
was reluctant to move on. The silent, immobile child in the hospital bed pulled her
back to the ward at every opportunity and
she knew that her anxieties were not only for
Emma herself. If the child recovered she
guessed that the physical damage would
eventually heal and be forgotten. What
brought the tears pricking at her eyes was
the utter isolation of this survivor and the
knowledge that the damage that inflicted
would last forever. She shook her head
irritably and squared her shoulders to try to
settle her emotions, when she became aware
of another presence by the bedside. She
jerked herself back to reality to find a tall,
elegant Asian woman in a black trouser suit
and a silky scarf around her shoulders looking at her speculatively. She put down her
briefcase on the floor and pulled up a chair
from the next bed and sat down next to Val.

'Are you a member of Emma's family?' the
woman asked with a smile which faded as

Val Ridley explained who she was and how CID could find no trace of family for Emma.

'I'm from social services,' the woman said. 'Razia Qureshi. I was going to call the police later this morning to check out Emma's exact situation. If there are no relatives on hand we'll have to make an emergency care order and take over parental responsibility for her. The hospital will need consent for further treatment of a child. Strictly speaking they shouldn't have operated on her at all without consent, but no one bothers too much when it's a life or death situation. The doctors do what they have to do.'

Razia Qureshi nodded slightly to herself, as if confirming her own judgement, and ran a hand across her immaculate dark hair.

'I feel very bad about this,' she confided, her face sombre now. 'We should have seen it coming.'

'What do you mean?' Val asked, astonished.

'I didn't hear about the shooting until last evening, when my boss rang me at home. I'd been away for a few days. He wanted me to talk to the police straight away but I thought I would come and see Emma first.' She spoke with very little accent but what there was betrayed her Yorkshire birth.

'You knew about the family?' Val asked, her voice hardening. 'Social services knew about them?'

'I knew about them, personally,' Razia said, glancing down at the floor, uncomfortable with the admission. 'It was about six months ago and we had an anonymous complaint from someone in Staveley, some neighbour, she said, worried about the little boy. She thought the father was hitting him.'

'And was he?' Val asked sharply.

'I don't know,' Razia said. 'I went up there and saw all the children and the mother, who denied that there was anything wrong. In fact the children seemed well cared for, no signs of ill-treatment, happy, I thought. You have to understand that I have more than forty families on my casebook and with most of them there's no contest; they have serious problems, the kids are at risk, they're neglected or they're playing up, or there are all the signs of abuse of one sort or another. But I couldn't pick up any signs with the Christies except that the father was volatile, irascible – he came back in the Land Rover as I was leaving, demanded to know who I was and threatened me with violence if I ever came back. I can hear him now. "I'll effing kill you, you interfering cow," he said. "Paki cow," actually, though that's not the worst thing I've ever been called. We get a lot of abuse.' She smiled faintly. 'Not all of it racist.'

'I'm sure,' Val said, as Razia twisted her hands in her lap. 'But you never went back?'

'I told them I would be back, as a deterrent in case there was anything in it. I didn't like the father, obviously. But I never did go back. I put it on the back-burner, something to keep an eye on perhaps if I ever got the time. But I never found the time. There never is enough time in this job. And now...' She looked at Emma Christie, whose shallow breathing never faltered beneath the white bedding. Val swallowed down her initial anger.

'You couldn't have predicted this,' she said briskly. 'I don't see how anyone could.'

Razia shrugged. 'Maybe,' she said. 'If the newspapers get hold of it they'll pillory us, as usual.'

PC Gavin Hewitt shuffled uncomfortably in his canteen chair and gazed down at his industrial strength cup of tea.

'It's not always so easy to get out there as often as I should,' he mumbled at DS Kevin Mower. 'Omar' Sharif was on the opposite side of the table, listening to the conversation with a sceptical look in his dark intelligent eyes.

'But if there were problems with Christie's shotgun, surely that would be a high priority?' Mower insisted, holding the young uniformed constable in an icy glare. 'That's not kids in the bus shelter stuff, is it? That's serious?'

'Yeah, well, I did talk to him about it when the woman from social services complained, but he said she just panicked. He'd come in from doing a bit of rabbiting, the gun wasn't even loaded, he said. He reckoned she'd never seen a shotgun before and thought he was going to blow her head off with a high powered rifle.'

'That's what he said?' Mower asked, even more sharply. 'That's an odd way to put it, isn't it?'

'I suppose it is,' Hewitt admitted grudgingly. 'He obviously didn't like her snooping round, but I just thought it was the way he thought. Nothing significant.' He glanced at Sharif. 'I don't think he liked her being a Paki, either. He was obviously a bit of a racist. You know how it is? I reckon he could have deliberately tried to put the wind up her by waving the gun about, as a joke, like.'

'Not much of a joke,' Sharif said sharply. Hewitt looked at him without enthusiasm.

'Just what I thought at the time,' he said. 'No offence.'

'And you didn't think it was serious enough to take any further action on his shotgun certificate?'

'He was bloody meticulous about that gun,' Hewitt said, annoyed now. 'I inspected his gun cupboard, and it was all in order. If I was looking for people being sloppy with shotguns up there, it wouldn't be Gordon

Christie I'd be looking at. He never said, but I reckon he'd been in the army. He knew about guns and took good care of them.'

'And if the gun used in the shooting – an automatic pistol, by all accounts – if that was his, you'd no idea he had it.'

'Of course not,' Hewitt said angrily. 'You know as well as I do it's illegal to have a handgun. I'd have been down on him like a ton of bricks and so would my super. What do you think this is out here, the wild West?'

'Just checking,' Mower said, and there was no apology in his tone. 'What made you think Christie had been in the army anyway?'

'Just a feeling,' Hewitt said. 'He wasn't local, though I think his wife was. He had a Scottish accent, I think, though he never said where he came from. It was the short hair cut, the way he walked maybe – a bit military, know what I mean? But he was very cagey, never gave owt away. Answered your questions – yes, no, maybe – polite but nothing more. No words wasted, any road. Quiet, amenable enough, but I wouldn't have liked to get on the wrong side of him.'

'And now we know he had a violent temper, so violent he probably hit his son – if the complaint to social services is to be believed – and seems to have ended up taking out his whole family with a handgun which suddenly appeared out of nowhere. So just what was that all about?'

'You never know, do you?' Hewitt said. 'Some people just snap for no obvious reason at all.'

'People may snap but they don't usually have a powerful weapon to wreak this sort of carnage when they do.'

'Right,' Hewitt said unhappily. 'I told you. I'd no idea about the pistol. No idea at all.'

'And when they snap, there's usually a trigger,' Mower said, almost as if thinking aloud. 'They may be stressed out but something makes them snap. In Christie's case it doesn't seem to have been money. There was plenty of cash going through his bank account, cash in the house, some of it unexplained. The house is well furnished, the kids seemed well looked after, apart from this incident with Scott. People commented on it. But what we don't know is where he was getting those large sums of cash from. Did you get any clues about that? Did he have some sort of illegal scam going we ought to have known about? It can't just be avoiding VAT and income tax. This is big money we're talking about, for a self-employed odd job man. Who was paying him, and for what?'

Hewitt shook his head. 'As far as I knew he worked as a mechanic. She didn't work at all. The kids looked okay to me. I didn't have many problems up at Staveley. An occasional burglary and the teenagers mucking about in the bus shelter, that was about it. The Christies gave me no cause for concern. Apart from the visit by the social worker, egged on by some nosy neighbour, and to be honest I'd have been pretty upset if that had happened to me and my family.'

'Well, it looks as though the nosy neighbour may have been on to something,' Mower snapped. 'But that wasn't the trigger, was it? It happened a while back?'

A good few months ago,' Hewitt said, returning to defensive mode. 'I can check the date if you like. I did pass it on, you know. It wasn't my decision to take no further action.'

But more senior officers would have relied on Hewitt to assess the seriousness of Christie's behaviour, Mower thought to himself, and Hewitt obviously hadn't thought it was serious at all. He sighed.

'Do you want me to check the date?' PC Hewitt persisted.

'Not now, later,' Mower said irritably. 'So, not shortage of money. What about sex? Tell me about Mrs Christie. Was she on the razzle? Was there any sign the marriage was in trouble?'

'How the hell would I know that?' Hewitt protested.

'Gossip,' Mower said surprisingly mildly. 'Chatter in the pub, in the post office. Intelligence gathering, Gavin. Isn't that what community policing is supposed to be about? Keeping an eye on things so we're not taken by surprise, so we pick up the bad apples before they get out of hand. Did you know Mrs Christie? Did you ever talk to her? Or did you ever hear anyone talking about her?'

Hewitt furrowed his brow in thought. 'I saw her when we had the complaint from the social worker, but I don't think she said a word. He made all the running on that one. And I think I saw her fetching her kid from playgroup a couple of times. I used to stop for a chat with the mothers at the gate now and again, listen to the gossip, know what I mean? Linda is ... was, I mean, quite a good-looking blonde, so you'd notice her in a crowd. She was quite a bit younger than Christie, I reckon. I suppose you could call that intelligence gathering.'

'Fancied her, did you?' Mower asked cynically and the younger man flushed slightly.

'I didn't mean that,' he said.

'No, but did you mean she was fanciable?' Mower pressed, in spite of the discomfort the question obviously caused Sharif's Muslim sensibilities. It was time the lad toughened up, he thought, as he waited for Hewitt to reply.

'Well, yeah, she could have been,' Hewitt conceded. He thought again. 'I did see her once talking to Gerry Foster... He's got a bit

80

of a rep for playing away, come to think of it.'

'And who's Gerry Foster?'

'The landlord at the Fox and Hounds. Big bloke with dark hair, a beard. If you want someone who keeps his finger on the pulse up here, Gerry Foster's your man. He hears it all, I reckon. Much more than I do, as it goes.'

'Well, I might just have a chat with Mr Foster next time I'm up here,' Mower said. 'In the meantime keep thinking in case there's anything else you've missed on your intelligence missions. So far it looks as if you've been wandering round Staveley with your eyes tight shut for all the intelligence you've gathered.'

'Yes, sarge,' Hewitt mumbled, swallowing his fury. But if Hewitt thought murdered children deserved anything less than his full attention then he was making a huge mistake, Mower thought, and he knew DCI Thackeray would back him up every inch of the way on that.

Late that evening, Michael Thackeray himself was standing by the tall window in the sitting room of the flat he shared with Laura Ackroyd, gazing at the moonlit garden outside. He felt rather than heard Laura come up behind him before she put an arm through his.

81

'You can't blame yourself for everything that goes wrong,' she said quietly.

'Not everything,' he said. 'But some things I'm responsible for. There's no getting away from that.'

'It's the little boy, isn't it?'

'The longer he's missing, the less chance of finding him alive,' Thackeray said, the fear which haunted him clenching his stomach like a vice.

'Why would the father take him away in the car if he wanted to kill him?' Laura asked. 'It doesn't make sense.'

'He seems to have gone off to school; his sisters hadn't, for some reason. His school-bag's not in the house, theirs were still hanging on the kitchen door. Men who kill their families generally don't like to leave anyone out,' Thackeray said. 'It seems to be almost a point of honour – if they go, everyone has to go.' He shuddered before turning to Laura and kissing her on the cheek, holding her very close for a moment.

'It's late. Come and eat,' she said and he followed her into the kitchen where a small table was set for two. But as he turned his attention to the curry she had kept hot in the oven, she could see that he was still pre-occupied with work. She watched him pick at his food for a moment before she gave in and turned the conversation reluctantly back in the direction of his thoughts.

'Why haven't you issued a photograph of Christie?' she asked. 'Ted Grant was going bananas for one this morning.'

'We can't find one,' Thackeray said. 'There were a few pictures of the children in the house, including the school picture of Emma and Scott we issued to the Press yesterday. But we can't find one of the parents.'

'No family albums? I thought everyone kept family albums,' Laura said, knowing she had strayed onto treacherous ground. She had never seen a photograph of Thackeray's wife and son from the time before his marriage disintegrated in tragedy. She guessed he had either destroyed them or hidden them away long ago.

'Not this family.'

'I did an interview with a psychologist today,' she said. 'I wanted to talk to him about what drives people to do these things.'

'Did you ask him if he knows how to prevent them doing them,' Thackeray said. 'That'd be a lot more useful.'

'You still think the father did it?'

'What else can we think?' Thackeray said wearily. 'If he didn't do it, where the hell is he? And where's the boy? There are so many holes in this whole scenario that I don't know what to think, to be honest. It'd be a whole lot clearer if we found the boy – one way or the other.'

Alive or dead, Laura thought, and she

knew that it was becoming increasingly un-likely that the fugitive pair would be found alive.

'How's the child in hospital?' she asked. 'Is there any change there?'

'The doctors seemed a little bit more hope-ful before I came away this evening,' Thack-eray said. 'But she's still not conscious. And even when she is, the chances are she won't remember much about what happened.'

'This psychologist at the university, he wasn't very optimistic about anything really,' Laura said. 'He said Christie sounds like the classic family killer – intense, controlling, wanting everything to be perfect, and then losing it completely when something runs out of his control. And the other cases I've looked at in the cuttings are all the same. Father is a perfectionist and can't bear any-thing to threaten his perfect family, so he kills himself and takes the family with him. Quite often the trigger is the threat of the marriage breaking down.'

She knew that she was not telling Thack-eray anything that he did not know already and that he was only half listening to her. But she felt an intense need to keep on talking. Anything to distract Thackeray from the thoughts which threatened to torment him all night.

'He said if the killer runs off with a child, or children sometimes, he tends to go back to somewhere the family's been happy together; the seaside, quite often, or a beauty spot. It's as if he wants to kill himself somewhere he has good memories...'

'This is Dr Prothero, at the university, is it?' Thackeray asked. 'I've talked to him before.'

'So you know it all? Sorry,' Laura said.

Thackeray shrugged.

'Usually when you search a house when something like this has happened you build up a picture of what the family was like,' he said. 'But in this case Kevin Mower said he wasn't able to get hold of anything personal in that place. It was as if Christie had somehow wiped the slate clean at some point, and then kept everything strictly impersonal. There was nothing there to give a handle onto either of the parents at all. No letters, no address books, no records of the children being born or growing up, nothing at all more than three years old. It's as if they parachuted into Staveley from outer space. And then – carnage.' His voice trailed away.

'Michael,' she said. 'You can't let this case damage you as well.'

'No,' he said, his eyes bleak. 'There's been enough of that, hasn't there?'

'I didn't mean that,' she said.

He got up from the table and stood behind her chair with his arms round her shoulders for a moment.

'Don't ever leave me, Laura,' he said. 'I couldn't survive without you.'

'I know,' she said. 'Truly, I do know that.'

Chapter Six

Ted Grant's bulging blue eyes told Laura Ackroyd that he was not likely to be deterred by her objections to his latest brainwave. He brandished the outline of her feature on family murders which she had printed out for him, and scowled.

'Human interest,' he said. 'That's what it needs. All this psycho-babble about fathers is all very well but our readers won't wade through that unless there's summat personal to hold their attention. This little girl in hospital's the perfect peg. All alone there, hanging between life and death because her father couldn't hack it. Get yourself over to the infirmary and see what details you can dig up about her condition. Is she going to make it or what? Where's her granny and her aunties and uncles? See if there's any chance of getting a picture. We can make a big appeal of it if she doesn't snuff it too soon. Where's the rest of little Emma's family when she needs them?'

Laura opened her mouth, took a deep

breath and eventually replied in the only terms that she thought Grant would understand.

'The police won't want us making the assumption that Gordon Christie was the gunman,' she said carefully. 'It's legally very dodgy to go there.'

'Well, don't say he was,' Grant snapped. 'Leave it open. She's still a victim with no family to support her. That's all you need. You can get round the legal issues with a few allegedlys and apparentlys, the odd well placed question mark, for God's sake. Is this the latest victim of a spate of family massacres? How much carnage lies in wait behind suburban front doors? That sort of thing. You're not working for the bloody police force, you know, even if you do choose to live with it.'

'Right,' Laura said, her cheeks flaming. She took hold of the article which Grant thrust in her direction and went back to her desk, careful not to slam the editor's door too hard behind her. Reluctantly she stowed her tape recorder in her bag, put on her coat and walked the short distance from the *Gazette*'s office to the Infirmary. She made her way through the long corridors to the intensive care ward on the top floor. When she looked through the glass in the heavy swing doors she recognised DC Val Ridley sitting beside a high bed where a small figure lay hooked up to the machinery which Laura assumed was keeping her alive. She slipped into the ward and past the empty nurses' station. Most of the staff were clustered around a bed at the other end of the ward where some major life and death procedure seemed to be taking place.

'Hi,' she said quietly to Val, who jumped, as if her mind had been a long way away, but her startled expression was soon replaced by a faint look of embarrassment and she glanced round at the nurses, who had still failed to notice Laura's arrival.

'How is she?' Laura asked, her eyes fixed now on the child's pale face with a mask over her mouth. Emma's eyes were closed and it was difficult to tell whether or not she was alive, although the monitors bleeped rhythmically above the bed.

'There's no change,' Val said quietly, following Laura's eyes. 'She's been slightly less deeply unconscious since yesterday, apparently, but she's not opened her eyes. It's still touch and go.'

'Are you on duty here until she wakes up?' Laura asked, slightly surprised that the police could spare an officer for what looked like a fairly fruitless vigil.

Val, usually so pale and composed, flushed slightly, 'Not officially, I just pop in when I've got the time,' she said. 'Stupid to let it get to me, I know, but I do so want her to survive...'

'It's a terrible thing,' Laura said quietly. 'But what's she going to wake up to?'

'Tell me about it. It haunts me,' Val said, and Laura realised from her stricken expression just how deeply affected she evidently was by Emma Christie's plight. Thackeray was obviously not the only officer to be taking a hammering from this case, she thought.

'Can't the *Gazette* make some sort of appeal for relatives?' Val suggested. 'There must be someone somewhere...'

'You'd think so,' Laura said. 'As it happens my editor wants me to write something about Emma for tomorrow, so maybe that'll help.' She wondered if her own reservations about what she had been ordered to do were oversensitive. Perhaps Emma needed publicity. But her doubts returned with full force as she saw a nurse bearing down on her from the other end of the ward with a fiercely disapproving expression on her face.

Are you a relative?' she asked.

'I'm from the *Bradfield Gazette*. I just wanted to know how...'

'Out!' the nurse snapped, without waiting for more. 'You've no right to be in here. It's Press intrusion. Gross intrusion. If you're not out of that door in ten seconds I'll send for security and have you thrown out.'

Laura shrugged and turned to go. Val Ridley stood up and followed her to the door.

'You were lucky to get as far as you did,' she said mildly as they made their way back out of the hospital side by side. 'But I'll let you know if there's any change in her condition. We need to find some relatives, we really do, and something in the paper might help with that. The poor kid will end up in care if no one comes forward soon and I couldn't bear that.'

Laura looked at Val Ridley for a moment and wondered what had made the normally cool and detached detective so emotionally concerned about the injured girl's future. But she knew better than to ask directly.

'I'll see what I can do,' she said. 'And thanks.'

Half an hour later Laura was sitting in Dawn Brough's neat sitting room holding a cup of tea and looking out of the picture window at the family's bleak winter garden where a few daffodils where just beginning to force their way through the half-frozen soil. She had driven up to Staveley for the second time that week, determined this time to find out more about the family whose life in the village had been so brutally curtailed. After parking briefly outside the Christie's cottage, which was still wreathed in police tape, she had turned the car and driven slowly back down the waterlogged lane where she had spotted Dawn closing the garden gate of the first small detached house in the new development between the village proper and Moor Edge. She had stopped and wound down her window.

'Have you got yourself lost?' Dawn had asked.

'Not really,' Laura said and introduced herself. For a second the other women's blue eyes clouded and she pushed untidy blonde hair away from her broad, open face.

'The *Gazette?*' she said uncertainly.

'I'm writing about Emma Christie,' Laura said. 'The police are trying to find the rest of her family but they're not having much success. There must be some relatives somewhere...'

'Poor kiddie,' Dawn said. 'It's wicked, what happened, isn't it? I feel terrible about it, actually. I'm lying awake at night wondering if there was something I could have done to prevent it.'

She must have realised from Laura's astonished expression that she had said more than she could leave at that.

'You'd better come in,' she said. 'I was just making a cup of tea.'

Having settled her visitor in her comfortable sitting room and plied her with tea and biscuits, a professional hazard, Laura thought wryly as she turned down the unwanted calories, Dawn sat down herself and sighed heavily.

'Linda didn't have many friends in the

91

village,' she said. 'It was just an accident that we got to know each other outside the school gate. You know? As you do?'

Laura smiled encouragingly, knowing nothing from experience about what went on outside school gates.

'Anyway, it turned out we lived close, and our Stephen was in the same class as Scott, and we used to arrange for the two little ones to play together sometimes. I'm furious with myself now. I should have seen this coming.'

'You mean you knew her husband was violent?' Laura asked, surprised.

'Not as violent as he turned out to be, obviously,' Dawn said quickly. 'But I knew he hit her. She tried to keep the bruises covered up but I saw her shoulder once, when she was wearing a short-sleeved shirt. It was black and blue. She started crying then, and said she'd had a fall but I knew it wasn't true and eventually she admitted he hit her. She said it didn't happen often, but I think she was lying. He was such a big man, really tall and broad with it, and she was so tiny really, in comparison. I think he bullied all of them. I'm sure he hit Scott as well, if not the girls.'

'He sounds a nasty bit of work,' Laura said. 'Did you tell anyone about what was going on?'

Dawn shook her head, looking miserable.

'Linda swore me to secrecy when we talked about it. She swore she could handle it. She said Gordon was under a lot of pressure, he'd had a bad time in the past, something about a previous job, and he'd get over it in time. She made out he was quite ill, not sleeping, having nightmares, all sorts, and it wasn't really his fault, but he didn't seem to be seeing a doctor or anything. I didn't really believe a lot of what she said, but what could I do? Anyway, she seemed much happier over the last few months, so I thought things must be getting better.'

'Why d'you think that was?' Laura asked, but Dawn just shrugged and looked uncomfortable.

'I couldn't say really,' she said. But Laura could tell from the faint flush which rose from her neck and her refusal to meet her eye that neat, conventional Dawn was lying.

'Do you think her husband was behaving better – or was there something else?' she persisted. Dawn twisted her hands in her lap for a second and then shrugged.

'It's not going to hurt Linda now, is it?' she said very quietly. 'I did think she might be playing away.'

'You mean she had a boyfriend? That seems a risky thing to do if her husband was so violent.'

'Maybe she saw it as a way out,' Dawn said. 'Why not? Why should she stay with a man like Gordon if she'd found someone better?'

'Have you any idea who it was?' Laura asked.

'Not really,' Dawn said. 'Though I wondered about Gerry Foster at the pub. I saw them talking at the Christmas do at the school. Gordon wasn't there that day and Linda looked quite relaxed and pretty... She was pretty you know, but so stressed out most of the time you hardly noticed ... but honestly, I don't actually know anything for sure. It's only me picking up hints, you know? Nothing definite.'

'Have you told the police all this?' Laura asked.

'No, I haven't. I spoke to them when it happened but the sergeant I spoke to rushed off when he discovered Scott was missing, and they've not been back.'

'I think you should tell them now,' Laura said. 'It could be important. If there was a boyfriend that could have been what triggered this whole catastrophe.'

'I suppose so,' Dawn said without enthusiasm.

'The other thing I wanted to ask you was whether Linda ever talked about her own family?' Laura said. 'There's Emma lying in hospital and no one seems to have shown any interest in her at all, no granny, no aunts or uncles. No one's been to visit or even contacted the hospital to see how she is. Surely one of the Christies had relations who would want to see Emma, even if they couldn't look after her. If she recovers it looks as though she'll be taken into care because there's no one else around. That's awful.'

'Linda did talk about having a sister once or twice, but she never said where she lived. I got the impression that they'd lived abroad for quite some time and lost touch with folk here.'

'You don't have any pictures of the family, do you? It would be good to have a photograph to go with the piece I'm writing about Emma.'

'I may have some snaps of the children taken when they were playing with mine last summer. I can't remember if Linda's in any of them but I'm pretty sure Gordon isn't. He never came round here and usually he was out when I went up to Moor Edge. I think that was deliberate. 1 don't think he liked Linda mixing with anyone, really. She had to keep her friends to herself. Hang on a minute, and I'll look in my photo album, see what's there.'

Laura waited patiently while Dawn rummaged in a cupboard in the hall and came back with a leather bound album which she riffled through quickly.

'There we are,' she said at last, handing

Laura the book. 'I thought I remembered taking a few snaps one hot day last summer, in the school holidays. They were all round here for tea that day.' She leaned over Laura's shoulder.

'That's my two, and that's Scott. And there's the two girls with their mum. There's another one of Linda but it didn't come out very well. My husband says I'm hopeless with a camera. He takes all the snaps when we're on holiday. We haven't got a digital yet.'

Laura looked at the smiling faces frozen in time, two of them now gone for ever and the other two lives evidently hanging by a thread, and felt an overwhelming sadness.

'Can I borrow these two?' she asked. 'It may just jog someone's memory even if the school photos we've already printed haven't. There must be someone out there for Emma, surely.' And she realised that she too had been hooked irretrievably by this tragedy.

The police patrol car cruised slowly up the twisting hill behind Staveley village, the two uniformed officers inside chatting companionably as they drove. To their left the land fell away and the stone roofs of old Staveley, interspersed with the occasional red tiles of new houses, were visible beneath the craggy hill which protected it from the prevailing westerly winds. To the right the land rose steeply, with brown clumps of dead bracken and thickets of spiny gorse clinging to the thin soil between outcrops of dark millstone grit. The driver slowed slightly where the road widened at a muddy entranceway partly obscured by bushes and a few straggly trees, which apparently led into the side of the hill.

'It's an old quarry, disused now,' the officer in the passenger seat said in response to his partner's interrogative glance.

'Has anyone looked down there?' the driver asked. The passenger shrugged.

'Doesn't look as if anyone's been down there. There's no recent wheel tracks.'

'Best check, if I can get in without getting stuck in t'mire,' the driver said, swinging into the narrow entrance and beginning to bump his way along a rutted and extremely muddy surface.

'You can clean t'mud off when we get back to base,' his partner said irritably.

'Happen,' the driver said. 'But what's that then if no one's been down here?'

He pointed at a car parked at the back of the hollow rocky bowl left by years of quarrying. 'Someone didn't want that seen, did they?'

'The chopper should have picked it up. They've been over often enough in the last few days.'

'Well, they didn't, did they?' the driver said

triumphantly, stopping the car and unbuckling his seat belt. 'Let's have a look, shall we? If it does nowt else, it'll get Sergeant Elsey off our backs. Though it's not the Land Rover we're supposed to be looking for.'

When they reached the car, a sporty looking Honda, they realised that the overhanging cliff of rock above them, plus a heavy covering of snow which still lingered on the shaded side of the quarry might well have made the car invisible from above. The driver cleared the remaining wet snow from the number plate, radioed headquarters for a check on the vehicle's ownership and peered through the car windows curiously. The vehicle was locked and the tax disc on the windscreen was up to date.

'Belongs to someone in t'village,' he said when the answer came back. 'A Stuart Weldon, of the Old Hall, Staveley. Happen we'd best go and ask Mr Weldon if he knew his car's been hidden up here. Seems a bit of an extreme way to avoid getting clamped, doesn't it? Most likely it's been nicked and dumped, and someone's planning to come back for it later when the heat's off.'

Laura Ackroyd put the phone down and ran a hand through her red curls in exasperation as she considered the unexpected intrusion. She had got home early with the intention of calling Michael Thackeray in private, away from the hubbub and intrusive curiosity of the newsroom. She wanted to know whether or not Dawn Brough had been as good as her word and contacted the police to pass on the revelations she had shared with Laura that afternoon. The last thing Laura wanted was to lay herself open to the accusation that she had gained relevant knowledge of the Christie case and not passed it on. Keeping her own career and Thackeray's judiciously separate was like walking a tightrope, she thought, and one of these days one of them would fall off. She just hoped the drop was not too damaging.

As she had opened the door of the flat at five thirty, the telephone was already ringing and she snatched it up slightly breathlessly, flinging her coat and bag onto the settee as she did so. The voice which greeted her, distorted by a mobile connection which came and went erratically, but still only too instantly recognisable, was one from the past she had absolutely no wish to hear again.

'Hey, babe,' carolled Vince Newsom, the former boyfriend whom Laura had ejected from her flat and, she hoped, her life, several years before. 'I'm on my way up the motorway to your neck of the woods, sweetie, to follow up this story of the poor little abandoned kid you wrote about yesterday. Nice one, that. Any chance of meeting up for a quickie this evening?'

Laura swallowed hard.

'No chance, Vince,' she said, with as much ice in her tone as she could inject.

'Oh, come on, darling,' Vince persisted. 'I could make it worth your while – one way or another.'

'Get lost,' Laura said.

'Oh dear,' Vince said, the connection sharpening so there was no doubt of the contempt behind the banter. 'Settled down, have we? You're not still with that gloomy copper you fancied, are you?'

'That's none of your business,' Laura said.

'I only meant I may need a bit of local input on this story,' Vince said, angry now. 'The *Globe*'s not ungenerous on that sort of help, and I don't expect the *Gazette* has upped its miserable rates of pay since I left, has it? I'm staying at the Clarendon, if you want to get hold of me.'

'I don't want to know, Vince,' Laura said. 'You'll have to do your own legwork on this one. And don't bother to call again.' She broke the connection angrily, knowing that she was unlikely to avoid bumping into Vince if he spent any time in Bradfield building up Emma Christie's plight into a full-blown London tabloid tear-jerker. And where the *Globe* led, the other papers would probably not be far behind. She smiled grimly. Emma's nurses hadn't seen anything in the way of Press intrusion yet, she thought. If

Emma did wake up, she might need a 24-hour guard to keep the *paparazzi* at bay.

Angrily, she threw herself into a little energetic housework, and after a frenzy of polishing and Hoovering, she began to prepare an evening meal for herself and, she hoped, Thackeray. Left to herself, she knew that she might rely on ready-meals and the microwave oven, but Thackeray was a traditionalist about food and although his timekeeping was highly unreliable, she did her best to satisfy his appetite for home-cooking. Tonight, as she had the time, she put a lamb casserole in the oven and peeled potatoes before she tried to contact him by phone again. But when she called CID she was put onto Sergeant Kevin Mower.

'He's in with the super,' Mower said. 'Can I give him a message?'

'One reason I was calling was to ask if Dawn Brough, Linda Christie's friend, had been in touch. I talked to her this morning and advised her to tell you lot what she told me about the family. Has she been in contact?'

'Not that I know of,' Mower said. 'Was there anything particularly significant?'

Laura hesitated for a second. She did not make a habit of passing on information to the police that she had picked up in an interview, but Dawn Brough's unexpected suggestion that Mrs Christie might have been having an affair struck her as too serious to ignore. She told Mower what Dawn had said.

'It may be nothing,' she said. 'She may have got it completely wrong. But I thought you'd want to check it out. It could be the reason for what happened, couldn't it? And the reason you've not found Gordon Christie and the boy? Perhaps he attacked his wife, and the girls got in the way, so he took the boy and ran.'

'Whoa,' Mower said, laughing. 'You're running away with yourself. But I'll pass it on and I'm sure we'll check it out. There's still no sign of Christie or the boy, so it's quite possible they're still alive somewhere. Let's hope so.'

But when Michael Thackeray finally came home a couple of hours later, he appeared even more pessimistic than usual and was dismissive of Laura's revelations.

'There's a pattern in these cases,' he said. 'And a hundred places up in the hills where Christie's body could be. And the boy's as well. They may not turn up till the spring when the sheep farmers let the flocks up onto the tops again and take a look at some of the more isolated barns. We've had forty men up there again all day today and all they've come up with is one apparently stolen car belonging to someone in Staveley who's away on holiday, according to his

102

father. We can't spare that sort of manpower for much longer if that's all they're going to come up with. We're going to have to scale the search down.'

'You don't think they're alive, do you?'

'Not really,' Thackeray said, his eyes bleak. 'There's not been a single sighting of Christie or the Land Rover since he disappeared. I thought at first he must have made a run for it with the boy, but now I'm not so sure. I'm more inclined to think he's driven the vehicle into one of the reservoirs, or into a bog. But you can't search the whole of the Pennines indefinitely. We all know there are bodies on those moors that haven't been found for fifty years or more, even though we know roughly where they're buried.'

Thackeray's expression was resigned and Laura longed to take him in her arms, but was even more afraid of the sort of rebuff which had been becoming more frequent recently. This case was getting to him in ways which she could only begin to guess at, and she could find no way to comfort him, or even persuade him to admit that anything was wrong.

'The nationals are beginning to take an interest in Emma Christie,' she said. 'I heard the *Globe* is sending someone up.'

'That's no bad thing,' Thackeray said unexpectedly. 'Someone may recognise her or her brother and come forward with some information. The *Gazette* and the local radio stations haven't been very effective so far. I'm beginning to think the family must have come from some other part of the country originally. No one in Yorkshire's taking a blind bit of notice.'

'Right,' Laura said cautiously. She knew that Thackeray would be less than pleased to discover that the *Globe*'s knight in shining armour would turn out to be Vince Newsom, but she didn't intend to tell him that tonight. His mood was dark enough already. Hopefully Vince would discover that an unconscious child gave him as little purchase on a dramatic story as it had given her, and that his stay in Bradfield would be both frustrating and brief. Laura sighed.

'What are you thinking?' she asked softly. 'Not about this awful case, but about us? I never know these days.' But Thackeray did not answer, his expression hardening and his eyes distant, and eventually Laura stood up and went to bed alone.

Chapter Seven

Jason Fearnley, cocooned like an Arctic explorer in his padded jacket and with a thick brown muffler covering his nose and mouth against the fierce north wind, wrestled his quad bike over the rough unfenced terrain beyond his small hill holding. He had lost three ewes, pregnant but no less silly for that, who had somehow scrambled clear of their walled field close to the farmhouse and wandered out of sight on the open moor, where in the summer they were let loose to graze.

'Damnation,' Jason said as the bike skidded almost out of control on the greasy surface, sodden with melted snow. The perilous economics of hill farming meant that the loss of any ewe and the lamb she was carrying was a serious anxiety. The loss of three would be a heavy blow. He brought the bike to a precarious halt on the edge of an outcrop of rock and scanned the moors which spread out in all directions, a patchwork of dark rock, last season's battered swathes of burnt umber bracken and pale, desiccated, moorland grasses. Hefted sheep would not wander beyond their normal

105

grazing land, but that allowed these three several square miles of familiar space in which to lose themselves; square miles that still harboured deep snow drifts and sodden bog at this time of the year.

Below him he could see the dilapidated drystone walls that hemmed in his small enclosed fields and the farmhouse where he had left his wife cooking breakfast. His stomach told him that it was past time to be back in the warmth of the house tucking in to a loaded plate and a mammoth mug of sweet tea, but there was little chance of that just yet.

'I should have fettled that wall before I brought them in,' he muttered angrily to himself, knowing that his present predicament was due as much to his own carelessness as to the sheep's inherent urge to wander. Suddenly something unusual caught his eye. Where the snow had drifted three or four feet deep against the remains of a wall that struck out across the moor, he could just discern an indeterminate bundle lying in the melting snow, a bundle which could possibly be a dead ewe, possibly a sack of fly-tipped rubbish, or just possibly something worse. He turned the bike and stormed and bounced down the slope, cursing himself under his breath for his lax husbandry. But as he got closer he realised it was not a sheep that lay huddled there, and he knew, with an uncomfortable lurch in his stomach, that what he had found was human and probably as dead as he feared his ewes might be.

An hour later DCI Michael Thackeray and Sergeant Kevin Mower leaned against the same drystone wall, watching the pathologist Amos Atherton crouching awkwardly above the huddled body of a young boy who, they all assumed, must be Scott Christie. Thackeray drew deeply on a cigarette, as if his life depended on it, while Mower seemed more interested in the damage being inflicted by mud and snowy slush on his shoes. He remembered being told to keep a pair of wellingtons in his car boot when he first came to Bradfield and realised yet again what a mistake it had been not to listen to that sage Yorkshire advice.

Atherton glanced in the officers' direction, puffing slightly as he eased his heavy frame into a more comfortable position.

'There's no sign of trauma,' he said.

'He wasn't shot?' Thackeray asked.

'No blood, no wounds.' Atherton's tone was irritable, as if he had expected to have made himself clear enough already. 'If he was out here for any length of time in the snow, the likely cause will be hypothermia. The way he's curled up tells you he was probably try-ing to keep warm, poor little sod.'

'And he wasn't carried here and dumped?'

Atherton scrambled to his feet and stepped

back from the body, his breath coming in steamy gusts.

'I couldn't swear to it, but the way he's lying says he was alive when he lay down there. His hood was pulled up, his arms round his knees, classic foetal position you'd adopt if you were still conscious but bloody cold. Of course, if he was carried out here and dumped you'll not find any trace of it now, with the snow almost gone and all this mud churned up. Get your forensic teams up here if you like, but I reckon they'll be wasting their time. They'll not find owt.'

'He's less than half a mile from the farm-house,' Mower objected. 'Surely if he was on his feet he'd have made it down there.'

'You ever been out in a blizzard up here, lad?' Atherton asked with some asperity. 'He'd not see a hand in front of his face for a start, let alone a house as far away as that. And a child as small as him would soon find it difficult to walk at all in deep, drifting snow. Once he was off the road in that weather he didn't stand much of a chance unless someone actually fell over him.'

'He'd just go to sleep, presumably?' Thackeray asked, hoping against hope that the falling asleep had been gentle.

Atherton shrugged.

'That's what they say,' he said. 'But they don't often wake up to tell you about it, do they?'

108

'But what the hell was he doing wandering around up here on his own? Was he really running from his own father?' Thackeray asked and Mower recognised the pain behind the question.

'He must have been running from whoever shot the rest of the family,' Mower said quietly. 'Whether it was the father or not.'

'So maybe Christie is up here somewhere,' Thackeray said. 'Maybe he lost track of the boy in the blizzard, and gave up and finished himself off. Or just lay down to die himself. We'll have to keep the search going now. The super won't be too enchanted with that. It's costing a fortune in overtime already.'

'If he's up here, where's the Land Rover?' Mower objected. 'A body's hard to find but a bloody Land Rover shouldn't be.'

Thackeray sighed, trying to fight off the black depression which had threatened to overwhelm him as he tramped across the soggy moor to Scott Christie's last resting place.

'Come on,' he said, suddenly pulling himself back into some semblance of normality. 'There's nothing more we can do up here.' He turned to Atherton who was packing his bag already.

'Let me know if anything unexpected turns up at the postmortem,' he said. He was thankful that this was one dissection he did not have to attend as it appeared to be an accidental death.

As they turned away, Jason Fearnley, who had been perched some distance away on his unwieldy bike watching the proceedings, wrapped himself up again in his muffler and tucked it into the collar of his jacket.

'Is that it then?' he asked. 'You don't need me any more?'

'We'll need a statement later,' Mower said. 'I'll get a uniformed officer to come and see you this afternoon, okay? It looks as if he simply got lost and died of cold.'

'If I've found my bloody ewes, I'll be at home,' Fearnley said sourly. 'At this rate, all I'm going to find is three more bloody dead bodies.' There was a glimmer of sympathy in Thackeray's eyes as he nodded his farewell to the farmer. It was a hard life on these hills, as he knew only too well from watching his own father's ultimately vain struggle to keep a small sheep farm going. Fearnley's permanent battle to wrest a living up here in all weathers could have been his own if his life had taken a different turn and an ambitious teacher at his school in Arnedale had not encouraged him – an unexpectedly bright country boy – not to any old university but to Oxford and towards, he had obviously hoped, life's glittering prizes. And much good that had done him in the long run, he thought bitterly, as he turned away and strode in sturdy boots down the hill towards the road and the parked police vehicles, leaving Mower slipping and sliding on Italian leather in his wake.

As they approached the road again they noticed a car they did not recognise parked on the muddy verge behind the police and emergency vehicles, and as they got closer two men got out, one carrying the paraphernalia of a photographer.

'Morning, Mr Thackeray,' the other said cheerily. 'Have you found anything significant up there?' Thackeray looked at the tall man in padded jacket and wellingtons and, although he looked familiar, he did not immediately put a name to the good-looking, tanned face beneath the floppy fair hair.

'Vince Newsom, the *Globe*,' the not-quite-stranger said, holding out a hand which Thackeray ignored. 'You remember me? I'm up here to do something on this Christie family murder.' He glanced up the hillside down which Thackeray and Mower had just slid and up which a couple of ambulancemen in bright green waterproofs were beginning to climb.

'Have you found Christie then?' Vince persisted. Thackeray turned away, his expression frozen, and left it to Mower to deal with Newsom.

'If you get in touch with the Press office at county HQ, there'll be a statement later,' the sergeant said briefly. The photographer had by now attached his telephoto lens and was snapping the huddle of police officers who remained partly hidden by the dry-stone wall half a mile up on the side of the hill.

'There's nothing for you here,' Mower said angrily, and turned to the car, while Newsom and the photographer shrugged and began climbing up the steep slope themselves.

'Bloody ghouls,' Mower said as he struggled into the driving seat and eased the zip on his padded jacket a fraction before trying to wipe some of the mud off his loafers with a paper tissue. He glanced at his boss and wondered why he was gazing out of the car window so fixedly.

'I don't envy the farmer working up there in this weather, either,' he said. 'Bloody nightmare.'

'It's a dying way of life,' Thackeray said, noncommittally.

'So what now, guv?' Mower asked as he started the engine and swung the car onto the narrow road, which wound a tortuous course from Staveley to the villages on the west-facing, Lancashire slopes of the Pennines.

'It looks as if we're back where we started,' Thackeray said. 'Just one body worse off. A family dead, a father missing.' He lapsed into silence as the scene at the Christie's house leapt in all its bloody detail into his mind's eye again, as it had been doing ever since he had first walked blindly away from it on the first day of this case. Mower took one glance at the frozen expression in Thackeray's eyes and said no more, concentrating on negotiating the sharp bends as the road dropped precipitately from the high moors back into Staveley village. As they slowed at the first of the stone cottages, Thackeray put a hand on Mower's arm.

'Stop at the pub,' he said.

'Any special reason?' Mower asked, with a crooked smile.

Thackeray's reasons for stopping at a pub did not include the normal everyday need Mower still felt, and cautiously indulged, for a pint or two of ale.

'I want to talk to the landlord. Something Laura picked up when she was doing interviews in the village yesterday.' Mower raised a laconic eyebrow at that. It was not often Thackeray acknowledged any exchange of information between himself and his girlfriend, in either direction.

'The possible boyfriend?' Mower said as he parked the car in the empty car park at the side of the Fox and Hounds. 'She did pass that on earlier. Maybe I forgot to tell you.'

It was eleven o'clock and the pub did not look as if it had opened its doors yet. But when the two men tried the main entrance they found it unlocked and inside Gerry Foster, the landlord, was busy behind his bar stacking bottled lagers on his chilled shelves. He looked up at his visitors without enthusiasm or any sign of recognition.

'Mr Foster?' Thackeray asked, pulling his warrant card from his inside pocket and offering it across the bar. 'DCI Thackeray. I wonder if we could have a talk about Linda Christie.'

Foster was as tall and as broad as Thackeray himself but his expression was difficult to read behind the dark beard, which hid his mouth and gave him a slightly piratical air of menace. His eyes remained deeply unfriendly as he surveyed his visitors.

'Oh, aye?' he said. 'And what about Linda Christie?'

'Are you married, Mr Foster?' Thackeray asked.

'I am,' the landlord said. 'You can't run a place like this on your own. My wife takes care of the catering. We're not one of these poncey gastro-pubs, but we do sandwiches and snacks. You have to these days. Folk want to eat while they drink in case you lot catch 'em over the limit on the way home.'

'Is your wife in?' Thackeray asked. The question was straightforward but Mower knew from the tension that it generated that it carried a heavy weight. There was a battle of wills going on between the other two men which he did not quite understand yet.

'She's gone to the cash and carry,' Foster said. 'Won't be back for an hour.'

'You're in luck, then,' Thackeray said.

Foster said nothing but Thackeray merely waited as the silence between them grew electric. In the end, the landlord shrugged in surrender and ran a hand across his mouth and beard.

'Some beggars been gossiping, have they? We thought we'd been pretty careful.'

'You were having an affair with Linda Christie?' Thackeray asked, though it was more of a statement than a question.

'If you could call it that,' Foster said bitterly. 'It was hardly *Footballers' Wives*. It was pathetic really, looking back. We got to know each other a bit last summer when we were both involved at the school. For me, it was more like running a branch of the Samaritans than owt else, as it goes. She was desperate for someone to talk to about Gordon and at first that's all we did. She'd come in here for a lemonade or summat after the meetings, something he wouldn't pick up on her breath, and I'd walk her back up the lane to see she got home safely.'

'But it went further than that?' Thackeray persisted.

'In the end, yes. We went up on the moors in the car, like a couple of teenagers. I knew it was stupid, I knew Gordon Christie was a stroppy bastard and he'd go ape if he found out. And my missus wouldn't have been best pleased, neither. But you know how it is. Two unhappy marriages and the chance offers? You take it, don't you?'

'Did you not think that you were putting Mrs Christie at risk?' Thackeray found it hard to keep the contempt he felt for Foster out of his voice. He bunched his fists inside the pockets of his coat until the nails dug into the palms.

'I didn't think he was such a mad beggar as he turned out to be, no,' Foster said. 'No one could have known that.'

'And you didn't think that this was something you should have told us when the worst happened up at Moor Edge cottage? Two dead, two missing and another life hanging in the balance and you said nothing when the village was full of police asking questions. Did you really not think it was relevant to Linda's murder?'

'It wouldn't have helped you find Gordon, would it?' Foster flashed back. 'He was an evil-tempered bastard. Summat like this could have happened any road, whatever I did. Whatever Linda did, for that matter. I told her to leave him. I told her to take the kids and get out. But she wouldn't listen. The man was paranoid. He was running from something, though she never let on what – if she even knew. He'd sit in here of

116

an evening wi' his back to t'wall, twitching every time the door opened. Strangers came in and he'd be off, not even finishing his pint half the time. He was a nutter, was Gordon Christie but nothing I said could persuade her to get out while she could.'

Foster shrugged, his face putty coloured and drawn beneath the beard.

'I tried to persuade her, believe me, I did,' he said, so quietly that the two police officers could barely hear him. 'But she wouldn't budge.'

'Do you think he could have found out about your relationship with Linda?' Mower asked. 'If you were so careful? Do you think she told him?'

Foster drew a sharp breath.

'That's not very likely, is it?' he said, his voice hoarse. 'That's the last thing she'd do. Apart from owt else, he'd have been as likely to come after me as her, and there was no sign of that, thank God. I've told you. The man's violent. The man's crazy. Anything could have set him off. He was like a volcano waiting to blow. But he didn't seem to be coming in my direction.'

'Well, I can tell you for a fact that someone did guess, so maybe Christie worked it out as well,' Thackeray said. 'Did you know he had a handgun?'

'No, of course not,' Foster said. 'I knew he had a shotgun. Linda mentioned him going after rabbits once. Lots of folk round here do that. But I knew nowt about any other guns.' He hesitated for a second. 'Not that he might not have known about them,' he said.

'What makes you say that?' Thackeray asked sharply.

'Well, she talked about them living in Portugal before they came here. The little lass, Louise, was born out there. But Linda hadn't liked the climate there, or the people, something made her unhappy, any road, and I think she persuaded him to come back to this country. She never talked about anything before Portugal. Except once, when she said something about the lad missing his father when he'd been in Ireland. Then she stopped dead, and wouldn't say owt else when I asked her what he'd been doing in Ireland. It was like a shutter coming down. She looked scared witless and she went off home that night without letting me take her up to the moor for our usual little rendezvous.'

'Was Gordon Irish?' Thackeray asked sharply. 'Did he have an accent?'

'He did, a slight accent, but I'd have said it was more Scottish than Irish. Linda never said where she came from but she sounded like born-and-bred Yorkshire to me. Not broad, like round here, but not your southerner, rhyming grass wi' arse. Know what I mean?'

Mower smiled faintly, possessing a few of the despised vowels himself, but Thackeray was still fixed on the landlord's story.

'She never said anything else about his background?' he asked.

'Nothing,' Foster said. 'But she did make me think I was right about something else. I always suspected he was ex-army, though he never said. I was in the Green Jackets myself for eight years, and there was something about him that made me think he'd been there, done that, know what I mean? If he was, it could be that's what did his head in. It happens, especially in Ireland. They're supposed to sort you out before they let you out again, but it doesn't always work. I've seen it before with mates of mine. What do they call it? Post-traumatic stress, is it?'

'Being paranoid doesn't mean they're not out to get you,' Thackeray said. 'Do you think someone was out to get Gordon Christie?'

'I haven't a clue,' Foster said. 'But he looked as if he thought they were. What I do know is that Gordon was out to get Linda one way or another. And it looks as if he succeeded, doesn't it? I only wish to God we'd had this conversation a week ago and maybe she'd still be alive.'

Later that afternoon the phone on Thackeray's desk rang and snapped his mind back to reality. He had been sitting in his office

119

ever since he had come back from a canteen lunch he had done no more than pick at, brooding over what the sudden reappearance of Vince Newsom in Bradfield might mean. His own contact with him several years earlier, when he had first met Laura Ackroyd, had been brief. Newsom had already left the *Bradfield Gazette*, and moved out of Laura's flat, by the time Thackeray had reluctantly recognised the attraction between himself and the red-headed reporter with the mischievous smile. But with his wife confined to a long-stay hospital and the events which had taken her there painfully carved into his psyche with an acid which only seemed to grow more painfully corrosive with time, he had not been looking for a relationship.

It was surprising, he thought wryly, how insidiously Laura's looks, her persistence and her personality had worn down his defences, and it would be even more surprising if Vince Newsom, who had also adored her in his way, would not still be bowled over when he saw her again. If he had not done so already. Surely, Thackeray thought, the first thing Newsom would do in Bradfield would be to renew that old acquaintance, for professional if not personal reasons. They were both journalists, after all. And at a time when he and Laura were living together at arm's length rather than in each other's arms, Newsom might seem as attractive as he had once done. He shook his head angrily. Laura would not make that mistake twice, he told himself. Would she?

He picked up the phone, which had continued to shrill impatiently.

'Thackeray,' he said.

'Atherton,' a voice snapped back. 'You took your time. You asked me to call you if I found anything interesting when I got the little lad's body back here.'

'And?' Thackeray asked.

'And – he was shot at,' Atherton said. 'Not shot, just shot at. There's a bullet hole in the left sleeve of his jacket which I didn't see when we were up there. Goes right through, but it's left a slight mark on his left arm. Someone shot at him and just missed, I'd say. He may not even have known he'd been touched. But I thought you'd want to know that.'

'Anything else?'

'I've not begun the post-mortem yet. D'you want to come down? It could be attempted murder.'

'I'll give that a miss,' Thackeray said wearily. He found all postmortems hard to stomach, but the dissection of a small boy was an event he felt more than justified in sparing himself. 'I'll get Kevin Mower to join you,' he said, and hung up.

Chapter Eight

Vince Newsom marched into the newsroom at the *Bradfield Gazette* the next morning as if he owned the place, which was exactly the way he had acted when he had worked there himself. Laura Ackroyd suddenly became conscious of his presence behind her chair, and spun round to find herself the recipient of an enthusiastic kiss on her cheek.

'There you are, babe,' Vince said cheerfully. 'Same old desk, same old stories? Tell me about it. I told you years ago you should come to London and look at you, still here.'

'And same old Vince,' she said sharply, taking in the fair hair falling across his forehead, the faintly tanned skin, the slightly jutting jaw and the unbelievably blue eyes which were as self-satisfied as they had ever been. 'It's obvious London suits you, anyway.'

'Couldn't be better,' Vince said. He glanced round the newsroom, where most of the reporters' eyes were fixed on him, mostly in horrified fascination, and pulled a bulging wallet out of his inside pocket.

'I'm taking the plunge at last,' he said to Laura more quietly. 'Got engaged to this amazing babe last month. Bought her a bloody great diamond, the lot.' He flicked a photograph of a young woman in her direction, a bland face with a token smile and long blonde hair, rake thin, professionally coiffed and made up and wearing an off-the-shoulder evening gown that Laura guessed would have cost more than her monthly pay cheque.

'Very nice,' she conceded, relieved to find that there might be a good reason for Vince not to make too much of a nuisance of himself while he was in Bradfield. 'Who is she?'

'Caroline Stewart Venables. Met her on a story I was doing in the Isle of Wight over Cowes week. Her father made a mint in property and has built himself a mansion down there. Swimming pool, gym on site, enough en suites for a footie team. Very *nouveau*, very nice.'

'You won't have any trouble getting on the property ladder then,' Laura said.

A look of satisfaction, quickly subdued, flashed across Vince Newsom's good-looking features.

'Daddy's buying us a house in St John's Wood,' he said. 'Period property, excellent location.' He glanced round the newsroom complacently. 'Never mind, hey?' he said.

'We'll be seeing you in *Hello* magazine, then?' Laura offered. 'Mind the curse doesn't get you. A spread in *Hello* followed by a quick divorce, you know how it goes?'

'Do I sense the presence of the little green monster?'

'I think on the whole I prefer what I've got,' Laura said, suddenly sickened by the exchange, although she was conscious even as she spoke that what she had got was by no means as certain as she had hoped it would be so long after she had thrown Vince Newsom and all his worldly goods out of her flat.

'Why don't you go and see Ted?' she suggested. 'I'm sure he'll be suitably impressed.'

'I will, I will,' Vince said. 'I just wanted to ask you if there's been any developments with this kid in hospital. Has she come round? Any relatives turned up?'

'Oh, dramatic developments,' Laura said contemptuously. 'They found her little brother yesterday afternoon, as dead as the rest of them. They only need her father now to make the complete set.' Vince shrugged and turned away and Laura watched him make his way through the crowded desks to Ted Grant's glass cubicle at the other end of the office where he was greeted with a shout of rude good humour that could be heard across the whole editorial floor. She smiled wryly to herself. Vince had always fulfilled the editor's criteria for a good reporter – brash, unscrupulous, and not too concerned with the actual facts of a story if they got in the way of a good headline. He was, in other words, just what she knew she could never be. She was as likely to survive in the cut-throat world of the tabloid Press as a butterfly in a tornado.

But at least Vince's arrival had one good side. Much as his presence would irritate Michael Thackeray professionally, the news of his impending nuptials might calm any anxiety he might feel about Newsom's more personal ambitions in Bradfield. Although she was not as certain about that as she hoped Michael would be. She had good reason to know that fidelity did not come high on Vince's list of desirable attributes, if it appeared there at all. And she had to admit that his presence revived memories of the exuberantly good times which had lit up their relationship at the start as well as the sour taste it had left at the end. She sighed and turned back to her computer screen, knowing that, one way or another, Vince Newsom's nuisance value could be high.

Superintendent Jack Longley looked up impatiently when his DCI came into his office in response to his summons.

'You took your time,' he said, taking in the tension in the younger officer's body language as he loomed towards him, shoulders hunched.

'Sit down, sit down,' he said. 'I think we

may have cracked this Christie business.'

Thackeray took the offered chair and looked at Longley in surprise.

'You're joking?' he said, swallowing down an intense surge of relief which he knew he could not explain in purely professional terms.

'Well, it's no thanks to our colleagues in Manchester, I have to say. And I tore them off a strip for some sloppy routines over there. But here's the report, just faxed through. The good news is that they spotted Christie's Land Rover two days ago, burnt out in Moss Side, where apparently, wrecked and burnt out vehicles pop up overnight like rosebay willowherb on every vacant bit of land. The fire brigade apparently knew nowt about it. The locals are so used to this sort of thing that they don't bother to report it half the time. Normally it's kids, nicking cars and setting light to them for the hell of it. So it was a good two days before the local bobby took a close look, took the trouble to check the reg – which was a tad discoloured by that time – and discovered we were interested in it. Even worse, it wasn't until they sent someone to remove it that anyone realised that there was a body inside. Burnt to a cinder. They got around to letting me know this morning.'

'Christie?' Thackeray asked quietly, making an effort to control his breathing. He

126

should not be gratified by any death, least of all that of a man he needed to speak to, for reasons which went well beyond police procedure. But he could not suppress a feeling that some sort of justice might have been done in Moss Side. But Longley had not finished, and sounded less than certain in his response.

'Well, it's likely to be Christie,' he said. 'But our contact in Manchester says there's not a lot left of whoever it is, certainly nothing to give a positive ID at this stage. The remains are in the morgue and will be looked at in detail today.'

'DNA?'

'Tricky, he thought.'

Thackeray pondered this for a moment.

'It's a horrific way to commit suicide,' he said, doubtfully. 'And difficult too. It's not that easy to set a car ablaze, especially if you're inside it. I suppose it could be murder, which would leave us with a very nasty problem.'

'We'll cross that bridge if we have to,' Longley said equably. 'Manchester's making inquiries around where the vehicle was found but it's not an area where witnesses beat a path to the door, apparently. Sounds a bit like the Heights, to me. You know the scene well enough. But I thought you'd want to get over there, see what the hell's going on, talk to the pathologist, if you can.

Hopefully this will wrap the whole thing up. In one way these domestic cases are simple enough to crack, but they're unpleasant. Let's hope the whole family's accounted for now, Christie shot them and then killed himself, and that'll be an end to it.'

'The pub landlord in Staveley suggested that Christie was ex-army. Reckoned he knew the type. But we've checked with the MoD and they've no record of him. What's more relevant, I reckon, is that the same landlord admits he was having it away with Christie's wife. He was a morose beggar at the best of times, apparently, so it could well be that which pushed him over the edge.'

'Well, maybe the coroner will want to know about all that, but it'll be of no interest to us any more if this really is Christie they've found, and it's a suicide', Longley said.

The superintendent handed Thackeray the file on his desk.

'It's all in there,' he said. 'Give me a bell when you've made your own assessment at the scene. We'll need to keep the Press informed. There'll still be a lot of interest in the little girl in the infirmary, even if this closes the case.'

'And the *Globe*'s sniffing around looking for some sort of tear-jerker,' Thackeray said. He forebore to tell Longley just who was in town from the *Globe*. 'Don't worry. I'll keep you up to date. This is one case I'd like to see resolved more than most.'

Longley nodded. He had seldom seen Michael Thackeray so stressed, but he knew that he would get nothing out of him about his own feelings. This was the most private of men and he suspected that the job was becoming more difficult for him as time went by, rather than less. And there was absolutely nothing he could think of doing about that except hope he made it through to retirement.

Thackeray and Sergeant Mower drove to Manchester in what could hardly be called a companionable silence. Mower knew his boss well enough to recognise when he wanted to be left to his own apparently gloomy thoughts, which he reckoned was increasingly often. For his part, Thackeray chain-smoked and stared out of the window at the continuous stream of lorries they overtook on the trans-Pennine motorway, lorries which threw up so much spray that it was almost impossible to make out the details of the rolling hills and moors the road swept across on its way from one conurbation to another. Once past the high reservoirs, almost invisible through the swirling rain and mist, and over the watershed, it was downhill into the overcast murk of Greater Manchester, where the glittering regeneration of the city centre spread little cheer in the small outlying towns of Victorian terraces, abandoned mills and edgy race relations which they passed through on the way.

They were met in reception at police headquarters by a crop-haired, chilly eyed young man who introduced himself as DI Mark Hesketh.

'Glad you came, sir,' he said to Thackeray without any sign of warmth when the introductions were made and he led them upstairs to the CID offices. 'We've made a bit more progress since I spoke to your super this morning. But if it's ID you're after, it's not going to be easy according to our forensics people. There's not much of this guy left. They're still working on the body and on what's left of the vehicle.'

'It must have been a fierce fire,' Thackeray said.

'Right,' Hesketh said, with slightly more enthusiasm. 'And the reason's not difficult to find. The petrol can was in the main body of the car with him. He must have doused himself with it and struck a match, as far as we can work out. The tank didn't go up until later, and that finished off the job pretty comprehensively, as it goes. Must have taken some bottle, that.'

'Unless someone else struck the match,' Thackeray said coldly. 'I assume you've considered that possibility?'

'You're thinking murder, not suicide?' Hesketh's surprise registered as little more than a raised eyebrow.

'I'm not thinking anything,' Thackeray said. 'You've found a Land Rover we've been seeking for the last four days, and a body which may or may not be the owner of the car, who may have killed himself in a particularly agonising way – or not, as the case may be. I don't know who he is or how he died, and nor, I suspect, do you. Did anyone see the blaze?'

Hesketh shrugged, obviously irritated by Thackeray's implied criticism.

'It's not an area where people volunteer much to the police,' he said. 'It's bandit country down there. We're still knocking on doors, without much result so far. Chances are the vehicle was torched in the early hours, three, possibly four days ago.'

'Was there a weapon of any sort found inside the Land Rover?' Thackeray asked, bringing Hesketh up short again.

'Should there have been?' he asked.

'If the victim was Gordon Christie we think he was in possession of an automatic pistol. If he'd wanted to kill himself, a bullet would be the most obvious way to do it. We've good reason to believe that he shot his wife and children before he disappeared.'

'Ah,' Hesketh said. 'One of those. We weren't aware of that, I don't think.'

'You should have been. We warned that the driver of the vehicle might be armed and that he might have a child with him, when we put out the call for it,' Thackeray said sharply.

'Right,' Hesketh said. 'A child? There's no sign...'

'We've located the child,' Thackeray snapped. 'He's dead, too. I think maybe we ought to start at the beginning again. Let me fill you in on Gordon Christie and then we'll look at your reports, and maybe what remains of the Land Rover.'

'Sir,' Hesketh said with ill-grace, unresponsive to the flash of sympathy in Kevin Mower's eyes as the visitors pulled chairs up, sat down around Hesketh's desk and began to go through the file that the Yorkshire detectives had brought with them. But before Thackeray had finished his succinct exposition of the tragedy at Moor Edge cottage, Hesketh's phone rang and he grabbed the receiver like some sort of lifeline. He listened in silence for some time.

'Right,' he said, at length. 'I've got the officers from Bradfield here with me now. We'll come over.'

'Something significant?' Thackeray asked.

'It was the pathologist,' Hesketh said. 'He's found a bullet-hole in the fire victim's skull. No sign of the bullet though. Something else to look for in the wreckage and at the site – though if it went through one of the windows we'll be lucky to locate it on the waste ground up there.'

'I'd keep trying, if I were you,' Thackeray said curtly, getting to his feet. 'So let's go and see your pathologist, shall we? And then see what's left of the Land Rover. If this is Christie and he shot himself, the gun should be in the wreckage and we're just left with the mystery of how the car went up in flames. If it's not, then we could be looking at another murder investigation.'

'There's another possibility if you know our scallies,' Hesketh said sourly. 'Someone found the body, nicked the gun as a useful accessory and then torched the Land Rover for a laugh. Not just one crime but several, and more to come if the automatic's on the streets of Moss Side now. All round, it's a pity you didn't keep your Mr Christie on your side of the Pennines, Mr Thackeray. With respect, of course.'

Dawn Brough sat in silence by Emma Christie's bedside, twisting a paper tissue in her hands until it disintegrated into damp shreds between her fingers. She knew she was doing neither Emma or herself any good by maintaining this intermittent vigil she had taken upon herself, but she had found herself drawn into town again that morning after she had dropped her own children off at school. She did not understand why she felt so driven to make the journey to the infirmary, except by owning to some sort of overwhelming mothering instinct that she could not explain to herself let alone her husband, who told her irritably that she was wasting her time and should concentrate on her own kids.

This morning she thought that Emma's breathing sounded more regular – normal even – than on her previous visits, and the screens and dials which flickered above the bed did not appear to her to be doing such a frantic dance today. But she did not know whether this meant anything and the nurses were too busy to be approachable and merely seemed relieved that the unconscious child had a visitor ready to sit beside the unwrinkled white covers of the bed and occasionally make contact with Emma's limp hand.

The one person Dawn had spoken to on her last visit had been DC Val Ridley, who had stood up when she arrived, as if ready to leave. She had looked at her interrogatively and Dawn had felt obliged to explain awkwardly who she was.

'She doesn't seem to have any family left,' she had whispered in embarrassment, but the police officer had smiled warmly at her.

'We've not been able to find anyone at all yet,' she said. 'I'm sure there must be someone, but maybe abroad or something. It's really good of you to take the trouble. I feel awful about her lying here all alone, too. She's bound to want her mother when she does wake up.'

Dawn had nodded, on the edge of tears, and had been thankful when Val had rushed off, promising to come back when she could.

'We need to talk to her, you see,' Val had said, as if in self-justification as she went, and Dawn guessed that there was more to it than that. Sitting by the bed again today, at one end of the busy ward, she occasionally glanced towards the door, half hoping that Val would appear again. But no one came or went except a couple of anxious-looking relatives who hurried down to the far end of the ward, where a huddle of medical staff were gathered around the bed of a young man swathed in bandages and high-tech equipment.

Dawn shuddered. She hated this place and wished more than anything that she did not feel this overwhelming need to be here. She glanced at her watch again. Soon she would have to leave to be in time to collect her own children from school. That was the only thing that seemed even more important at the moment than seeing Emma. At least, she thought, her younger child, Jenny, had not shown any apparent curiosity about the sudden disappearance of her friend Louise, but Stephen had taken the loss of Scott

Christie hard, asking about him constantly over the days when his whereabouts had been uncertain, and storming about the house like an angry whirlwind the previous evening when Dawn had gently explained to him that his friend would not be coming back. How could anyone do that? Dawn asked herself for the hundredth time, and for the hundredth time could find no answer.

She glanced back to the small figure in the bed beside her and drew a sharp breath in surprise as she realised that Emma's eyes were open and staring at her, though barely focused.

'Emma?' Dawn said quietly, taking the child's hand again. Emma did not seem to hear her. Dawn glanced up and down the ward, feeling herself trembling slightly, and eventually caught the eye of a harassed looking nurse.

'She's awake,' Dawn said, her breath coming quickly.

The nurse looked at Emma dispassionately for a moment, but the child's gaze never flickered as the adults bent over the bed.

'Maybe,' she said. 'I'll get the doctor to come over and have a look at her when he s free.

'Will she remember what happened?' Dawn asked, but the nurse just shrugged.

'They seldom do,' she said. 'And with the head wound it's even less likely. There may be brain damage...'

'It might be better not to remember,' Dawn whispered but found she was talking to herself as the nurse hurried away. She took Emma's hand and squeezed it gently, but there was no reaction and after a couple of minutes she closed her eyes again with a faint sigh, as if the effort of raising the lids, even for a few moments, had exhausted her.

'Come on, sweetheart,' Dawn said urgently. 'Come on, keep trying.' Dawn jumped as she felt a hand on her shoulder and turned round to face Val Ridley again.

'I thought you'd be going soon,' Val said. 'I can stay for a while now.'

'I must go,' Dawn said. 'But she opened her eyes a minute ago. The doctor's coming to look at her. I really think she may be coming out of it at last.'

'I hope so,' Val said. 'She's our only witness to what happened in that house.'

'She may not remember,' Dawn said.

'No, she may not, and in some ways I hope she doesn't. If it was her father with the gun it's more than she needs to know, isn't it? Better forgotten, though it'll make our job harder.'

She hesitated for a moment, her eyes fixed on the unconscious child again.

'What really bugs me is that if no one from the family turns up she'll end up in care. I'd hate that. It happened to me when I was ten.'

Dawn looked at her, suddenly under-standing why this quiet pale police officer spent so much time at Emma's bedside.

'It must be dreadful,' she said. 'But surely she can't be completely on her own. Is there no sign of her father yet? He might have some answers.'

Val hesitated for a split second and then shook her head.

'Nothing definite,' she said. 'One of the problems is we've no photographs of the wretched man. There was nothing in the house.'

'I found one,' Dawn said unexpectedly. 'I was hunting through for that reporter from the *Gazette*, Laura something? I gave her some pictures of the children taken in our garden, but after she'd gone I remembered my husband had taken some snaps at the school fête last summer and I thought Gordon was there that day. And there he was, just in the one snap, but definitely him, in the background but quite a clear likeness...'

'Where's this photograph now?' Val inter-rupted, suddenly galvanised. 'You haven't given it to the *Gazette*, have you?'

'No, not yet, it's still at home,' Dawn said, startled. 'You can come and get it, if it's so important. I've got to get back now to collect the kids from school.'

'Right,' Val said. 'I think I'd better do that, don't you?'

Chapter Nine

Sergeant Kevin Mower closed the file of reports from the Manchester police which he had been reading in Michael Thackeray's office and sighed.

'It makes no sense, guv,' he said.

'Not a lot,' Thackeray agreed. 'I thought we'd been lucky that they found both the bullet and the pistol in the wreckage yesterday. The bullet's badly damaged but a match with the gun in the Land Rover, but the gun in the Land Rover isn't the one used in Staveley. What the hell does that mean?'

'You think it was murder, not suicide? And whoever shot him left the gun to make it look like suicide?'

'As DI Hesketh said, it's certainly a possibility. But either way, we don't know who the victim was, so it's difficult to know where to go next.'

'What are the chances of getting usable DNA?' Mower asked. 'I thought with these new techniques they'd got, miracles were just about possible.'

'At a price,' Thackeray said gloomily. 'I couldn't get any promises out of the forensics lab. They'd do their best and it would take some time, was all they'd say. They can work from a single cell, apparently, but it's a time-consuming business. But as I said to the super, we do need to know if the body's Christie's, whatever it takes to find out. In the meantime they're looking at matches for the bullet and the gun on the files. If it's been used before, that may offer us a few leads. There's little enough else to go on.'

'You'd have put money on it being Christie,' Mower said.

'You'd have put money on Christie having driven up onto the hills and shot himself soon after the deaths at the house that morning,' Thackeray said. 'With the same gun. But he didn't. The whole thing's beginning to look a lot more complicated than we thought at first. While we're waiting for something definite from the labs, we'll do a complete review of all the evidence we've got so far in case there's anything we've missed. If we don't do it ourselves we'll have county breathing down our necks wanting the thing either cracked or closed. We all thought we were dealing with a particularly nasty domestic but if that body isn't Gordon Christie's we could have a major murder investigation on our hands and very little of the basic work done.'

Before Mower could respond there was a tap on the door and Val Ridley put her head round.

'Something important, Val?' Thackeray asked.

'Two things, sir,' she said, passing Thackeray a buff envelope. 'Dawn Brough, the Christies' neighbour, found this for us.' Thackeray took the photograph out of the envelope and studied the picture of a group of adults and children smiling with more or less enthusiasm at the camera against a background of balloons and candyfloss.

'That's Gordon, behind Linda and Scott,' Val said, pointing to a partially obscured figure at the back of the picture, caught full-face but looking away from the camera and probably unaware of being photographed.

'We'll get it blown up,' Thackeray said sharply. 'At this moment we don't even know whether Christie is alive or dead, but if we discover he's alive that will be very helpful. Well done, Val. And the second thing?'

'I've just come from the infirmary,' she said. 'Emma Christie looks like she's regaining consciousness. She actually opened her eyes yesterday and spoke a few words this morning, the doctor said. He also said that she probably won't remember what happened that morning but it's just possible she will. She could be the witness we need.'

'We'd better have someone at the bedside soon, then,' Thackeray said. 'Someone's going to have to tell her about the rest of her family, but only when the medics think it's wise.'

'I'd like to be there, sir,' Val said. 'If you can spare me?'

Thackeray looked at the pale, blonde young woman, an efficient officer who generally kept her private life and her emotions well concealed, and wondered what caused the barely disguised pleading in her eyes. What was Emma to her? he wondered.

'You can't be there twenty-four seven,' he said quietly. 'Organise a rota with uniform to start as soon as the doctors think it's sensible. As soon as she's able to talk we need to know what she's got to say.'

'Sir,' Val said and went out looking even less cheerful than when she had arrived.

'She's taking this case badly,' Mower said. Thackeray nodded but made no comment. Val Ridley was not the only one taking this case badly, he thought. He glanced down at the photograph of Christie and his wife and son with cheerfully smiling friends and shuddered slightly. The man was tall and dark-haired, as they had been told, and he wondered if he was only imagining a threatened look in his eyes, something of the desperation of a trapped animal, as Christie stood there hemmed in by lightly clad summer revellers who seemed to be in a different dimension to the one he inhabited. He passed the picture to Mower impatiently.

'Get it enhanced and copies made. If that body's not Christie's, we'll need it. We'll have even more urgent reasons to find him.'

Dawn Brough felt slightly guilty about the red-headed reporter who had chatted to her over tea at her house. She had promised her a photograph of Gordon Christie if she could find one, but now the police had taken possession of the only snap she had discovered. She picked up the phone and rather tentatively called the *Gazette* and eventually found herself put through to Laura Ackroyd.

'I expect the police will issue it to the Press eventually,' Laura said, annoyed that she had been pre-empted by Val Ridley. 'When was the school fête exactly? Perhaps one of our photographers was there.'

'Oh, yes, there was someone,' Dawn said. 'But I don't expect they caught Gordon. He was really – what do you call it? – camera shy?'

'What was he wearing that day?' Laura asked. 'Can you remember?'

Dawn thought that over for a moment.

'It was a hot day,' she said hesitantly. 'We were lucky for once. Usually it rains. He had a green shirt, a polo shirt with a collar, short sleeves, that's in my picture, and dark jeans, I think. And he had Scott in tow most of the time. The little lad had a green T-shirt as well, paler green. Scott was quite fair, but

Gordon was dark. Dark hair, no beard or anything, and tall. Don't get him mixed up with Gerry Foster from the pub if you're looking at pictures. He's dark too, but he has a beard.'

'Yes, I've met him,' Laura said. 'Okay, I'll have a look through our own pictures here and see if I can find him. You never know, we might get an exclusive out of it in spite of the police.'

'What exclusive's that then, doll?' a voice she didn't want to hear came from behind her as she hung up. She turned round irritably.

'Are you looking for a job here or something?' she asked. 'Don't the *Globe* want you any more?'

'What do you think?' Vince said, his eyes roaming across the newsroom restlessly. 'I just came in to see Bob Baker, but he doesn't seem to be around.'

'He's on a day off, I think,' Laura said, unable to keep a note of satisfaction at the crime reporter's absence out of her voice. Anything which interfered with Vince's plans was good news in her book.

'I'll treat Ted to a lunchtime pint, then,' Vince said easily. 'Care to join us, honey, or are you too deep in your little exclusive?'

'Thanks, but no thanks,' Laura said, thinking that there were no two people she would less like a drink with today, or any day, but Vince merely grinned at her over his shoulder as he drifted away. He still treats the place as if he belongs here, Laura thought angrily. She guessed she was not the only one who resented the assumption that the *Bradfield Gazette* was a branch office for the *Globe*. Only Ted and perhaps Bob Baker would find that flattering.

She sighed, glanced out of the office window, and turned back to her computer screen without enthusiasm. It was a dark, damp day with more than a hint of rain in the air and it matched her mood. Watching Thackeray get dressed that morning, insisting that he had to make an early start as he brought her a cup of tea in bed with a smile that was no more than perfunctory, she had wondered for the hundredth time why the loss of his wife, which should, she had hoped, have liberated him from his past at last, had instead thrown him into a mood of icy non-communication which was gradually tearing her apart.

'Do you feel like going out for a meal tonight?' she had asked. 'There's that new Italian place?'

'I'm not sure what time I'll get away. Don't worry about me, I'll get something on the way home if I'm late.'

'I do worry about you, Michael,' she had said quietly. 'All the time, as it goes.' But he had merely looked at her, his blue eyes unfathomable, before turning on his heel and closing the bedroom door behind him. And when she had heard the front door of the flat close behind him she had buried her head in the pillows again and wept.

Once the lunchtime drinkers had left the office she walked over to the far corner of the newsroom where Phil Halliday, the picture editor, sat hunched over his computer juggling images of Bradfield United's latest disastrous midweek performance around the screen. He barely glanced up as Laura approached and, when he did, his expression was mournful.

'Looks like they're for the drop again,' he muttered as he zoomed in on a shot of United's goalkeeper sprawling in the mud as a scoring ball sailed into the net for the fourth time during the previous evening's match. 'Pillock,' Phil said as he stabbed at his keyboard viciously and blanked the screen. 'Not a win in seventeen games. So what can I do for you, love?' he asked.

'How long do you file stuff in that system of yours?' Laura asked.

'How long do you want me to have filed something?'

'One of our photographers went to a school fête out at Staveley last summer, June or July probably. Would you still have all the shots he took?'

'You don't know which photographer, I

suppose?' he asked, and shook his head when Laura said she didn't.

'Well, you might be lucky. I'm not as religious as I should be at culling stuff. The memory's so good I tend to leave things on I probably shouldn't. The truth is I still hanker for the old picture library where we stored stuff for years. It was surprising how often it turned up trumps when someone or something resurfaced years later.'

'Staveley primary school?' Laura said.

'Summat to do with the family who was shot?' Phil asked.

'We may have the father in a picture,' Laura said. 'The police are very slow at issuing a photograph of him.'

'Right,' the picture editor said, evidently galvanised at that. She stood behind him while he searched his indexes and files for what seemed like forever before stabbing at the keyboard in triumph.

'Bingo,' he said as a couple of dozen tiny images appeared on the screen. 'There's another set as well, by the look of it. Do you want to have a look at them while I go and get a sandwich. Click on each image to enlarge it and then on Next. Okay?'

Laura slid into Phil's vacated chair with a feeling of excitement and began to flick through the photographer's record of a sunny afternoon last summer. But she worked quickly, focusing only on green shirts, and

147

eventually she knew that in that sea of happy faces she had tracked down Gordon Christie in not one photograph, but two. In the first, he too was smiling as he glanced down at the fair-haired little boy whom Laura recognised as his son, Scott. In the second, he had been caught by the camera full-face and was looking much less happy in a crowd of people that included his wife and all his children and, ironically, the burly bearded figure of Gerry Foster, the bad-tempered landlord from the Fox and Hounds. It looked, Laura thought, as if he had realised he was being photographed that time and did not like it much.

She made a note of the reference numbers of the two photographs and saved the file again, deciding not to print anything out until Vince Newsom was safely out of range. Finding the pictures was a modest triumph, and as it was now too late to get them into the paper today she decided to keep the knowledge to herself for the moment and reveal it at the next day's editorial conference, to which Vince would certainly not be invited. She didn't win many brownie points with Ted Grant but this, she thought, might earn her one or two.

PC Gavin Hewitt pulled up outside Staveley Old Hall and looked at the high electronically controlled gates with disfavour. Any idea of pulling up in the cobbled yard with a screech of brakes, in the old *Starsky and Hutch* style he secretly favoured, had to be shelved as he climbed out of the panda car and pressed the bell on the stone gatepost. When he had explained his business to a disembodied voice in the house, the wrought iron gates swung slowly back and he drove in.

Hewitt was old enough to remember when the old hall had been just that, a dilapidated stone manor house, its roof sagging under the weight of its ancient tiles, its woodwork beginning to rot after centuries of withstanding the Pennine gales, one or two of its mullioned windows torn out and replaced with PVC, and what was left of the house surrounded by a cluster of outbuildings left to fall into ruin when most of its farmland had been sold off to other landowners, leaving the house without much purpose in the rural landscape. In the early Nineties, when Hewitt had been a teenager in Staveley, the house had been bought by a young couple whom the locals dismissed contemptuously as hippies, and who had made a half-hearted attempt at modernisation, which seemed to require an effort out of all proportion to the results visible to the sceptical villagers. Three children and many botched attempts at small-scale farming later, the couple had sold off the chickens and goats and pigs, split

149

up and acrimoniously moved on, and the house had stood empty for a few more years until the tentacles of the property boom reached even these outlying areas of unfashionable Bradfield and attracted renewed interest in the hall's ancient stone walls and picturesque situation on the lower-lying edge of the village, with nothing but miles of wild open moors beyond its walls.

Hewitt had moved on himself when he joined the police force, his family had scattered and he had had little reason to revisit Staveley until he was appointed its community police officer in the early years of the next century. Staveley had seemed to him familiar enough when he came back, apart from the cluster of new-build properties on the village edge. But the Old Hall, he had thought, was something else. It had moved into a new dimension: re-roofed, re-windowed, re-pointed, tastefully extended here and there, its boundary walls made more than proof against intruders, the gardens made over, gravelled and decked and water-featured out of all recognition, and one of the barns reclaimed to house an indoor pool and conservatory terrace, which would not have looked out of place in Hollywood.

Hewitt didn't know how or even where Bruce Weldon had made his pile, but he had no doubt that the pile was substantial. This was the second time since the tragedy at

Moor Edge cottage that he had driven through those smoothly oiled electronic gates: he had been impressed the first time when he had asked Weldon about his contacts with Gordon Christie as an odd-jobbing mechanic, and he was still impressed, as he got out of the car, to be met by Weldon himself, in riding gear, striding across the gravel to face him, his crop tapping rhythmically against his glossy boots as he approached, followed by two black labradors who snuffled at Hewitt's uniform trousers wetly, but amiably enough, but cowered away when Weldon called them off more sharply than Hewitt thought was strictly necessary.

'Constable Hewitt,' Weldon said. 'What can I do for you? Have you found Gordon Christie yet?'

'No, we haven't, sir,' Hewitt said. 'We're still looking, as far as I know.'

Weldon glanced up at the high fells which were visible beyond the stone wall and a stand of rowan and birch that had been planted to the north of the property as a wind break.

'There's a lot of room up there to hide yourself if you really try,' he said. He glanced at his watch. 'I'm just off out for a hack. What can I do for you?'

'Well, I don't suppose it's anything really, sir, but we had a call from someone in the village this morning saying they thought they'd heard gunfire last night. In this direction, they reckoned. I don't suppose you heard anything yourself, did you?'

'I didn't,' Weldon said shortly. 'But the walls of this place are bloody thick. They knew how to build in the old days, even if they didn't have a clue how to keep a place like this heated. I was watching a film last night and went to bed about eleven. I didn't hear anything untoward. I expect it was someone out after foxes. It'll be lambing time soon enough.'

'In the house by yourself, sir, were you?' Hewitt persisted.

'Just me and the dogs,' Weldon said shortly. 'I don't keep live-in help. Just a housekeeper and a cleaner who come in daily.'

'Right,' Hewitt said. 'And your son's still away, is he? I wanted a word with him about his car...'

'I've spoken to him about that,' Weldon said, his impatience becoming more obvious. 'He reckoned a friend of his left the car there for a joke. He'd parked it at the Fox and walked home because he'd had a few. You should approve of that.'

'Well, ask him to give me a call to confirm all that, would you sir, when he gets back? Just for our records. He'll be back soon, will he?'

'I've really no idea,' Weldon said, and Hewitt wondered if he had imagined the

152

faintest flicker of anxiety in his eyes. 'Stuart lives here but I'm not his keeper. He comes and goes as he pleases. Doesn't tell me what he's up to half the time. Now can I get on with my morning, please? I've a friend waiting for me at the stables in Broadley. I'm already late.'

'Right, sir,' Hewitt said, making his way back to his panda car slowly while he cast an admiring eye over the immaculate frontage of the old house, the sparkling panes of glass in the mullioned windows reflecting back the morning's grey clouds and an occasional gleam of weak sunshine. He drove out of the gates, closely followed by Weldon, with the dogs on the back seat of his latest model 4x4, and watched in his mirror as the gates slowly swung shut behind them. Weldon overtook him in the village and roared off down the hill towards the town while Hewitt pulled up outside the shop and called in to his station.

'Summat odd about these gunshots,' he said to his sergeant. 'I reckon CID will want to know. I spoke to Mr Bruce Weldon at the Old Hall, who said he'd heard nowt last night, watched a film and slept like a baby, he reckoned. But if you look closely at one of the downstairs front windows, I'd swear that there were two bullet holes in it. Now what's that all about, d'you reckon?'

It was mid-afternoon by the time PC

Hewitt's report had filtered through to CID at Bradfield police headquarters and onto Sergeant Kevin Mower's desk. He took it straight into DCI Thackeray.

'Worth a trawl, guv?' he asked.

'What do we know about Weldon? Anything?' Thackeray asked.

'Nothing on record,' Mower said. 'I checked. The son's had a few brushes as a young lad, public order offences, one assault, obviously had a drink problem at one time, but nothing for years now. I had a word with Hewitt to see what he knew about them but apparently Staveley gossip just laughs at the father's efforts at being a country gent – the green wellies, the riding, the dogs. He seems to fancy that being lord of the manor goes with owning the biggest property for miles around, but no one takes him seriously. They take his money when it's offered for the church roof or computers for the school, and otherwise ignore him.'

'Do we know where the money comes from?'

'He claims to be a retired businessman. Hewitt reckoned he made a packet in Manchester, but he doesn't know how. Stuart Weldon doesn't seem to work either, although he's always got a number of flash cars on the go, some of them top of the range sporty numbers. A Lamborghini amongst them at one time, allegedly, though that seems a bit unlikely.'

'Well, I think it's worth asking Greater Manchester if they know anything about Weldon. If there's any suspicion he's living on the proceeds of crime we can take it further, look at his accounts, and the rest. We still don't know where Gordon Christie was getting large sums of cash from. And you could go up and have a look at these alleged bullet holes. See what you think.'

'Right, guv,' Mower said. But when he and DC Omar Sharif returned from a sortie to Staveley later in the afternoon, it was only to report a number of frustrating negatives. Weldon had not been at home when they had arrived, although the motherly looking housekeeper had let them in willingly enough and even shown them into the sitting room where Hewitt had thought he saw damage to the window. But when Mower, who barely knew a daffodil from a petunia, had stood apparently admiring the garden outside while in fact inspecting the small panes of the windows, he had found nothing unusual except a single rectangle of glass held in place by putty much softer and newer than the rest. In response to Mower's inquiries, the housekeeper confirmed that she had heard no shots because she had left Weldon's house as usual soon after six.

'You had a broken window,' he had said mildly to the woman as she stood close

155

behind him, and watched him press his thumbnail lightly into the soft putty.

'We think it was cracked by gravel thrown up by one of the cars,' she said, with an easy smile. 'The glazier came to mend it this morning. They're very quick if it's anything to do with security.'

'So when do you think it happened?' Mower persisted.

'Well, I only noticed it this morning, but it could have been any time over the last couple of days. I cleaned the windows on Monday but Mr Weldon generally opens the curtains before he goes to bed so I wouldn't necessarily have noticed.'

'But surely he would,' Sharif had broken in quickly. 'A broken window's not something you'd miss, is it?'

'I noticed it this morning and sent for the glazier straight away,' the housekeeper said firmly. 'Mr Weldon hadn't mentioned it, and I didn't bother him with such a little thing. He was in a hurry to go out. He leaves the general running of the house to me.'

'You don't live in, do you?' Mower had asked.

'No, I come up every day. I live over Wilton way. I drive up, work and get off home again. I've a family of my own to look after. I don't want to be at anyone's beck and call all hours.'

'So you wouldn't have heard these shots

we're interested in?'

'Oh, no, I go home at six. Mr Weldon didn't mention anything, though. I expect it was someone out shooting vermin. It's surprisingly countrified round here, you know, although we're so close to Bradfield and the motorway. That's why Mr Weldon likes it, I think. He and Mr Stuart travel quite a lot.'

'Right,' Mower had said. 'And Stuart Weldon's travelling now, I understand?'

'I believe so,' the housekeeper said. 'He's always off somewhere. I've not seen him for t'best part of a week now. But that's not unusual. They keep themselves to themselves, the two of them. I get on with my job and they get on with their affairs. Best way, I always think, with this sort of job. You don't want to get too involved, do you? I don't, any road.'

'Did you know Gordon Christie? The man whose family were shot? I believe he did some work for Mr Weldon.'

The woman shook her head slowly.

'I was thinking about that when I heard. A terrible business, wasn't it? I think I did see him when he came to do some work on the mowers last summer, but I don't think I'd recognise him if I bumped into him in the street. I don't take much notice of what goes on with the outdoor staff. I've got enough to keep me busy indoors.'

And with that Mower had had to be

content. But when he and Sharif were back in the car and heading down the steep hill towards the centre of Bradfield, he glanced at his companion.

'Did you believe her?' he had asked.

Sharif shook his head. 'I might have done,' he said. 'She seems straightforward enough. But when you two were over by the window I noticed something else. Right opposite the window there were two patches of new paint on the wall. Just where a couple of shots would have knocked lumps out of the plaster. The housekeeper may not know owt about it, but I reckon someone took a couple of pot shots through that window, maybe at someone inside. And Mr Bruce Weldon obviously doesn't want anyone to know about it.'

'And the question then is whether an honest man would be as reticent as that,' Mower had said thoughtfully. 'I think the Weldons merit a closer look after all.'

Chapter Ten

The photograph was spread across three columns of the front page of the *Globe* in colour which was, in reality, no colour at all: a pale face with a bandaged head against a white pillow with only the blue of the half-open eyes to indicate that Emma Christie was no longer quite as deeply asleep as she had been for almost a week. But the picture, and its accompanying headline 'I want my mummy' exploded like a grenade amongst Bradfield's police and hospital managers and reverberated around the newsroom of the *Gazette* where Ted Grant was apoplectic at being out-foxed by Vince Newsom. 'How the hell did he get that?' was the question on everybody's lips to which there was no obvious answer. Vince Newsom, whose by-line graced the exclusive story, was keeping his head down this morning, if he was still in Bradfield at all.

'Did anyone see him on the ward?' DCI Michael Thackeray demanded of DC Val Ridley when she responded to his summons to his office. Sergeant Kevin Mower watched proceedings from the back of the room where he half-perched on the windowsill as if distancing himself from what was going on.

'Apparently not,' Val, who had just returned from the hospital halfway through the morning, said defensively. She looked even paler and more tense than usual and Mower felt a niggle of anxiety himself as he realised how this case was taking its toll in unexpected ways.

'It was very busy in there yesterday,' Val

went on. 'There'd been a bad smash on the M62 and they had two patients brought in around teatime. It's not impossible to go in and out without being noticed. The nurses are often too stressed out to notice who's coming and going. They have more important things to do.'

'And we had no one there? You haven't set a rota up yet?'

'The doctors didn't think it was worth it yesterday. She'd slipped back into the coma. I went in after work for half an hour about six, but she seemed deeply unconscious then. You said...'

'Yes, I know what I said,' Thackeray came back quickly. 'I said take the doctors' advice. But what that means is that Newsom could have walked in and out yesterday pretty well any time without being challenged. He must have had this photograph by yesterday evening for it to appear in this morning's paper.' If he had learned nothing else from Laura Ackroyd, he thought, he had absorbed some knowledge of how newspapers were produced.

'He could have done. But he may not have needed to,' Val suggested. 'He might have paid someone else to take pictures, someone on the staff maybe. Someone who could wait for a good moment and snap her when her eyes were open.'

'Is the child actually conscious or not?'

Thackeray asked angrily. 'Or is this stuff in the *Globe* a complete invention?'

'She's not really conscious,' Val said. 'She's opening her eyes occasionally but she's not actually saying anything coherent yet. Just mumbling. The doctors aren't that optimistic, really. The *Globe*'s just making things up.'

'Surprise me,' Thackeray said with unusual venom. Anyway, get the hospital security people on the case, can you Val? They should be able to keep the Press out, at least. And we'll take over as soon as there's a chance she can tell us something useful.'

'I suppose the upside, is that the publicity may flush some relatives out of the woodwork,' Val Ridley offered. 'I can't understand why she's still all alone in there. She must have some other family. I don't know why no one's come forward.' She sounded slightly distraught at the thought.

'It's probably because as far as we can see Gordon Christie doesn't exist officially,' Kevin Mower offered from his slightly detached vantage point against the windowsill. 'Or any of the rest of the family, for that matter. Social services haven't been able to find a birth certificate for Emma, which implies that they're not really called Christie at all. Granny is hardly likely to come running to the rescue if she doesn't even recognise the child's name, is she? The question then arises as to what or who Gordon Christie was going to such lengths to hide from. And whether, in the end, someone caught up with him.'

'They've still not identified the body in Manchester?' Val asked.

'The latest is that they've found some possibly usable DNA samples from it, which they may be able to match with samples we can provide from the Christie's house – hairs from his hairbrush, that sort of thing,' Thackeray said. 'But it will take time. Days, if not weeks. So we still don't know if Gordon Christie's dead or alive.'

'So we keep looking?' Kevin Mower asked. 'On the assumption he's still out there somewhere.'

'I'll talk to the super this afternoon about issuing the photograph. That should help,' Thackeray said. 'We can't assume he's dead on the evidence of what was in that car. And if he isn't dead, he may well still have a weapon. So yes, we keep looking for Gordon Christie. He's either a deranged killer himself or the victim of a particularly vicious killer who's wiped out most of his family. Either way he's not likely to be very rational and, with a gun in his hand, he could be very dangerous. I want him found.'

Laura Ackroyd drove out of town to Staveley with a feeling of familiarity. As she had hoped, her discovery of pictures of the Christie family at the previous summer's school fête had gone down well enough with Ted Grant, in spite of his early morning tantrum at being scooped by Vince Newsom's coup on the front page of the *Globe*. Slightly to Laura's surprise, though, Ted had decided not to run the *Gazette*'s photographs immediately, but to send Laura back up to the village to research a long feature for the following day.

'Get me quotes from the family friends, try to get hold of the kids who were at school with Emma, I want to know what people feel when summat like this happens in their community, you know the sort of thing. Find out if the funerals are going to be in the village church and if the school will close for the day. All that background stuff.'

'Right,' Laura had said, without too much enthusiasm.

'And when you've got the lie of the land brief Phil and he'll organise some pics to go with these.' Ted gestured at the shots taken the previous summer. 'Before and after the tragedy, that sort of thing.'

'What are the police saying about their search for Gordon Christie?' Laura had asked Bob Baker, the crime reporter, who had also been called in for this particular discussion. He had looked at her oddly, and she knew she had carelessly asked the wrong question.

'I thought you'd be up to date on that, in your position,' Baker had said with a smirk. Laura flushed slightly and did not pursue the point. There might have been a time when Michael Thackeray would have discussed his problems with her, but for the moment those times seemed to be over, and the reminder turned her cold inside. And as Baker followed her back into the newsroom at the end of the meeting, she realised she might have betrayed far more than she had intended.

'Cooling off a bit, is it?' Baker whispered in her ear. 'Couldn't have anything to do with Vince Newsom turning up again, could it? He told me about the thing you two used to have going. Smart cookie, Vince. You could do worse. I'd really like to know how he got that picture of little Emma, wouldn't you?'

'It's an awful picture,' Laura said. 'It breaks every rule in the book. And I've about as much interest in Vince Newsom as I have in something that crawled out from under a stone.'

'Right,' Baker said, with a smile which was closer, Laura thought, to a sneer. 'I'll tell him that then, shall I, next time I see him?'

'If he's stupid enough to still be hanging around Bradfield after this morning's effort, you can tell him anything you like,' Laura had said as she packed her tape recorder into her bag and pulled out her car keys. She turned her back on her tormentor, but Baker could not resist the last word.

'I'll give Vince your love then, shall I?' He had laughed uproariously at his own joke as Laura turned away, but as she drove out of town she was still thinking far more about her own problems than she was about her assignment. She desperately needed someone to talk to but Vicky Mendelson was still away, and her grandmother – who in any case had always maintained a sceptical detachment from her relationship with 'her policeman' – was in Portugal on a visit to Laura's parents and a much needed rest in the sunshine. She felt suddenly alone and vulnerable in the very place she had always regarded unequivocally as home.

'Damn you, Michael,' she said to herself as she pulled into the deserted car park at the Fox and Hounds. She got out of the car and slammed the door with a satisfactory thud, a substitute, she knew, for a well-aimed kick at her increasingly exasperating lover. 'Damn and blast you.'

She glanced around. It was a cold morning and a light rain was falling, casting a steely sheen across pavements and roofs but blotting out the hills beyond the huddle of houses and cottages. Most people, she guessed, would be indoors if they were at home at all. But a light shone through the misted window of the shop, and the door of the pub was open. She decided to tackle Gerry Foster first, but when she went into the bar there were no customers in sight, nor even anyone behind the bar. She took one of the high stools at the counter and cleared her throat to attract attention.

Eventually a woman emerged from the rear of the bar without much evident enthusiasm for her solitary customer. Laura asked her for a coffee, was told it was not available and settled for an orange juice instead.

'Is Gerry around?' she asked when the glass was put in front of her and the woman had closed the till with a heavy hand.

'He's out,' the woman said. 'Who wants him, any road?' Laura explained who she was and the woman's pale features under straggly blonde hair, became even more tense.

'Gerry'll not have anything to say to the *Gazette*,' she said.

'He seemed happy enough to chat last time I spoke to him,' Laura said.

'Oh, he did, did he?' the woman said as if that did not surprise her.

'Are you Mrs Foster?' Laura persisted.

'For my bloody sins,' the woman said. 'Janine. They say the wife's the last to know, don't they? I expect the news'll be in t'bloody *Gazette* next, will it? Everyone else seems to know about it. P'raps you'd like to print an advertisement, would you?'

'Sorry?' Laura said, taken aback by this unexpected tirade. 'I don't know what you mean.'

'You mean you're not here to ask him about his little fling wi' Linda bloody Christie? Confessions of murdered woman's lover? All over t'front page? Isn't that what you've got in mind?'

Astonished by this, Laura took a sip of orange juice to give herself time to collect her thoughts. Dawn Brough's vague suspicions, which she had passed on to Thackeray as no more than that, must have turned out to be accurate after all.

'I'm sorry, Janine,' she said. 'I really didn't know about that.'

'Well. You're t'only one for miles around, then,' Janine said wildly.

'Will your husband be back soon?' Laura asked cautiously.

'I've no idea,' Mrs Foster snapped. 'He buggered off this morning after we had a blazing row and I've no idea where he's gone. He's left me to open up on my own and there'll be no food at lunchtime if he's not back to mind the bar. He's turning into a waste of space, is Gerry. It's been the same since he came out of the army. Can't settle to owt for five minutes. This is the third time we've tried to run a business and it'll be

167

t'last as far as I'm concerned.'

'D'you think he's blaming himself for what happened to the Christies?' Laura asked quietly, knowing all too well the coruscating effects of guilt when a child has died.

'I've no bloody idea,' Mrs Foster said again. And I can't say I really care. He's made his bed, he'll have to bloody lie on it, won't he. But he'll be doing it without me, the way we're going.'

'Did you know Linda Christie?' Laura asked.

'By sight, that's all,' Mrs Foster said. 'I knew her husband, and a right miserable beggar he was an' all. Pity is he didn't turn the gun on himself first off. I can't say that would have surprised me

Laura sipped her juice with a sigh. She would not write about Linda Christie's extra-marital affairs although she knew if Vince Newsom got hold of the same information he would not share or even understand her scruples. But the vision of a deeply depressed man whose suicide would apparently not have surprised his neighbours was a haunting one. She wondered why no one in the village had thought to offer him any help before he cracked so irretrievably.

'It's not something I really need to know for the piece I'm writing, Janine. What I'm trying to find out is what effect something like these shootings has on a village like Staveley. Does it affect trade, somewhere like this, for instance? Do people come to their local to talk about it?'

'Well, I can tell you that, any road,' Janine Foster said with a grim smile. 'Our regulars have abandoned us and the place has been packed full of gawpers, coming up to look at the Christie's house. There's a pile of flowers outside the front gate, I'm told, but I don't reckon they've been left by anyone from t'village. What's the point of leaving teddy bears for dead children? It's just these ghouls who pop in and out, peering in folk's windows, taking photographs. It's like living in one of those reality shows on telly. And you're just another version of that, any road, aren't you? Give the public a few extra snippets in case they can't get up here in person? It's disgusting, if you ask me. Why can't you leave us be?' It had obviously not needed the *Gazette*'s two-penn'orth to bring the horror tourists out in force, Laura thought, and felt faintly relieved at that.

'I'm sorry you feel like that,' Laura said. 'But people do need to know some of the details when something as horrific as this happens. And it's better if it's in the paper rather than through gossip. I don't think the interest will die down till they've found Gordon Christie. Or even till after the trial, if there is one. People must still be very worried, especially in the village, if they think he's still out there somewhere with a gun.'

'Of course people are worried,' Janine Foster said. 'The mothers won't let their kids out of their sight. They're standing outside the school in all weathers to take them home themselves instead of letting them walk. But it's all just a nonsense panic, that, isn't it? If he's made a run for it he'll be miles away by now. And it was his own family he obviously decided to knock off, not just anybody's children. It wasn't – what's the word? – random. I reckon some folk just like scaring themselves silly. It gives 'em summat to get excited about.'

Laura drained her glass and glanced at her watch. It was just coming up to midday.

'Do the primary school children go home for lunch?' she asked.

'Aye, some of 'em do.'

'So I might catch a few parents outside the school about now?'

'You might,' Janine Foster said grudgingly. 'But don't say I sent you.'

Feeling far more depressed than when she had arrived, Laura walked down the village street, feeling as if the blank windows of the cottages were watching her progress with a malevolence she had not fully anticipated. The school, a low Victorian building which still had 'Boys' and 'Girls' set in stone above two separate entrances, huddled against the side of its neighbouring church as if sheltering its inmates from the fierce Pennine gales, which Laura knew would lash it from the west. And on the other side of the tarmac playground a small group of mothers were huddled under umbrellas, talking to a tall man in a suit who seemed inadequately protected from the drifting, misty rain. Half a dozen pairs of eyes turned implacably in her direction as she approached and there was no response to her tentative smile.

'Can I help you?' the man asked, obviously used to taking charge of a situation in which the group of women seemed uncertain. Laura explained who she was and what she was doing in Staveley and felt the whole group stiffen and become even more defensive.

'I'm Frank Garside, the headteacher here,' the man said. 'You'd better come in out of the rain and we can have a chat. But I don't really know what I can tell you apart from the fact that the whole village is devastated, and I'm sure none of the families here will want you going around asking questions, and quite possibly upsetting people, even more than they're upset already.'

One or two of the mothers nodded at that.

'People were really shocked by the photograph in the *Globe* this morning,' Garside went on, steering Laura across the playground towards the school door. 'If I come across that reporter, I won't be slow to tell him so, either. But I suppose the *Gazette* is something else, being local. I certainly hope so.'

Laura waited impatiently for Thackeray to come home that evening. The time she had spent in Staveley that morning, and the longer hours she had spent at her computer trying to organise her impressions for the next day's paper, had distressed her in way which she had not anticipated. Frank Garside had been kindly and levelheaded, but did not disguise the fact that the loss of two of his pupils and their baby sister in such horrific circumstances had destabilised his school. The children were disturbed, he had said, and the staff who had known the Christie family were deeply saddened by what had happened. If Emma were to die too, he had said, it would be a blow he wondered whether his little community could cope with. Counsellors and therapists and the full bureaucracy of the caring professions had been mobilised already, he said, but he had sounded sceptical about how far any of that would help children traumatised by the loss of their friends.

'What I can't get to grips with is why now?' he had said helplessly as he plied Laura with tea in his tiny office overlooking the playground where some children were splashing through the puddles to meet their parents by the gates.

'What do you mean, why now?' Laura asked.

'Well, according to some of the children, Emma and Scott had told them that they were moving. I wasn't too happy about it when I heard, though Mrs Christie hadn't told me anything officially. You never want to lose pupils in this game. Our future depends on keeping numbers up.'

'Moving?' Laura had said. 'You mean moving away?'

Apparently. Emma had told one of her friends that they were going to live by the sea. She was happy about that, because they'd lived by the sea before, when they were abroad, I think. She was quite excited at the idea.'

'Do you think they were going abroad again?' Laura asked.

'I've no idea,' Frank Garside said. 'It's just a bit of children's gossip really, and there's no way of checking if it's true now, is there? Not that I thought it was out of keeping with that family. Linda was a pleasant enough woman, but Gordon I didn't like. He was an edgy, moody character, quite unpredictable. There was a suggestion once that he'd been hitting Scott. I couldn't tell social services that we'd noticed any evidence of abuse, but quite honestly it wouldn't have surprised me very much. I'm quite sure he could lash out if he was provoked. But Scott obviously adored his dad, whether he deserved it or not.'

Garside sighed and glanced out of his window again to watch some of the boys who had braved the weather to kick a ball around.

'There's only seventy children here,' he said. 'We're like a big family. Most of the parents know each other, there's cousins as well as brothers and sisters from the more long-established families in the village. This thing has hit us all like a thunderbolt.' And that, Laura knew as soon as the words were out of Garside's mouth, was her headline.

She had spent another hour or so in the village, chatting to some of the mothers bringing their children back to school after lunch, and trudging up to Moor Edge cottage to look at the rain-bedraggled bunches of flowers that had been left in the lane where the blue and white police tape still flapped forlornly in the wind. She had driven back to the office depressed by what she had seen and realising all too well just why Thackeray had seemed so deeply affected by this case. It was, she thought, a sort of violation not just of the family who had died but of all the families in the village; a denial of all that being a family was supposed to

174

mean. In some ways, she had ended her article, it must be easier to come to terms with the violation of children by a stranger than to see a father or mother turn so violently against those they were expected to cherish and protect. And that thought, she *knew*, must be tearing Michael Thackeray apart.

She would have liked to talk to Thackeray about the emotions her day's work had aroused, but she knew she would be treading on ground that was far too sensitive to venture near. And when he finally came in, late and drained, she offered no more than a brief description of how she had found the pictures of the school fête in the files and her subsequent researches, in response to his perfunctory inquiry.

'It's difficult to get away from the feeling that a peaceful village like that should be immune from violence,' she said. 'It seems like an intrusion.'

'There's no such thing as a peaceful village any more, Laura,' Thackeray said. 'With modern transport and communications, the whole of the North of England's one big village now. Criminals and crime touches everyone.'

'I suppose so,' Laura said as they ate and watched the TV news. 'The headteacher did say one odd thing, though. Apparently Emma told her friends she was going to move away. To the seaside, she said. And Scott had mentioned it, too. Did you know about that?'

Thackeray looked at Laura for a moment without speaking. Then he shrugged wearily.

'Nothing about this case surprises me any more,' he said. 'I don't think we know anything about that particular bit of information, no. But Gordon Christie was obviously very keen to keep his life private when he was alive, and I found out this afternoon that he's got friends – or maybe enemies – who want to keep it just as private now he's apparently dead.'

'What do you mean?' Laura asked, surprised herself now.

'Nothing I can tell you about,' Thackeray said quietly. 'Forget it, Laura. You just concentrate on the state of Staveley and leave the elusive Gordon Christie to me. But if you want an opinion, off the record, of course, I don't reckon we'll ever discover what really went on at Moor Edge cottage. There's too many filthy fingers in this particular pie.'

Chapter Eleven

DCI Michael Thackeray was knocking impatiently on Superintendent Jack Longley's office door the next morning, almost before his boss had taken his coat off and settled his substantial frame behind his desk.

'Come in, Michael,' Longley said mildly, although it was obvious that Thackeray's mood was very far from contented. And Longley himself seemed paler than usual, lines of tiredness etched into the corners of his mouth and fleshy bags under his eyes looking like crumpled purple tissue paper in the harsh morning light.

'What can I do for you?' Longley asked, in a tone which suggested that he knew and would not welcome the answer.

'I've been thinking about what you said yesterday afternoon, sir,' Thackeray said. 'And I've concluded that what's being suggested will seriously hamper my investigation.'

'How's that?' Longley prevaricated. 'As far as I can see the investigation's pretty well closed.'

'No, sir, it's not,' Thackeray said flatly. 'It's nowhere near closed. We've two murder victims already, a third child shot at and left in the snow to die, which is tantamount to murder, in my book, and possibly a fourth if you count the body in the burnt out Land Rover. And there's another child still on the critical list. Are these so-called friends of ours seriously suggesting we offer the coroner no more information than we could have offered on day one – murder followed by suicide? End of story? Because on the evidence available I don't believe that's all there is to it, and the very fact that our friends are trying to interfere makes me even less willing to believe it.'

'Calm down, Michael,' Longley said. 'You're jumping the gun. All they've asked is that we don't publish pictures of Gordon Christie just now. And as there's a strong possibility that the charred remains of Gordon Christie are lying in a morgue in Manchester, we've no particular reason to release his photograph anyway. So where's the problem?'

'Well, for one thing I think there are other pictures of Christie floating around. It's only a matter of time before the Press get hold of something. And for another, the spooks obviously know about Christie and it doesn't look as if they're proposing to tell me what they know,' Thackeray said. 'Was he one of theirs?'

'If this is domestic murder, you don't need

to know that,' Longley said.

'The coroner might not take the same view,' Thackeray said. 'We've not found a suicide note and he'll want some questions answered. We've no idea what provoked Christie into this massacre, if in fact it was him who fired the shots. It might have everything to do with something in his past history. And so far we've uncovered absolutely nothing about that: not who he is, where he's from, what he did in his previous life. It's a blank sheet, which, by the sound of it, someone in London could do something to fill in if they chose to.'

'Let's wait to see whether Christie's dead or not, shall we?' Longley said.

'And if he's not? If it's not his body in the Land Rover, then what? If he's still out there somewhere with a weapon and someone else is shot? Who carries the can then? You can be damn sure it won't be the spooks. They'll jump straight back into their holes and leave us up to our necks in the mess.'

'You're exaggerating, Michael,' Longley said.

'No, sir, I don't think I am. I don't like this. In fact, I think it stinks. What are they trying to cover up? It makes no sense. Was Christie on their payroll? Why was he using what's obviously an assumed identity? He was not who he claimed he was and we've got absolutely nowhere trying to find out who he really was. Was he a criminal lying low for some reason? Was he on some sort of witness protection scheme that went wrong? They don't usually try to give an entire family a new identity, do they, but this lot have been expunged from the records as far as we can see. How did they do that? It's not easy to achieve without official help.'

'You know no one will fill in that sort of detail, even if they could,' Longley said.

'All we know is that the family have lived abroad, the kids said so, the mother said so, though we can't find so much as a single passport in the house. Incidentally, we now know the children were talking about moving on again. So what's that all about? Was he sent abroad for his own safety? And if so, why the hell did he come back? If they don't want his picture published, what are they still trying to hide?'

'You'll get no answers, Michael, you know that. If Christie was "disappeared" officially, he'll stay that way, and we'll have to make the best we can of that.' Longley looked as if his conclusion was as unpalatable to him as it was to his DCI. But he shrugged resignedly, while Michael Thackeray clenched his fists in frustration.

'Does county approve of that?' Thackeray asked.

'Do you think I'd be taking this line without their say-so?' Longley said. But Thackeray still looked mutinous.

'Even if Christie really is dead, we still need to make some effort to make sense of this,' he insisted. 'There will still have to be inquests and our esteemed coroner is not a fool. Whoever Gordon Christie is – was, maybe – his family didn't deserve what happened to them. And there are rumours flying around which may come out at the inquest, whatever anyone tries to hide. One or two people have suggested he was ex-army, but the Ministry of Defence say there's no record of him. But what about the SAS? What about Special Branch? What about Five? There's more than one organisation out there that probably know who Christie really is. I need some support here. I need some backup from you or the chief constable. At least we have a photograph now so there's some chance of finding out his real identity. But not if some bastard in London thinks he can put a lid on the inquiry like this.'

'Wait until you've got the bloody DNA results,' Longley said, more impatient now. 'Until we identify the body in Manchester we don't know where we are. When we've got those results we'll review where we're at.'

'If our friends don't subvert the DNA tests as well. I don't suppose that would be too difficult to do. A little mix up in the lab, maybe?'

'Now you're beginning to sound completely paranoid, Michael,' Longley said, his colour rising. 'Never mind our friends. *I'm* telling you to wait. Wait for the forensics. Wait for the child in hospital to wake up. Follow up any other leads, by all means, but leave Christie himself on the back burner until we know if he's alive or dead. Sorry – unfortunate turn of phrase – but there's absolutely no point in alerting the media with Press conferences and photographs and all that ballyhoo if there's a chance we have to announce a day later that the object of our inquiries has been dead for almost a week. We'll look like right idiots.'

And we'll look like an efficient police force if it turns out he's a supergrass some London crime syndicate has caught up with?' Thackeray's scepticism was a fierce as he dared make it. 'Or he's an IRA informer that the security services were supposed to be protecting? Whatever our friends say or do, you can be sure the truth will come out in the end. The Press are already digging around. I happen to know that the *Gazette*'s pulled a picture of Christie out of their archives. There are probably others knocking about that the *Globe*, for one, will do their damnedest to get their hands on now they've picked up on Emma Christie's situation. It'll be our faces the thing blows up in if they get a hint of a cover-up.'

'I'll bear that in mind,' Longley said. 'But

we still wait for Manchester and the forensics. That's final.'

'Sir,' Thackeray said. He eventually shrugged in resignation. 'There's some evidence that someone took pot shots at a man called Weldon who lives in the old manor house at Staveley,' he said. 'We could see where that takes us if the rest of the inquiry's on hold.'

'Has Weldon made a complaint?' Longley asked.

'No, that's the odd thing about it. He seems to have done his best to make sure no one knew it had ever happened. But just for once a uniform had his wits about him and noticed the damage.'

'Check Weldon out,' Longley suggested. 'And Michael...'

'Sir?'

'Try to keep this case in perspective,' Longley said. 'I know it's difficult when children are involved.' Thackeray did not reply and when he had left the room Longley sighed, knowing he had wasted his breath. Then he picked up his phone.

'Get me Ted Grant at the *Gazette*,' he said.

DC Val Ridley opened the door of the intensive care ward quietly and glanced across at Emma Christie's bed. What she saw there sent her heart jerking wildly and her knees threaten to collapse under her. She took a deep breath to steady herself, cursing her

183

own vulnerability to this pale, silent child, and made herself put one foot after another in the general direction of the bed. The head of the bed, which had been horizontal for the whole time she had been stealing time from her duties to visit Emma, was now slightly raised and with it, Emma's bandaged head. Even across the breadth of the room Val could see that Emma's eyes were open. She hurried to the side of the bed where a nursing assistant appeared to be re-arranging Emma's position.

'She's awake,' Val said, her breath catching embarrassingly in her throat and making her voice husky. But the sound was enough to make the young black woman in blue hospital uniform start in surprise, and something she had been holding dropped to the floor with a clatter.

'You made me jump, you came up so quiet,' the nurse said, looking flustered.

'Sorry,' Val said. 'I was just so pleased to see her sitting up.' She looked at the child more closely and realised that although her eyes were open her expression was dazed.

'Hello, Emma,' she said, but Emma's eyes simply flickered for a moment in her direction and there was no other response.

'Has she said anything?' Val asked. The nurse shook her head and Val wondered why she appeared so anxious.

'No, I don't think so,' she said. 'I was just

checking.' She ducked down quickly on the other side of the bed from the police officer and picked up whatever it was she had dropped, before turning away. But Val was too quick for her, and she hurried round the bed and took hold of the woman's arm so that she could see clearly what she was holding in her hand.

'You're hurting me,' the nurse said in a fierce whisper, obviously not wanting to attract the attention of any of her colleagues who were working further down the ward.

'And you're not hurting Emma, taking photographs of her?' Val asked, taking the small camera from the woman's hand. 'How much did the *Globe* pay you for this then?'

The nurse did not reply, turning her head away as Val opened the camera and exposed the film to the light.

'Would you like a child of yours all over the front page of that rag?' Val asked, furious now. 'And what will the hospital say when they discover you've got a lucrative little sideline like this?'

'It's not illegal,' the nurse said.

'It may not be illegal but it'll lose you your job,' Val said, her voice harsh.

'You don't need to do that, you don't need to tell anyone. There's no harm done. I hadn't even taken anything this morning.'

'And you won't be taking anything any other morning, either. I'll make sure of

185

that,' Val said.

There were tears in the woman's eyes now. 'You don't know what it's like bringing children up on your own these days. The things they want. He offered me £100, just for taking one little snap. Would you say no to that? It did her no harm. No harm at all.'

Val glanced at the child in the bed, who appeared to be watching their whispered altercation with something like fierce concentration, and suddenly her anger evaporated and she felt drained of emotion.

'It meant my boy could go on the school trip to the Lake District,' the nurse said, sensing her advantage.

'If he contacts you again, ignore him,' Val said wearily. She knew that now Emma was awake she should be able to arrange for her to be watched day and night. 'If I report you, you'll be in deep trouble, you know that, don't you?' The nurse nodded and glanced up the ward where a colleague was looking curiously in their direction.

'I'll do that then,' she said. 'He won't contact me again I don't suppose now he's got what he wanted. He looked like that sort of bastard.'

When the nurse had hurried out of the ward, Val took the chair alongside Emma, who was still following every move with those unnervingly blank blue eyes.

'Can you hear me, sweetheart?' Val asked.

'Are you really awake?' Emma did not respond and Val picked up her limp hand and hunched over the bed as if in pain herself.

'Come on, sweetie. We want you to get better,' she said. It was, she thought, the only thing worth achieving in this messy, heartbreaking case, although that sentiment was not one which she would ever share with any of her own colleagues. Outside the ward, the nurse Val Ridley had confronted watched through the glass pane in the ward doors and was quite sure she saw Emma Christie's lips move. She edged away into a side room, closing the door behind her as she pulled out her mobile phone. When Vince Newsom responded she asked him a single question.

'She's awake. How much if I tell you everything she's said?'

Laura flicked through the first edition of the *Gazette* to the centrefold where, as expected, her feature about Staveley's reaction to the tragedy in its midst was spread across two pages. She skipped through the text and was pleased to see that it had not been much mangled by the sub-editors, and then glanced at the colour photographs which accompanied the article. To her astonishment, the photograph she had located in the electronic archive showing Gordon Christie at his children's school fête was not amongst them. It seemed to have been replaced by another picture of the same event which included all the rest of the family, but not the father, whose whereabouts, as far as she knew, were still the subject of urgent police inquiries.

Angrily, she picked up the paper and marched, pink cheeked with hair flying, through the newsroom to Ted Grant's office, watched by one or two startled faces amongst the reporters who were not completely glued to their computer screens. Grant's door was open and he waved her into his sanctum without much enthusiasm.

'What happened to our exclusive picture of Gordon Christie?' she asked before the editor had chance to inquire why she was there.

'Ah,' Ted said. 'That's a long story.'

'I thought it was the whole point of the story,' Laura snapped back. 'Seeing that Vince Newsom beat us into the ground yesterday with his snatched picture of Emma Christie. Not that I think much of snatching pictures of unconscious children, but ours was legitimate enough. It was taken in good faith. Here I am spelling out the impact of the apparently happy dad who goes berserk with a gun, the shock it's caused to a whole community, and we have an exclusive – and legitimate – picture of the same happy dad with his kids last summer. What went wrong?' The words tumbled out and her cheeks became even more flushed before she had finished this breathless tirade.

Laura had never seen Ted look abashed. It was not an emotion she thought he ever experienced, and certainly never expressed. But for the couple of seconds it took for the expression to flicker across his face, this was the only word she could find to describe her boss's feelings.

'The police don't want his picture published just at the moment,' Grant said, his embarrassment abating as quickly as it had appeared. 'Superintendent Longley was bending my ear soon after eight o'clock this morning, before the first edition went to press. I don't know how he knew we had pictures of Christie...'

He left the sentence hanging and Laura suddenly felt very cold. Had she mentioned the pictures to Thackeray? She could not remember. She pushed the thought out of her mind though she knew that it would not go away.

'Why on earth doesn't he want the picture published? It might help find the wretched man.'

'Apparently they might have already found him, dead. They're waiting for forensic evidence to prove it one way or the other.'

'So? He might reasonably ask us not to use

the pic as a sort of wanted poster, but that's not what I was doing. My piece was quite different. And the picture of Christie and the children made perfect sense in that context.'

Ted Grant flushed and hauled himself out of his chair.

'It was a good feature, Laura,' he said as if the words were being squeezed out of him like toothpaste from an almost empty tube. 'Don't fret about the picture. We'll use it later when we know for sure what's happened to Christie.'

And with that she had to be content as she followed Grant out of his office and watched him begin one of his threatening perambulations around the newsroom, breathing down necks and grunting approval or disapproval as he read what was being written on the various screens. He could have done his reading by calling up reporters' files from the comfort of his own desk computer, but that, she knew, would not have had the same demoralising effect he enjoyed so much.

Somewhat wearily, she got on with the rest of her day, but she never succeeded in shaking off that chilly worry in the pit of her stomach and as soon as Thackeray came home that night, looking grey and tired, she could no longer contain the question which had been niggling her all day.

'Did you tell Jack Longley that we had a picture of Gordon Christie?' she demanded, almost before he had taken his coat off.

He looked at her blankly for a moment and then shrugged.

'I might have done,' he said. 'It didn't matter, did it? Wasn't it today it was going in the paper?'

'Only it didn't,' Laura said, her anger bubbling over. 'Jack Longley pressured Ted Grant into holding it out. It ruined my story.

'I'd no idea he was planning anything like that. And I must say, I'm surprised Ted Grant agreed,' Thackeray said. 'But Jack's under a lot of pressure on this case. We all are.'

'Well, I'm sorry about that,' Laura said. 'But I don't see why you have to indulge in stupid censorship like that. What on earth's the point? There'll probably be other pictures kicking about and they'll end up on the front page of the *Globe*, no doubt, when Vince Newsom gets his sticky fingers on them.'

'That's what all this is about, is it?' Thackeray asked, turning away. 'You and Vince Newsom?'

'No, of course it isn't,' Laura said. 'But I think you could treat anything I tell you off the record as carefully as I do when you let things slip.'

'I try not to do that,' Thackeray said quietly. 'It's much more embarrassing for

191

me when our professional lives get entangled than it is for you.' He spoke with a cold objectivity which chilled Laura's blood, almost as if she herself were a nuisance he could do without.

'You should be at a few of my editorial conferences if you think that,' Laura said bitterly, smarting still from some of Bob Baker's jibes. 'I suppose that's why you didn't tell me that you'd already found Gordon Christie's body,' she added bitterly.

'I didn't tell you that because I don't know yet whether or not it's true,' Thackeray said. 'A body's been found in his burnt out vehicle. They're trying to identify it from DNA but it's not easy. It may be him. We really don't know. Maybe Jack decided to fill Ted Grant in on where the investigation has got to. I simply don't know that either.'

Laura looked at him, her eyes full of scepticism.

'It's not a good enough reason to pull the picture,' she said. 'Why would we? It was harmless enough. It was a fantastic illustration for my piece. Why shouldn't we run it?'

'I don't know what Jack Longley said to your boss, Laura,' Thackeray said, his own anger boiling over. 'You'll have to believe me. I thought you understood how much I hate this case. I don't want anything which will make it more awful than it already is. I want it over and done with. And I really don't care how many pictures of Gordon Christie you publish in the *Gazette* so long as the man's safely dead.'

Laura pulled up short at that, recognising the pain behind Thackeray's anger, and knowing it was a pain that she could never fully share and had so far failed to assuage in any significant way. She swallowed down her own irritation.

'It's horrible, I know,' she said reaching out a tentative hand to touch his arm. 'I've seen something of it, too, you know. But you mustn't let it get to you.'

'Easy to say,' Thackeray said, ignoring her outstretched hand as he turned away. And with a sudden stab of fear Laura wondered if, after all they had been through together, this would be the case that destroyed them.

Chapter Twelve

DC Val Ridley knocked on the DCI's office door soon after nine the next morning and found, as she expected, Michael Thackeray and Kevin Mower reading the *Globe*'s latest front page with muted fury. Thackeray looked up as Val came in.

'Any idea where he got this from?' he

asked. 'She's not just asking for mummy now but her sister as well. Allegedly.'

Val took a deep breath, almost overcome by the anger that had hit her as well as soon as she had read the headline in the paper someone had thrust in front of her in the main CID office: Vince Newsom's new instalment of the Emma Christie story.

'The bastard's inventing it, with a bit of help from one of the nurses,' she said.

'Are you sure?' Thackeray snapped.

'No, I'm not sure, sir, not one hundred per cent sure. But I took a camera off her yesterday after the picture first appeared and I read her the riot act. That's the same picture. No one's managed to get a new one, at least. There's been someone at Emma's bedside ever since yesterday's story appeared. I organised it as soon as I realised she was coming round. I saw Emma yesterday evening myself and it's true, she is coming out of the coma, but she's not coherent. She's mumbling a lot, but I can't make out what she's trying to say and the ward sister says nobody can.'

'So this is all a fantasy?' Kevin Mower asked. 'That's a bit much, even for the *Globe*, surely?'

'I've just come back from the hospital. Nothing's changed overnight. The nurse I took the camera off isn't on duty this morning, which is why I thought I'd better see you. I wanted permission to chase her up, look at her mobile phone records maybe. It's quite possible she's ignored me completely and is still feeding Newsom this garbage. She certainly seemed to think she's found a useful source of extra income and I'm pretty sure he couldn't have got to Emma himself. I talked to uniform about setting up a rota to keep an eye on her as soon as I realised what was happening yesterday with her trying to get another photograph, and I also put the fear of God into hospital security. Uniform aren't too happy about a 24 hour watch.'

Thackeray sat back in his chair and sighed.

'I'll talk to uniform,' he said. 'But I doubt if the nurse has committed anything you could call a crime, though she may well be in trouble with the hospital authorities. It's invasion of privacy, though, a particularly nasty instance of it, and embarrassing for us. If we're doing nothing else right in this case we should at least be able to keep Emma Christie safe. It's not impossible that if the killer is still alive he might want to finish what he started, I suppose. As Vince Newsom so helpfully suggests in his story. Whoever the killer is, he may think Emma will remember something about what happened once she's fully conscious.' He thumped a fist onto the offending newspaper with a force that surprised the two younger officers. It was rare to see Thackeray express overt emotion, although Mower knew better than most the turmoil he concealed beneath his controlled public face.

'You're assuming the killer isn't lying in a morgue in Manchester, then?' Mower said. Thackeray looked at him bleakly for a moment without answering.

'We can't assume that,' he said. He turned back to Val Ridley. 'Talk to your nurse again, and close that loophole. Tell her you're investigating breaches of hospital security which might put the child in danger. And if you let drop that her phone calls can very easily be traced it may bring her to her senses.'

'Shall I tell hospital security about the camera incident?' Val asked. 'It could lose her her job.'

Thackeray hesitated for a second, staring down at the *Globe*'s front page again.

'Tell her that if Vince Newsom prints any more information that he's obviously gained from an inside source, we'll have to make a full report to the hospital. So far this is harmless stuff as far as we're concerned: true or not, it doesn't really impinge on the investigation. But if Emma really does wake up and remembers anything important about the shootings then it will need to be kept confidential, and her security will be absolutely vital. We may have to move her somewhere else. You can tell the hospital that.'

'Right, sir,' Val said.

After she had gone, Thackeray looked at Mower with obvious anxiety.

'Like everything else in this case, it all hangs on the forensics from Manchester,' he said. 'If Christie's dead I don't think we need to worry about Emma. If not...' He shrugged.

'We can't just move her out of intensive care,' Mower said.

'Not without very good reason,' Thackeray agreed. 'And probably only to another hospital which might be just as leaky. Talk to uniform for me and make sure they know that her security is not just a babysitting issue. It's a whole lot more important than that.'

DCI Thackeray allowed himself to be driven up the steep hill from Bradfield to Staveley with far more ambivalence than he would have admitted to DS Kevin Mower, who was at the wheel. It was true that he had felt an urgent need to get out of his office after a steamy hour fending off Superintendent Longley and the Press office, all incandescent at the morning's *Globe* frontpage. Vince Newsom's latest effort had provoked a spate of excited calls from other London papers which probably had reporters tailgating each other up the fast lane of the Ml in the direction of Bradfield by now. But halfway through the morning, CID had received a report from PC Hewitt in Staveley which had brought Thackeray some relief from the pressure of outside interest in the case. It had been Mower who had spoken directly to the breathless constable, sceptically at first but then with increasing interest as the main point of what he had to say had emerged from the avalanche of words.

'So why didn't we pick this up in the house-to-house inquiries?' Mower had asked sharply when Hewitt had finished.

'The old boy's been on holiday, hasn't he?' Hewitt said. 'But I spotted him this morning when I went up on my regular patrol, and I suddenly remembered we hadn't interviewed him.'

'Good man,' Mower was forced to concede. 'I'll be up to see him myself later.' And when he had passed the information on to DCI Thackeray he was not entirely surprised when his boss had decided to come to the village with him to interview Donald Wright of Lane End, Staveley, just back from a few days' break in Torquay.

Wright was at home when they knocked on the door of a substantial stone house behind the church, and he answered the door so promptly that he might have been waiting behind it.

'Mr Wright?' Thackeray asked, offering his

warrant card. 'DCI Thackeray and Sergeant Mower, Bradfield CID.'

'Major Wright,' the short, dapper man with silver-grey hair, a small moustache and a military-looking blazer responded. 'Royal Engineers, retired.' Thackeray wondered just how long he had been retired. It was almost impossible to judge Wright's age, but he guessed that it was many years since the man studying their ID with elaborate care had donned a uniform. He was obviously fit and trim and his face was tanned, the blue eyes still sharp, but as he showed them into his neat and tidy sitting room he moved slowly and the hands that picked up a decanter of whiskey and waved it in their direction shook slightly. When Thackeray and Mower refused the offer, Wright poured a generous measure for himself and was sipping contentedly even before he sat down.

'You don't mind if I do?' he asked. 'There's not too many pleasures left at my age, you know. My wife died last year and I find the time hangs heavily.'

'I'm sorry to hear that,' Thackeray said. 'It must be some time since you left the army?'

'I did longer than many,' Wright said. 'Saw a lot of good men sacked, you know? War service didn't save them. I was at D-Day my-self – just got my commission in time. Then in Germany.' He fell silent for a moment, apparently staring intently at something they could not see, and then, after another sip of his whiskey, straightened up in his chair. Thackeray waited patiently, wondering what memories haunted the old man and letting him take his time to return to the present.

'I'm sorry,' he said. 'You don't want to listen to an old buffer like me maundering on. I thought I'd told your constable all you needed to know. Sent for the top brass, has he? A bad business, this shooting. Had Christie hung on to a pistol from his time in the service, do you know? Too many of them get away with that, in my opinion. Always did. There's a few World War Two pistols still rusting at the back of drawers, you know?'

'Did Christie tell you he'd been in the army?' Thackeray asked. 'We weren't sure about that.'

'I don't think he ever told me,' Wright said. 'I just assumed he had. Behaved as though he had. Walked like a soldier, and a good one, I'd guess. Said something about Belfast once, I think, but he didn't give much away. Taciturn, I suppose you'd call him. Maybe not allowed to talk openly about what he did. Crossed my mind. But I thought it was strange that two ex-soldiers had ended up in Staveley quite recently.'

'Two?'

'Gerry Foster at the pub was in the Royal Green Jackets as a young man. Came out seven or eight years ago, he told me. Served in Northern Ireland, too, of course.' Wright's eyes clouded again for a moment. 'Nasty business, that. Never went there myself. Desk jockey by that time. But I was in Aden briefly. Don't suppose you remember that. Trouble in Arabia's nothing new. It's been going on for years.'

Kevin Mower, less tolerant of an old man's tendency to live more in the past than the present, broke in impatiently.

'So what about Christie? Hewitt tells us that you saw him just before you went off for your holiday. Is that right?'

'I've not lost my marbles yet, Sergeant,' Wright said sharply, somewhat to Mower's surprise. He was not used to being put in his place quite so abruptly and Thackeray smiled faintly at his discomfiture. 'I think I only spoke to Christie a couple of times while he lived here. Knew his wife by sight, of course. Saw her with the children. I like to get out and about every day for a brisk walk. Keeps the ticker in good shape.'

'Where did you see Christie last?' Thackeray asked quietly, becoming impatient with Wright's meandering thought processes himself. 'In the village, was it?'

'I was up on the footpath that takes you onto the Pennine Way eventually. It passes the back of Christie's cottage, but a hundred or so feet above it I suppose. Rough terrain. Christie's Land Rover had stopped just before the end of the lane and he was leaning out of the window talking to Bruce Weldon and his son, what's he called – Stuart?'

'You're sure about that?' Thackeray asked.

'There's nothing wrong with my eyes, thank God,' Foster said sharply. 'Hearing's a bit dodgy. Have to turn the television up, you know? But the vision's A1. Anyway, I know Stuart. I've bumped into him once or twice at the diabetic clinic I go to. Doesn't say much.'

'And when was this exactly? Can you remember the day you saw him with Christie?' Mower asked, impatient again.

'I went away on the 14th, so it must have been the 13th,' Wright said, without hesitation. 'The previous day was Monday and I don't walk as far on Mondays because I go down into Bradfield to a lunch club for ex-officers I belong to. Get the 0900 bus, do any business I need to do in town, back on the 15.15. Doesn't leave much time for a long walk, especially at this time of the year. So I'd say the 13th. At around fifteen hundred hours. I have my lunch while I listen to the one o'clock news, finish the chores and then normally go out about fourteen hundred. I'd been right up to the top of Pollock Hill that day and was on my way home when I saw them, at least an hour's walk, so about fifteen hundred hours would be right.'

And was it a long conversation they were having? Did you notice that?' Thackeray asked, taking the major's accuracy as read, and thinking what a reliable witness he would make if these facts ever needed to be spelled out in court.

'The Weldons were on foot, standing close to the driver's window. I couldn't see their car so maybe they'd walked up from the house and met Christie coming down the lane. But that's speculation. I'd no idea what they were saying, of course. I was far too far away to hear them. But it looked like a pretty animated exchange, if you like. A bit of arm-waving going on. And I recall Bruce Weldon thumping the bonnet of the Land Rover quite sharply. And Christie drove off very fast, considering the other two were standing quite close to the Land Rover. Bit close to the toes, I thought.'

'So it looked as though they'd been having a row? An argument of some sort?' Thackeray asked.

'Certainly could have been. What do they call it? Body language? It was the body language. It didn't look friendly. If they'd been a group of Arabs I'd been watching in Aden I would have put their conversation down as argumentative, even though I couldn't hear it.'

'Had you ever seen Christie with the

203

Weldons before?' Thackeray asked.

Major Wright thought for a moment.

'I'm not a great pub man, myself. My wife and I preferred a less smoky atmosphere for one thing. But I pop into the Fox for a tot now and again. I'm not a beer man. Christie was usually in there in the evenings, as I understand it, but he wasn't a man given to casual conversation. Always sitting in the same corner, back to the wall. But I did see him exchange words with Bruce Weldon once when I was in for a snifter after a meeting of the parish council. Weldon took him outside for a chat. I thought nothing of it. Why should I? Christie's done odd jobs for most of the village over the last couple of years. He's a good workman, knows his trade. Fixed my old mower for me when it packed up on me. Cornered the market in repairs since he's been here. I just assumed Weldon wanted to talk to him about a job.'

'Did you ever get any indication, from anyone, that Christie might be violent?' Thackeray asked.

Wright shook his head. 'I can't honestly say that I was privy to much village gossip,' he said. 'Nor my wife. We don't have close friends in Staveley. We moved here when I retired because of the access to the hills, which we both liked. Our friends are scattered – York, Richmond, on the south coast ... a lot of people in the services don't put down roots, you know. I got the impression that Christie was a bit like that. But it was only an impression. He looked like the sort of man who would pack his kit and be off somewhere new at a moment's notice. A lot of soldiers have to be like that when they're in the service, and I suppose it's a hard habit to shake off. Total mobility, we used to call it. I don't think it's much good for the soul, or for family life. I rather doubt it.'

'Well,' Thackeray said, when they had finally taken their leave of the major. 'There's a few things Mr Bruce Weldon seems to have forgotten to tell us. Well worth a word, I think.'

'See if we can catch him now, shall we?' Mower asked.

'Oh, I think so,' Thackeray said, thinking of his office waiting for him at HQ, almost like a prison cell, and glancing up at the sky, which was an unseasonable blue with only a few clouds being whipped in from the west on an almost spring-like breeze. He took a deep breath. Bradfield was out of sight from Staveley, which nestled in a hollow sheltered from the east by a rocky spur of heather-covered hillside, and Thackeray was suddenly filled with an overwhelming desire to escape from the steep, cramped streets and the clatter of construction in the little town in the valley where the new century was catching up rapidly on the remnants of the nineteenth almost as though the twentieth had never been. Thackeray suddenly felt old and tired, and he was aware of the unspoken questions in Mower's dark eyes as he waited for him to implement his decision.

'Leave the car here,' Thackeray said. 'I feel like a walk. We'll have a bite to eat at the pub afterwards.' Mower concealed his surprise and glanced down at his Italian loafers. Walking for him was an unfortunate necessity, certainly not undertaken for pleasure. He glanced at the car and shrugged before setting off in step with Thackeray down the steep hill towards the Old Hall.

Bruce Weldon was at home and they were shown into his sitting room by the housekeeper and greeted politely enough though without enthusiasm. The two dogs with him looked up at their master inquiringly and sank down again when he glanced in their direction. While Mower was openly admiring the man's Armani suit and tie, impeccably covering a slim-hipped broad-shouldered figure in a way that only serious money can buy, Thackeray was more conscious of the hint of strain on the tanned face and around eyes which did not echo the smile with which Weldon waved them into comfortable armchairs.

'Is this about the Gordon Christie business again?' Weldon asked with only the smallest hint of impatience. 'I thought I'd told Gavin

Hewitt everything I knew about the man.'

'We thought you had done that,' Thackeray said. 'In fact, you could say we hoped and expected you had. But it now seems there's a little more that you could have told us.' Even the faint hint of a smile left Weldon's face at that and the two officers were left in little doubt that this was a man who did not like to be crossed.

'I don't think so, Chief Inspector,' he said brusquely. 'I had very little contact with Christie.'

'But you had some contact, not long before the killings, on the 13th in fact, according to a new witness we've been talking to.'

'I don't think so,' Weldon said. 'What day of the week would that have been?' He pulled an electronic organiser from an inside pocket and thumbed a few buttons before shaking his head. 'Tuesday the 13th? I was in Leeds all morning in meetings. As I recall I came home about 1.30, got changed and just got over to Broadley in time for a ride before dark.'

'So you weren't talking to Christie in the lane leading to his cottage that afternoon?'

'Certainly not,' Weldon said. 'As I just said, I was only here for half an hour, at most. I distinctly remember the hurry I was in to get Broadley by 2.30.'

'And your son, Stuart? Was he at home that day?' Thackeray persisted.

Weldon shrugged an elegant shoulder.

'I don't recall seeing him when I came in,' he said.

'But that would have been before he went away on his current trip?'

Weldon glanced at his organiser again before he nodded.

'Yes, Stuart didn't go away until later that week, Wednesday or Thursday, I think. As I told PC Hewitt, we lead separate lives. I don't always know where he is or what he's doing. That's the way he likes it.'

'But he could have gone away on the same day that Gordon Christie apparently went berserk with a pistol?'

'That was the Wednesday, wasn't it? Yes, he could have done. That day or the next.'

'And have you heard from him?' Mower asked. 'Do you know when he's coming back?'

'I haven't, no,' Weldon said, and Thackeray wondered if he was imagining the faintest flicker of anxiety on Weldon's impassive features.

'But you spoke to him about his car,' Mower broke in. 'You told PC Hewitt you had mentioned it to him...?'

Weldon hesitated for a fraction of a second. 'No,' he said. 'I told Hewitt I *would* speak to him about it. When he gets in touch. He's never been good at keeping in touch. His mother used to complain about

208

it when he was away at school.'

'And his mother is...?'

'Divorced ten years ago,' Weldon said, curt now. 'She lives in Spain.'

'Right,' Thackeray said. 'Would you let me know when your son turns up, please, Mr Weldon? I'll need a word with him, too.'

'Fine,' Weldon said. 'Though I can't imagine why. I'd have thought your top priority would be to find Christie, if he's still alive. Or are you assuming he's lying dead somewhere on the moors? It could take months to find a body up there, I suppose.'

'We're making no assumptions, Mr Weldon,' Thackeray said, recognising he was wasting his time and getting to his feet. 'I won't disturb you any longer, but I would like to speak to your son, when that's convenient. Please?'

'I'll tell him when I see him,' Weldon said without enthusiasm. The dogs wagged their tails tentatively as the visitors went to the door but Weldon quelled them with no more than a glance. Everything in this man's life, Thackeray thought, was controlled with the likely exception of his son, and he wondered why Stuart was the exception.

Walking back up the village street to the Fox and Hounds after the electronic gates had closed soundlessly on Weldon's immaculate gravelled entrance, Mower grunted in frustration.

'What did you think?' Thackeray asked.

'Lying through his teeth,' Mower said. 'But clever with it. He's admitted he was in the village at about the right time that day but with enough people to confirm that he was elsewhere most of the day. You can bet no one will be prepared to swear exactly what time he arrived in Broadley.'

'What I find really odd is the absence of the son,' Thackeray said. 'Where the hell has he gone, and why? It might have nothing at all to do with Christie, but the timing says different. I think we need to talk to Stuart Weldon quite urgently, don't you?'

Chapter Thirteen

DC Val Ridley sat by Emma Christie's bed and watched the child intently. She had been moved downstairs to a side room off the main children's ward that morning, and was now sleeping peacefully without the aid of all the technical paraphernalia which had kept her alive for almost a week. The knot of anxiety which had clenched Val's stomach for all that time was gradually beginning to unravel and she was beginning to wonder where all her carefully nurtured detachment had gone. She had learned early in her career that whatever emotion she felt was safest concealed from thicker skinned colleagues who regarded any show of feeling as a sign of weakness. But somehow Emma Christie, this slight, ashen-faced figure with her head still swathed in bandages, had crept beneath her defences and left her vulnerable to the curious looks of Kevin Mower and even the DCI as she had found herself spending far more time at the child's bedside than duty demanded.

Part of her self-defence had always been to keep memories of her own childhood safely locked away, but Emma's uncertain future had inevitably reminded her of the time she had spent in a children's home when her parents' marriage had split up, and of the merciless bullying she had suffered from the other children there. She had wondered wildly, waking once or twice in the middle of the night in something approaching panic, whether she could adopt Emma if no relatives came forward to take care of her, only to dismiss the idea as foolish and impracticable in the icy light of dawn. She was single, she worked long hours and, if she was honest, she had to admit she did not really know either her own capacity to be a mother or anything about Emma herself, she told herself irritably as she watched the white coverlet that covered the child almost imperceptibly rise and fall in time to her shallow breathing. Emma awake and smiling and playing happily in the sunshine was just a figment of her own imagination, Val thought dispiritedly. It was a seriously unlikely prospect when the news was eventually broken to her about the fate of the rest of her family. She had even wondered, in the dark hours before daylight filtered through the curtains, whether wanting Emma to recover was not a cruelty too far. She might have been better off if the bullet that had grazed her brain had penetrated more deeply and killed her.

Val reached out gently and touched Emma's limp hand, imagining for a moment that she felt a response, before withdrawing as if she had been stung when the door opened behind her. One of the nurses she recognised from the intensive care ward put her head round the door looking worried.

'Oh, she's got you with her, has she?' the woman said.

'Someone's going to be here with her all the time now in case she starts to talk. Is there a problem?' Val asked, suddenly filled with suffocating anxiety again.

'There was, possibly,' the nurse said. 'Or maybe we're getting paranoid. An Asian woman came up to the ward upstairs without any obvious reason for being there, and shot off again when I asked her who she was looking for. I lost track of her by the lifts so I think she must have come down to this level.'

'Have you told security?' Val asked quickly.

'Yes, I have and they say they haven't seen her leave the building. They're looking at the CCTV tapes now. She's pretty conspicuous: she was dressed in the whole long black number, with her face covered. You could only see her eyes.'

'No guarantee she was even female, then,' Val said, almost to herself, beginning to be seriously worried now. 'Don't worry about Emma. I'm staying here until I'm relieved at four. But I'll pass it on to my people, just in case.'

When the nurse had left she went out into the corridor and called Kevin Mower on her mobile.

'You could hide a sub-machine gun under those long black robes,' he said sharply.

'More likely a couple of cameras,' Val said. 'It wouldn't be the first time a journalist has dressed up as a Muslim woman. Didn't that BBC man do it in Afghanistan?'

'Is it Vince Newsom of the blasted *Globe* again, d'you think?' Mower snapped.

'I don't really know what to think,' Val said. 'It could be some perfectly innocent visitor who got lost. This place is pretty confusing if you don't know your way around it. The CCTV should show us whether she's left the building or not.'

'If not, ask security to search the place until they find her,' Mower said. 'The brass will go potty if there's many more stories in the *Globe* like this morning's.'

But when Val got through to hospital security she found that they had anticipated police concerns and confirmed the justice of them. There had been no sign of a fully veiled Asian woman leaving the building, but in a cubicle in the women's lavatories near the main entrance they had found a black enveloping *jilbab*, discarded and bundled up in one of the rubbish bins.

'So someone dressed entirely differently could have left the building?' Val said angrily. 'When I'm relieved here I'll come down and look at your tapes and see if there's anyone I recognise.'

'Or maybe they've not left the building,' the security officer at the other end of the phone said with a hint of satisfaction, as if anticipating some sort of police failure on his patch. 'No way of knowing, love, is there, if you can't tell us who we're looking for? Not our fault.'

When Val hung up, she returned to Emma's bedside to find the girl looking at her with intensely blue eyes sunk into their dark sockets.

'Hi,' Val said. 'How are you feeling?'

'Where's my mummy?' Emma whispered, and closed her eyes again.

Michael Thackeray drove home that evening

214

with a sick feeling in the pit of his stomach. He had left his office an hour before after a fraught meeting with Superintendent Jack Longley and had then taken a detour via one of the new town centre bars before picking up his car from the police car park. He knew the man he was meeting by sight, but little more. His opinion of him, which was very far from friendly, had been honed by the very public display of his work over the last couple of days and by a sharp memory of what Laura Ackroyd had told him about her stormy relationship with her former live-in lover. His worst expectations were more than met by the sight of Vince Newsom in the flesh, as he swept into the bar a quarter of an hour after the time they had agreed to meet. The DCI had tracked him down earlier at the end of his mobile and insisted on talking to him face to face. The mobile was still attached to Newsom's ear as he glanced round the bar and was only snapped shut when the reporter apparently recognised Thackeray.

Newsom had draped his camel overcoat over the back of a chair and sat down opposite the DCI, flicking his hair out of his eyes and grabbing the cocktail list from the centre of the table. The bar had been Newsom's choice of rendezvous and Thackeray felt out of place in his slightly crumpled dark suit amongst the sharply dressed young couples enjoying after-work drinks at what he regarded as vastly inflated prices. Newsom glanced at Thackeray's glass, half full of gold liquid, with a look of near contemptuous inquiry.

'Another?' he asked. Thackeray had shaken his head. The sweet fruit cocktail had already furred his teeth and settled like lead in his stomach. Vince Newsom shrugged and ordered a *Margarita* and, while he waited for it to arrive, he leaned back in his seat and eyed the policeman with frank curiosity.

'Well,' he said at length. 'How's Laura? Still as spikey as ever from what I've seen of her.'

'I didn't come here to talk about Laura,' Thackeray said, knowing he risked sounding pompous.

'So why did you come here?' Newsom retorted as the waitress put his salt-rimmed glass in front of him. 'A bit of a briefing on this Christie case sounds good to me. Why haven't you found your man yet? Dead or alive?'

'You'll have to put questions like that to the Press office,' Thackeray said. 'What I wanted to talk to you about, off the record for the moment, although we can do this down at the nick if you prefer, is where you're getting your information from.'

'Oh, come on, Chief Inspector,' Newsom scoffed. 'You know as well as I do if you're still shacked up with Laura that we're never going to tell you that. It's for me to know and you to find out – if you can.'

'If your source is one of my officers you can be sure that I will find out, and they'll be out of the force before their feet can touch the ground,' Thackeray said.

'My lips are sealed, chief inspector,' Newsom said with a smirk.

'The other thing I want to know – and this is even more serious – is whether you tried to gain access to Emma Christie again today.'

'Again? Who said I'd ever gained access to her?' Newsom countered, his face darkening. 'Although if she's awake now, I assume she can have visitors? D'you think grapes or jelly babies would be best?' His flippant tone infuriated Thackeray but he choked back his anger.

'Until we find whoever shot her I'm responsible for the safety of that child,' he said. 'This isn't a game. Her life could still be in danger. I'll ask you again: did you try to see her today?'

'No, I didn't,' Newsom said and, although he did not want to, Thackeray believed him. 'But surely you're joking, aren't you? You think her father would come back and finish the job off?' Newsom's tone was incredulous now. 'In which case you must think Christie's alive? And armed? Well, that's tomorrow's story, no problem. "Emma

Under Threat From Mad Dad". How'd that suit you as a headline?'

'I didn't say that,' Thackeray countered angrily, realising he had said too much. 'And if you allege I did, I'll deny it.'

'Oh, I don't need to quote you, Michael,' Newsom said easily. 'You know that. We wouldn't want you booted out of the force before your feet touch the ground, would we? What would sweet Laura do then, poor thing?'

Thackeray had got to his feet then, steadying himself for a second on the table before straightening up. His stomach churned and he had to make a distinct effort not to use the fist bunched at his side to wipe the smirk off Newsom's face.

'Talk to the Press office,' he said at last, through gritted teeth.

'Oh, sure,' Newsom scoffed. Are you going so soon?'

Thackeray had walked away stiffly, his face a rigid mask of fury; with Newsom's final jibe ringing in his ears.

'Give my love to Laura. Tell her I miss her.'

What Thackeray could not know was that when he had gone the reporter had picked up his glass and sniffed the mixture suspiciously before tasting it. He savoured the fruit cocktail with distaste, which was quickly followed by a faint smile of triumph.

218

'Alkie,' he said under his breath. 'I thought so. Oh, Mr Thackeray, you just made a big mistake. And I'll have you for it.'

Laura had given up trying to tempt Thackeray's palate onto the wider shores of culinary adventure. Years of traditional Yorkshire cookery – heavy on meat and potatoes and light on herbs and spices – and snatched snacks on long, erratic shifts had left him deeply suspicious of the unfamiliar and the exotic. She had tried to educate his taste buds out of their rut and steer them in a more southerly or easterly direction but had reluctantly had to accept that the road to this particular man's heart involved traditional fare, however unhealthy: steak, sausages, battered fish and mountains of chips and mashed potatoes.

This evening she had picked up a steak at the supermarket on the way home, peeled potatoes and prepared mushrooms for what she knew was his favourite meal, but realised with foreboding as soon as he walked through the door and flung his coat down on the sofa that even this might fail to lighten his mood.

'A bad day?' she asked, as he came into the kitchen behind her and kissed the back of her neck.

'Not good,' he said.

She turned the heat down under the pans

and turned towards him, taking in the deep lines that were developing around his mouth and the dark circles under his eyes. He was having far too many bad days, she thought, but knew that until he had resolved the mystery surrounding the shootings at Staveley he would be haunted by what he had seen at the cottage that day and would never discuss with her or anyone else. But as she ran a hand down his cheek she realised that tonight there was something else.

'What's happened?' she asked, steering him into the living room and pouring two drinks, one tonic with vodka and one without. She handed him a glass.

'I just had a drink with that bastard Vince Newsom,' he said. The unexpectedness of that piece of information threw Laura for a moment and she looked at Thackeray in astonishment.

'Whatever for?' she asked.

'Someone tried to get in to see Emma Christie this afternoon. I thought it might be him.'

'And was it?'

Thackeray shrugged. 'He says not,' he said. 'But I wouldn't put it past him, would you? You know what the *Globe*'s like. You know what he's like. You, better than most. In some ways I'd rather it was him. Someone else might be worse.'

'You mean she might be in danger?' Laura

asked, shocked.

'I don't know anything about this case any more,' Thackeray said. 'I don't know who shot them, I don't know where Gordon Christie is, I don't know whether he's dead or alive, I don't really know who he is and what he was doing in Staveley, and all I get from upstairs is obstruction.'

'What do you mean, obstruction?' Laura said. 'Where's the obstruction coming from?'

'I don't even know that. And I certainly shouldn't be telling you all this. It seems pretty obvious to me that Christie and his family were hiding from something or someone. But whether they were hiding from the authorities or being hidden by them is totally obscure. And no one, it seems, wants to tell me one way or another. I had a session with Jack Longley this afternoon and he more or less told me to leave Christie's background alone. It wasn't relevant, he said, though I know he was just repeating what he'd been told to say.'

'That's outrageous,' Laura said quietly. 'Where's upstairs, in this case. If not Jack Longley, who? The Chief Constable, or somewhere else?'

'Oh, somewhere else, undoubtedly,' Thackeray said. 'If county had him on some sort of local witness protection scheme there'd be no problem in telling me now, even if I'd been out of the loop earlier, for security reasons. This is coming from elsewhere. County's being leaned on and it's making the whole inquiry twice as difficult as it need be. There are still leads to follow but no encouragement to follow them.' Thackeray thought back to his latest fractious meeting with Longley when he had outlined the suspicions that Bruce Weldon and his absent son had aroused, suspicions that Longley had dismissed with little interest. 'Wait for the forensics,' he had said yet again. 'Don't waste time or resources until we know whether he's dead.'

'That's appalling.' Laura's outrage brought Thackeray back to the present with a jump.

'So what's going to happen, then?' she asked. 'You'll never resolve it satisfactorily? You'll simply have to settle for half the truth, or less? What sort of justice is that to that woman and her children? And everyone else in that village who's been devastated by all this.'

'There's a distinct possibility that Gordon Christie is already dead,' Thackeray said quietly. 'You don't know that either, officially. We're waiting on forensics. But if the body that was found in his Land Rover turns out to be his, that'll be the end of it. A quick inquest, no known motive for the violence, end of story.'

Laura looked at Thackeray in disbelief.

'Covering up what, exactly?' she asked.

'I don't know. Maybe nothing at all. Maybe the case is just what it seems – the man flipped and shot his family.'

'And maybe not,' Laura said flatly. 'You couldn't leave it like that. There's too many loose ends.'

'If Special Branch or the spooks are involved, I may have to,' Thackeray said.

'I don't believe this,' Laura said. 'I reckon someone in Staveley knows more than they're saying about the Christies. Someone's covering up. I'll find out even if you can't. I'll go up there again tomorrow...'

'Laura, don't even think about it,' Thackeray said wearily. 'Either there's nothing at all to find out beyond what we already know, in which case you'd be wasting your time. Or there *is* something, and it's far too dangerous for you to be asking questions. Leave it alone, Laura. This is one case you mustn't interfere with. It's far too risky.'

'I want to write something about it,' Laura said, her face taking on an obstinate look that Thackeray knew well. 'If you can't do any digging up at Staveley, I can. I'm sure I can find out what was going on. I can't bear the thought of anyone getting away with anything with two children dead, and another one probably orphaned. You must understand that.'

Thackeray flinched at the spark of anger in

her eyes. He had felt like that himself once but more and more felt that passion being leeched out of him by bureaucratic obstruction he did not understand.

'I seriously thought of resigning this afternoon,' he said. He pulled a piece of paper out of his inside pocket. 'I got as far as writing the letter.' He handed it to Laura and she read it in silence.

'Oh, Michael,' she said. 'You can't possibly end it all like that. You can't just walk away.' He took the paper from her and put it back in his jacket pocket.

'Maybe not,' he said. 'Maybe I'll wait for the forensic results from Manchester and see where that leaves us. We're in a sort of impasse anyway until we know whether or not the man in the Land Rover is Christie. As Jack Longley says, there's plenty of other crime to be getting on with.' He shrugged wearily.

'You couldn't possibly just junk your career over this,' Laura said fiercely. 'You're too good at what you do.'

'It wouldn't be difficult right now,' Thackeray said quietly.

Laura pulled a face but did not argue any further. She could see the tension in Thackeray and knew no way to defuse it. Sex used to be the answer, she thought, remembering the passion that had brought them together in the first place, but she no longer found that worked.

'Do you want to eat now?' she asked.

'I'm not hungry,' he said.

Chapter Fourteen

'There's no point in duplicating their inquiries.' Superintendent Jack Longley's expression was not one which left much room for argument and the sick feeling in Thackeray's stomach intensified. He closed the brief report from Manchester police that Longley had handed him minutes earlier and took a deep breath, knowing he risked the super's infrequent but fearsome anger if he argued any further. But somewhere here, he knew, there were lines which had to be drawn, markers which had to be put down, or his job would become impossible.

'Manchester are happy with this, are they, sir?' he asked. 'They don't want any help from this end? They don't want us to help find the link there must be between their body and a vehicle belonging to Gordon Christie?'

Longley sighed heavily.

'You've read the report,' he said. 'All the evidence points to this being gang-related and Manchester-based. The gun was one used in a Manchester killing, believed to be a contract shooting of a gang leader. It's not the gun that killed the family in Staveley. True, we don't know who the victim is yet. There's no DNA match on the national database. But we do know it's not Gordon Christie because there's no match with his DNA either. On the two major issues, the gun and the body, there are no connections between the murder in Manchester and the Christie shootings. Let Manchester get on with it, Michael. It's not as if we're short of other investigations, or overloaded with detectives sitting around with nowt to do. It's a question of priorities and resources and that's my decision. Scale it back.'

'But this unknown victim just happened to die in Gordon Christie's Land Rover.' The two men stared at each other for a moment, both rigid with unspoken anger.

'They'll follow that up when they know who the victim is,' Longley said, more temperately than Thackeray really expected. He knew how far he was pushing his luck. 'If Christie abandoned the vehicle anyone could have picked it up. We'll leave it to Manchester to pursue that. They'll keep us informed. In the meantime, we're still left with the problem of finding Christie. That's our only priority now in this case. Our top priority, especially if he's still got a gun.'

'And this softly, softly approach has

absolutely nothing to do with our friends in London?'

'Never mind all that. Find Christie,' Longley said. 'Leave the rest alone.'

'Not easy, without a photograph,' Thackeray persisted. 'A photo-fit, something to give the Press.'

'I'll pursue that higher up and let you know,' Longley said.

'Sir,' Thackeray conceded, getting to his feet abruptly and spinning on his heel. He did not slam Longley's door behind him but he might as well have done. His discontent was clear enough as he left the office and Longley sat for a moment in silence before picking up his telephone and asking to be put through to county headquarters to pass his own uneasiness on up the line. But what worried him most was how close Michael Thackeray seemed to breaking point. And he wondered whether the strain written all over his DCI'S face was due solely to the unpleasantness of the deaths in Staveley, or to something deeper.

Kevin Mower watched Thackeray come down the stairs from Longley's office with unfathomable eyes. He followed the DCI out of the main CID office and into his own without waiting to be invited, closed the door and leaned against it, feeling the wood press hard against his spine as Thackeray took his chair behind the desk, leaned back and closed his eyes.

'Are you all right, guv?' Mower asked. Thackeray opened his eyes again and offered the sergeant a slightly grim smile.

'Not really,' he said. He passed the file he had brought down from Longley's office to Mower and pulled out his cigarettes. Mower could see that his hands were shaking.

'The body in Manchester isn't Christie,' he said. 'So we're back to square one. Find the bastard. And leave the rest alone. Manchester will handle the shooting at their end. We haven't the resources to waste time on looking at Christie's background.'

Mower took the report and raised a sceptical eyebrow.

'And what about the child?' he asked. 'Do we take the attempt to see her seriously? Or put it down to coincidence? I've got Sharif going through the hospital CCTV tapes to try to find whoever dumped the supposed Asian woman's gear, but it's like looking for a needle in a haystack. Do you know how many people go in and out of that place in a day?'

'I can imagine,' Thackeray said wearily. 'Keep the watch on Emma Christie. I want to know as soon as she really can talk. And we need to keep the Press away. Vince Newsom swears innocent on this one, but I don't really believe him. He'll try anything to get a story and he's still around.'

'And so are plenty of others, according to the Press office,' Mower said. 'Poor little Emma still seems to be a good story, by the tabloids' standards.'

'The *Gazette* won't hold back either,' Thackeray said wearily. 'They're sitting on a photograph of Christie the super's asked them not to use, but Ted Grant's not going to hold on for ever without a bloody good reason. Why should he? We're making out this man could be dangerous if he's alive and pulling our punches when it comes to finding him. It makes no sense. I feel as if I'm being asked to handle this case with one hand tied behind my back.'

'So where now, guv?'

'Well, we know now that at some point Christie and the Land Rover got separated, but we've no idea where. He may have driven it to Manchester himself, or abandoned it somewhere else and someone nicked it. But we know he must have left Staveley in it with the boy and it seems unlikely he'd head into Bradfield. He'd be much more likely to head west to get out of sight quickly, and the boy's body was found in that direction, so talk to uniform and get the search on the moor roads extended as far as they can go. And circulate farmers and shepherds up there again. The sheep are in-bye at this time of year...' He smiled faintly as Mower looked puzzled.

'They bring them down from the high ground for the winter,' he said. 'To save them getting trapped in the snow. And to keep them fed during the bad weather.'

'Right,' Mower said, thinking that this was really more than he wanted to know about sheep.

'Even so, someone might have seen some unusual movement up on the fells, tracks even. If this man really is ex-army he may fancy his survival skills even at this time of the year. But there's a limit to the length of time you can survive up on the tops in this weather. Talk to as many people in the isolated farmsteads and hamlets as you can.'

'He may be lying dead up there.'

'That's still a possibility,' Thackeray said.

'I'd still like to know who the hell he is,' Mower grumbled.

'We'd all like to know that, but until the spooks tell us – if ever – we may have to manage without that information. It doesn't mean we can't track him down. You can bank on that, at least.'

And to judge by the fury in Michael Thackeray's eyes, Mower thought as he left the DCI's office, his boss would not be averse to scrambling around the sodden moors and crags himself in search of this particular quarry. In fact it might make him feel much better.

After spending the morning reinvigorating

the hunt for Gordon Christie, Kevin Mower picked up his leather jacket, slung it over his shoulder, and left the CID office alone. Outside police headquarters he pulled out his mobile phone and made a call. Laura Ackroyd answered almost immediately, sounding surprised to hear who was at the other end.

'D'you fancy a quick drink?' Mower asked.

Laura hesitated for a second, and then agreed to meet him in the Lamb, the pub closest to the *Gazette* office.

'I haven't much time,' she said.

'Nor me,' Mower agreed. He broke the connection with a faint smile. There remained at the back of his mind the conviction he had come to years ago that Laura Ackroyd deserved someone better than the morose and complex man he worked for who was apparently less willing to commit himself than he had ever been. Laura deserved fun and laughter and a good time, he thought, although he knew it was more than his career was worth to make such a suggestion to her. Romance with a senior officer's partner had almost put paid to his prospects in the force once already, and he had no wish to repeat the experience which had brought him from the Met to this alien county, where his boss understood the over-wintering habits of sheep as well as he knew the predilections of the druggies and prostitutes on the run-down estates and backstreets of Bradfield.

'In-bye,' he muttered scornfully, as he crossed the town hall square and headed towards the Lamb. 'What sort of a word is that?'

Laura was there before him, her copper hair pulled back severely and an anxious look in her green eyes.

'Hi,' she said without much enthusiasm. 'What's going on?'

'You tell me? The DCI's acting stressed out and you look the same.'

She shrugged and her face closed tight.

'We're okay,' she said. 'I meant why are we having this drink? Just for old times' sake or is there something special?'

'Gordon Christie,' Mower said. 'The boss is hunting him round the sheep folds of the Pennines without so much as a snapshot to go on.'

'But Dawn Brough found you a picture, didn't she? What's the problem with that?'

'Let's just say it's been mislaid, or so I'm told,' Mower said. 'Funny how that happened after the funny fellers started taking an interest. Could you get me a copy of the one you found in the *Gazette* archive?'

'Well, I'm sure Ted Grant will give Michael a copy if he needs it...'

'No,' Mower said quietly. 'Not Ted to the DCI, just you to me, on the quiet. I need a copy and I'm not too keen to let anyone at the nick know I've got it.'

Laura looked at him in silence for a long time.

'Don't do anything silly, Kevin,' she said at length, knowing she was echoing Thackeray's warning to her of the evening before and that Mower was as unlikely to take any notice as she was herself.

'Just a few inquiries,' he said as lightly as he could manage. 'Nothing desperate. I hate the idea of Christie getting away with this because the powers that be are locked in some sort of internal turf war of their own. I guess the DCI feels exactly the same but he's stuck in the middle of it. I've got a bit more room for manoeuvre.'

Laura thought of Thackeray's letter of resignation which, as far as she knew, he still had in his jacket pocket and she shivered suddenly.

'It'll be difficult for me to run a print off without anyone noticing,' she said quietly. 'What about email? Have you got a colour printer?'

'Yes, that would be fine,' Mower said. 'I'll give you my personal email address. I don't want this going to the office.' He wrote it down for her on a page from his notebook.

'Delete the file when you've printed it,' she said. 'I'll do the same at my end.'

'That's not infallible, but let's hope no

one's ever so keen to find out how I got the picture that they decide to ransack my hard disc,' Mower said. 'I don't know what's going on around this case, Laura, but I don't like it.'

'Nor does Michael,' Laura said. 'That's pretty obvious.'

Laura went back to the newsroom in a thoughtful mood and, after checking that no one was close enough to see her computer screen, sent DS Mower the picture he had requested. She did not seriously expect any repercussions in her own office even if her email came to light, but she knew that what Mower seemed to be considering would take him into perilous territory. That he was prepared to take the risk convinced her that Michael Thackeray was not alone in his anxieties about just how the Christie case was being run and she too began to wonder what was being covered up by the shadowy figures who seemed to be manipulating what ought to be a simple manhunt for a domestic murderer. There must be, she concluded, much more to it than that.

She finished the feature she had been working on and then crossed the newsroom and tapped on Ted Grant's half open office door. He waved her in with an impatient gesture.

'I was thinking of going up to Staveley

again this afternoon, and then checking at the hospital to see how Emma Christie is,' she said.

'You think there's still mileage in that?' Grant asked without great interest.

'The nationals are up in force now. They seem to think there's still a story there.' She had seen the London pack assembled outside police headquarters the previous day harassing the *Gazette*'s Bob Baker for more crumbs of information than the force seemed prepared to divulge.

'Aye, well it would be good to get one over on Vince Newsom, though you'd better come up with something with a bit more substance to it than he's had so far. The police are denying that the kiddie's said anything coherent yet.'

'Well they would say that, wouldn't they?' Laura shot back with more asperity than she had intended and Ted gave her a quizzical look.

'Not getting much pillow talk on this one, then?'

Laura did not reply.

'Aye, well, you can have another snoop around if you like. Bob Baker's off today so he'll not come up with anything for tomorrow's paper. You'll get a human interest story out of it, I dare say, if nowt else.'

With that less than enthusiastic encouragement Laura drove up to Staveley through a drifting drizzle, which reduced visibility far enough to demand headlights soon after lunchtime and left Staveley shrouded in a mist that blotted out the dark humpbacked hills beyond the village completely. She parked at the pub and went into the bar, where Janine Foster, looking even more faded and distraught than the last time she had seen her, was serving one of the handful of customers who had decided to cheer up a dismal afternoon with a pint of Tetleys. She glanced at Laura with hostility in her eyes.

'You again,' she said. 'Can't the newspapers leave us alone?'

'I don't suppose they'll do that until Gordon Christie's found,' Laura said, ordering an orange juice. 'Have you had the tabloid pack in?'

'Some beggars from London came careering around t'village yesterday,' Janine said. 'It's like being in a bloody zoo.'

'Is your husband around?' Laura asked. 'He seems to have known Christie as well as anyone did.'

Janine Foster looked at Laura and smiled without mirth.

'Not as well as he knew Linda, though,' she said. 'Any road, he's not here. He got a phone call early on and said he had to go out. Didn't have the decency to tell me when he'd be back, did he? So I'm here on my own again, trying to run the place solo. We can't go on like this much longer. One of us'll have to go.' She suddenly seemed to notice that several of the customers were listening avidly to what she was saying and lowered her voice slightly.

'To be perfectly honest, I'd be glad to get away. There's a lot of unpleasantness going on in Staveley since the shootings. I've been getting phone calls, and no one's at t'other end. Heavy breathing sounds like a joke, doesn't it, but it can be right scary.'

'Is this just aimed at you or is your husband getting the calls as well?' Laura asked, recognising the fear at the back of the woman's eyes.

'He says he doesn't, but he's been getting summat. He's worried about summat. I've heard him arguing with someone on the phone more than once but he just says it's a dispute with the brewery and I'm not to worry. But that's all my eye. It doesn't make sense. I'm wondering if the calls I'm getting are really for him, and they just hang up because it's me that answers. I don't know what to think any more. This used to be a good place to live but since the shootings it's fallen apart. People are blaming each other, saying someone should have noticed that things were going wrong with the Christies, that social services should have done summat when they thought Scott was getting thumped... They're even blaming Gerry, as it goes, since it got out about his affair with Linda.'

'It's got around, has it? How did that happen?' Laura asked. 'It's not been in the Press.' Which, she thought, was increasingly surprising with Vince Newsom snooping around the village. It might only be a matter of time before Gerry Foster's liaison with the dead woman was spread all over the front page of the *Globe*.

Janine glanced away and Laura knew that she herself must have told someone who had passed the gossip on and it had mushroomed, as these things do.

'These things always get out, don't they?' was all Janine would say.

'Did it get out before the shootings?' Laura asked quietly. 'You said last time I was up here that people knew, that you found out from gossip. Is that what tipped Gordon Christie over the edge? Was that the way it happened? You found out, Gordon found out and then it all went so horribly wrong at Moor Edge?'

Janine pursed her lips and shook her head, and Laura knew she would get no further. If Janine had tipped off Gordon Christie about his wife's infidelity it was something she was not going to admit to a reporter, or, Laura guessed, to the police. But the fact that she must be hoping pretty fervently that

Gordon himself was dead, or at least too far away to ever reveal that piece of information, perhaps explained why she took Laura's empty glass with a hand which was shaking convulsively. Janine turned away abruptly to deal with another customer who had brought an empty pint glass and a look of naked curiosity to the bar, and Laura shrugged and turned away herself, feeling watched as she made her way out into the drizzle again.

She walked slowly up the steep village street, guessing that her progress was also being observed from the blank windows of the cottages on either side by eyes which would not be friendly if they recognised her as a reporter. At the end of the lane leading up to Moor Edge cottage blue and white police tape lay tangled in the bushes and ragged grass which had grown up against the drystone walls. Picking her way carefully along the muddy track, where traces of fresh snow gleamed in the shadier hollows and wet slush filled the ruts, past the new houses with their postage stamp gardens where Dawn Brough lived, she trudged as far as the Christies' cottage, wishing she'd put on the boots she kept in the back of her car. Her shoes were sodden.

The police tape was still in place here, across the gate and doorway, but there was no sign of life. Someone had closed the

239

curtains across the front windows, although whether out of respect for the dead or to give the police teams who had worked inside some privacy she could not guess. And outside the gate there was a small heap of bouquets, the flowers wet and wilting now, a brown teddy bear sodden amongst the crumpled cellophane and ribbons.

What a waste, she thought, knowing without having seen the horror that had lain in wait for Michael Thackeray, how devastating it must have been for him to have walked through that cottage door a week before. What a bloody waste.

She was about to turn away when she became aware of someone behind her. Her heart thumped wildly for a second as she spun round and then calmed as she recognised the man she had been hoping to speak to at the Fox and Hounds.

'You made me jump,' she said.

'Sorry,' Gerry Foster said. 'I come up here a lot.'

'I suppose you would,' Laura said dryly. Foster's face darkened.

'It wasn't like you think,' he said. 'Linda was a lost soul. She didn't know what to do, or where to turn. She couldn't live with Gordon, she said. He was sick. The bloody army does that to some people. They can't get over it.'

'So he'd been in the army, had he?'

'Oh yes,' Foster said.

'So you offered Linda the proverbial shoulder to weep on, did you? Didn't it cross your mind that Gordon Christie might go bananas if he found out? Everyone seems to have known what a moody beggar he was, long before all this.' She waved at the cottage where she guessed that traces of the massacre would still be visible to anyone who chose to go and look.

'You don't think something like that could happen,' Foster said. 'You can't imagine anything like that.'

'Right,' Laura said with a sigh. She supposed Foster was right. No one could anticipate such horror.

'I just went into the Fox,' she said. 'Your wife was wondering where you were.' Foster scowled again.

'As if she cares.'

'Well, you can't spend the rest of your life mooching about up here,' Laura said briskly. 'It's over now.'

Foster glanced away for a second and then held out a hand in Laura's direction, as if pleading for help.

'I've been trying to get up the courage to go inside,' he said. 'I wanted to find something of Linda's, a keepsake, like. Does that sound daft?'

Laura's expression softened slightly at the lost look in the big man's eyes.

'No,' she said. 'Not daft.' Foster hesitated again.

'Will you come in with me?' he asked.

It was Laura who hesitated now, appalled and tempted in equal measure at the idea of seeing the scene of the murders.

'I loved her, you know,' Foster said, glancing away. 'I even got to know the kids a bit, because they were hers. At school things, and that. We've only got the one lad and he's away at college now. I got involved in village things because of Linda's kids, not mine. It's not as if we're locals. It was summat to do to get away from Janine at first. We've been rowing for years. Oh, you don't know what it's like...' Laura shook her head impatiently, not wanting to listen to the intimacies of another failed marriage.

'How can you get into the cottage?' she asked. 'The police must have locked it up.'

'I've got a key,' Foster said. 'Linda had one cut for me. As a precaution.'

'A precaution against what, for God's sake?' Laura asked, surprised.

'In case Gordon started hitting her and she needed help. She said she didn't want to call the police, but she'd call me on her mobile, if she could, and I could come up. It's only five minutes away from the Fox, after all – if you're quick.'

'And did she?' Laura asked. 'Call you, I

mean? Did you come up here to confront Gordon?'

'No, I never got a call. Maybe she tried that morning, the mobile signal's not too good round here, I don't know. But I never got a call. The first thing I knew about it was when the police cars and the ambulances came rushing through the village. It was too late then.' Foster wiped the moisture from his face and Laura guessed that it was not just the rain he was wiping away.

'Come on then,' she said. 'I'll come in with you. But we'd best be quick. If the police found us in there they'd be furious.' What they were doing might not be illegal, she thought, but it was certainly unwise.

'I don't think they come up now,' Foster said. 'I think they've finished here.' He ducked under the police tape and walked up the short pathway to the front door of the cottage. Laura followed him, feeling slightly clammy inside her hooded jacket. She had been close to violent death before, but she knew as well as Michael Thackeray did that the involvement of children made this a crime scene of unrivalled horror. She would not, she thought, set foot in the family kitchen where the deaths had taken place. That was more than even her sharp reporter's curiosity wanted to explore.

Christie opened the front door and led the way. The hall was dimly lit and airless, all

243

the doors closed, the curtains on the landing window amongst those which had been pulled shut, and there was a fusty and slightly metallic smell in the air which Laura guessed was not only the result of the closed windows and doors. She shuddered slightly.

'Do you know which room is which?' she asked, but Foster shook his head.

'Upstairs is probably best,' she said firmly, and she followed him up the stairs and watched as he opened one bedroom door after another, glanced inside and closed them again.

'Those are the kiddies' rooms,' he said. 'You don't want to see.' Laura nodded. There was no way she could write about this clandestine visit to the murder scene without exposing herself to Thackeray's legitimate fury, and she was already regretting her decision to come inside.

'This is Linda and Gordon's room,' Foster said, opening the final doorway.

'Find something you want to take and let's get out of here,' Laura said, getting a glimpse of an unmade double bed, the floral duvet still flung on to the floor where the last occupant had left it, a blue nightdress in a crumpled heap beside the pillows. She felt slightly breathless. She watched Foster walk across to the dressing table and pick up and put down one or two items which had been left there. She could see that most things had been dusted with a white powder, no doubt to pick up fingerprints.

'Don't let anyone see you've been in here,' she warned. 'Don't leave any traces.' Foster grunted what might have been assent or protest but he kept his hands to himself until he picked up a scarf from a pile of clothes on the dressing table stool and suddenly buried his face in it. Laura watched in silence. There was nothing she could say to this man she believed, and who obviously believed himself, had precipitated this catastrophe. She knew, after living with Michael Thackeray, exactly how guilt might blight the rest of his life.

Downstairs, she thought she heard a door close and she froze, hearing only her own heartbeat.

'There's someone here,' she whispered, ears straining.

'There can't be,' Foster said, spinning round, the scarf in his hand.

'Maybe just the wind,' Laura said. Foster pushed past her and went into one of the bedrooms at the back of the house while she waited on the landing.

'Jesus,' she heard him say. Reluctantly, almost holding her breath to ward off the pain, she crept silently past the two unmade bunk beds, the stacks of toys and books, and the children's clothes neatly laid out as if ready to put on, and joined him at the window.

'What is it?' she asked.

'There's someone down there,' Foster muttered. I saw a movement by the shed and look, there's footprints in that snowy patch by the back door.' He pulled his mobile phone from his pocket and flicked it on and off again with an exasperated sigh.

'There must have been dozens of police people in and out,' she said.

'There was a fresh snowfall yesterday,' Foster said. 'Look, it's not melted by the back door. It didn't snow a lot, but you can see how the older prints are almost covered and there's just that fresh lot heading across the yard.'

'Christie, do you think?' she breathed. 'No one would think of looking for him back here.' She glanced back at the main bedroom and wondered wildly if the fugitive had slept there.

'Let's get out,' Foster said. 'This was a crazy idea. The whole thing's crazy. I wish to God I'd never got involved.'

They made their way out of the cottage silently and locked the door, and Laura noticed as they hurried back into the lane that Foster was still clutching Linda Christie's scarf in one hand. She could even smell a faint trace of her perfume.

'We need to tell the police,' she said.

'Don't be bloody daft,' Foster snapped as they hurried through the mud and slushy snow to the relative safety of the village. 'They'll want to know what the hell we were doing up here.'

'We have to tell them,' Laura said, and if Foster had known her well enough to recognise the stubborn set of her jaw, he would have known that she would not be shifted on this. 'I'll think of a way,' she said. 'If Christie's there with a gun they have to know.'

'If Christie's there with a gun, I don't think I want to be here at all,' Foster said. 'No one ever told me it would turn out like this.'

'What do you mean?'

'Never mind,' Foster said. 'I'm away from here before I'm the next one with a bullet through the back. I never signed up for that.' And leaving Laura in his wake, still wondering what he meant, he strode off in the direction of the Fox and Hounds. By the time Laura had picked her way through the slush back to her own car, Foster had passed her, driving a Toyota estate at breakneck speed up the winding road which led to the open moors and eventually to Lancashire.

Reluctantly, Laura drove off in the opposite direction, stopping only at an isolated phone box on the way back into town. She put her hand across the mouthpiece as she told the 999 operator that she had seen suspicious movements at the Christie's cottage just ten minutes ago, and hung up sharply when she demanded her name. As she dropped down the hill into the centre of Bradfield and joined the main stream of traffic she saw two police cars, blue lights flashing, heading in the opposite direction. That, she thought, with no particular pleasure, was the best she could do.

Chapter Fifteen

Kevin Mower negotiated the slightly bewildering dual carriageways which led around the centre of Leeds and found a parking space at the back of the Civic Hall. It was there that the two universities and the infirmary kept a sedate distance between their ancient pursuits and the trendy business developments around the shopping centre and the river which had catapulted the old Yorkshire manufacturing city into an icon of twenty-first century glitz. He glanced at his street map and followed the instructions he had been given to a red brick street corner pub which did not seem to have been touched by anything much in the way of development since the 1970s.

There were no smart loft apartments in this quarter, he noticed, just terraced houses, many of which appeared to have been converted into student homes, no doubt with young people crammed into every available nook and cranny. Term, he could see, was in full swing, and he passed groups of youngsters evidently making their way home, clutching bags of books and carriers of shopping. What was left of the local population seemed to be a mixture of white and Asian, none of them showing much sign that they were sharing in the booming prosperity for which the city had become well-known.

He pushed open the door of what announced itself in lettering engraved into the opaque glass of the windows to be the lounge bar and peered inside, where a sparse early evening cluster of men were hunched over their pints with the rapt attention of serious drinkers and did not so much as glance up as he entered. He could feel the multi-coloured carpet stick under his feet and the tang of liquor was overlaid by that of stale cigarette smoke and the greasy taint of ancient chips.

The person he was seeking was sitting in a corner close to the bar. Mower held out a hand, which was only taken reluctantly by the burly, grey-faced man in jeans and a dark anorak.

'Good to see you again, Harry,' Mower said. 'It's been a long time.' Harry Maitland wiped the froth off his upper lip and grunted by way of a greeting in return. Mower glanced at his drink, which was only half finished.

'I'll get you another,' he said. 'What is it? Tetleys?' He got another grunt in response which he took for assent. Fresh glasses on the table, Mower pulled up a stool opposite Maitland and took a draught of his own lager.

'How's it going in the security business?' Mower asked. 'You must be in demand with things the way they are. The IRA never came close to this lot, did they? And they were bad enough.'

The man looked at Mower with chilly slate-coloured eyes, around which the whites were too redly veined to look healthy. They had never been close when they had served together in the Metropolitan Police and this unexpectedly renewed acquaintance, re-newed at Mower's request, reminded the sergeant just how much he had always distrusted the former soldier who had been his colleague at Paddington Green for a brief and not very productive period of his career.

'Business?' Maitland said. 'Swings and roundabouts, innit?' The voice still betray-ing his South London origins and the deeply ingrained cynicism Mower remem-bered. In spite of the dim light at the back of the lounge bar, Mower could see just how unhealthy the man looked, and that his dark blue anorak was stained at the front and frayed slightly at the cuffs. The security business Maitland had gone into after he left the Met under a cloud was clearly not going anything like well enough for a man who, he recalled, had disliked hard work but been fond of his Scotch and his girls. Pints of Tetleys did not seem his style.

'The IRA was a doddle compared to this lot,' Maitland said with an approximation of confidence in his voice. 'The financial geezers down the road are wetting themselves.' But somehow Mower did not think that the financial geezers were turning to Maitland's security and investigation company for help against Al Qa'ida. A bit of surveillance on behalf of jealous spouses and business partners would be more likely the bread-and-butter of his world, and not much of that either, by the look of it.

'So what can I do for you,' Maitland asked, without enthusiasm. 'At the usual rates, of course.'

Mower smiled faintly at that.

'Just an ID problem,' he said. 'I thought you or some of your mates might come up with a solution. I think there's an army connection.'

'The British army's a bloody big institution,' Maitland said.

'Yes, but not the bit you were in,' Mower countered. And that's the bit I'm interested in. Irish connections. Possibly undercover. You know the sort of thing.'

'Could bring me a lot of grief, that,' Maitland objected, but he did not reject the photograph which Mower pulled out of his inside pocket and handed to him.

'The bloke in the green shirt there,' Mower said, 'does he look familiar, at all?' Maitland peered at the picture in the dim light for a moment but shook his head.

'Never seen him before in my life,' he said. 'It's fifteen years since I came out. It's too long ago. You can see he's a good bit younger.'

'D'you know anyone else who might give me a name?' Mower persisted. 'Anyone else you could show it to? You must still have some contacts.'

Maitland grunted and started on his second pint.

'Not if they're still in the service,' he said shortly. 'More than their pension's worth to chatter.'

'Someone who came out more recently then?'

'They keep at you even then,' Maitland said. 'They could make life very uncomfortable if they thought you'd been blabbing.'

'People do, though, don't they?' Mower countered. 'Write books, even.'

'Line their pockets,' Maitland said. 'But ID-ing someone? That's dodgy. Very dodgy.'

'We can't trace this bloke back more than three years when he turned up in Yorkshire with a wife and three kids and absolutely nothing in the records to pin him down. Before that it's a blank. A very carefully contrived blank, as far as I can see.'

'If the powers that be fixed him up with a new ID, it'll stay that way,' Maitland said.

'We want the bastard for multiple murder,' Mower said angrily. 'We're getting precisely nowhere with the powers that be. He shot his wife and kids.'

Maitland stared at the smeared table top in front of him for a moment or two and then shrugged.

'He'd not be the first to flip,' he said. 'There's supposed to be resettlement, counselling, all that stuff, but if it happens at all I don't reckon it does some of those lads much good. There's a lot of stuff buried in their heads, especially if they were in Ireland for any length of time. What do they call it these days? Post-traumatic stress? There's a lot of it about. An epidemic, if you really want to know.'

'Right,' Mower said.

Maitland picked up the photograph and put it in his inside pocket.

'I know someone who might just know, though God knows if he'll be prepared to help,' he said. 'Leave it with me. I'll have a word. Get back to you if I get anything. But 'don't hold your breath.'

'I won't,' Mower said, thinking that he had flogged some dead horses in his time but few more lifeless than Harry Maitland. He wondered whether his flagging career was the result of his evidently massive apathy or whether the apathy sprang from his sagging fortunes at work. Either way he reckoned that the photograph of Gordon Christie, apparently relaxing at the Staveley school fête, would get no further than Maitland's inside pocket. His trip to Leeds and the cost of a couple of pints of Tetleys ale, he concluded as he got up to go, had been pretty much a waste of time.

Michael Thackeray heard Laura's key in the lock as he was packing a couple of polo shirts into an overnight case. For a moment he stood by the bed, rooted to the spot, shirts in hand, and his heart thumping uncomfortably as he waited for her to dump her bags and come into the room behind him. He did not turn round, even though he heard her sharp intake of breath as she realised what he was doing.

'Where are you going, Michael?' she asked. He dropped the handful of clothes into the bag and turned slowly towards her, seeing the raw anxiety in her face.

'I've been told to take a holiday,' he said, his voice unnaturally low. 'I had this major row with Jack Longley and he told me to get away for a couple of weeks...'

'He's suspended you?' Laura asked.

'No, not exactly. Just a holiday, but without the option.'

'And you're going to accept that? In the middle of a murder inquiry?'

Thackeray sat down on the edge of the bed as if his legs would no longer support him. His face was very pale and he avoided Laura's eyes.

'I don't have any choice, Laura,' he said. 'He didn't give me any choice. And in any case the murder inquiry's running into the sand. Manchester's in charge of the body in the Land Rover, the search for Christie can quite easily continue whether I'm here or not. In fact, the chances of finding him at all, never mind alive, are getting more remote by the day. We had a report that someone had been seen at the cottage yesterday but we didn't find anything significant. It was probably just some ghoul peering in the windows to look at the blood on the floor.'

Laura shivered slightly, knowing that there had been more than one person who could be classified as a ghoul at Moor Edge the previous day.

'But there are so many unanswered questions around Christie,' she said.

Thackeray shrugged. 'Maybe. But as I'm effectively blocked from digging around in his past, I might as well not be here. I'll be better off out of it.'

Laura had never seen Thackeray look so defeated.

'I'll come with you,' she said, taking his hand. 'I'll call Ted first thing in the morning and tell him I need a week off. We could go to Portugal to see my parents. Joyce is still out there but they've got plenty of space. It would do us both good to get away for a bit.'

But Thackeray shook his head.

'Somewhere else then? Somewhere we can be alone...?'

'I've booked a flight,' he said. 'I need to be on my own for a while. This business with Longley has made me ask myself a lot of questions about the future. I need to think about where I'm going, if I'm going anywhere at all in the police force any more.'

Laura thought of the resignation letter Thackeray had written and put in his pocket and guessed that he might be planning to put it in the post on the way to the airport.

'You can't let these bastards defeat you,' she said.

'That's not what Jack Longley says. He says I'm wasting my time even thinking about defying the spooks, and I'd just better get over it if I want my career to go on much longer. He was pretty clear about that.'

'Don't do anything stupid, like resigning,' she said. 'That would be a total waste. They need people like you.'

'Not if we get in the way, apparently,' Thackeray said.

'I don't believe this,' Laura said, feeling almost as defeated as Thackeray looked but determined to keep on fighting with all the means in her power. 'I'll get your so-called holiday on the front page tomorrow, if you like, ask what the hell's going on with this case, a mother and two children dead, no sign of the father, and now the senior investigating officer effectively off the case. It's unforgivable, Michael. You must see that. I can easily stir Ted Grant up on this, get him into crusading mode, get him to make an issue of it.'

'Don't do that, Laura. Please,' Thackeray said. 'There's no way that would help me. It would wind up the brass at county and turn them against me like nothing else could. You'd kill my career, such as it is, stone dead.'

'If they haven't killed it stone dead already,' Laura said. 'Those bastards.'

Thackeray turned away and zipped up his bag, glancing at his watch.

'Leave it, Laura,' he said. 'I must go if I'm going to catch my flight. Give me some time and space, a week at most, and I promise I'll sort my head out, I'll be in touch.'

'And you don't need me for any of that?' she asked, unable to keep the bitterness out of her voice now. 'I'm superfluous to requirements in a crisis, am I?'

'Don't,' he said. 'Please don't.' He tried to take her in his arms but she slid out of his grasp and turned away angrily, her face flushed, copper hair flying.

'Are you going to tell me where you're going?' she asked as he moved out of the bedroom with his bag. 'Am I not allowed to know that, even?'

'I'm not sure yet,' he said. 'I'll call you tomorrow.'

'You've got a flight booked but you're not sure where it's going?' she flashed. 'You're kidding me.'

But he did not reply. He shrugged tiredly, picked up his coat in the hall and closed the front door quietly behind him, leaving Laura to fling herself into a chair and gaze at the silk flowers in the Victorian fireplace with her eyes full of tears. She was as sure as she had ever been sure of anything during the years of their stormy relationship that it was not just his future career Michael Thackeray was planning to reconsider on his enforced holiday; it was also his future with her. She wondered, in fact, if he would ever come back.

Chapter Sixteen

DS Kevin Mower and DC Val Ridley walked down the stairs from Superintendent Jack Longley's office in silence. The interview they had just had with him, in his self-appointed new capacity as senior investigating officer for the Christie family murders, had left them seriously dissatisfied. Neither of them had yet even begun to come to terms with the fact that DCI Thackeray had suddenly left police headquarters without any explanation apart from a two line note on the CID noticeboard that morning to say that he had gone on holiday. And their unease had only been compounded when Val's conviction that she had achieved a breakthrough in the investigation had been dismissed by Longley with little sign of interest.

'I'll get them to look at the forensics again,' he had conceded. 'There may be evidence of someone else being in the house but it will be difficult to pin it to that morning even if there is. But I wouldn't get too excited about what the child says, any road. A ten-year-old with a severe head injury's never going to make a credible witness, is she? Look into it, by all means, but don't waste any time over it. What I want is Christie found. It's a hundred to one that this case begins and ends with Gordon Christie. There's been enough time and resources wasted on chasing up other so-called leads.'

Back in the main CID office Val flung herself into a chair and ran her hands through her short fair hair in something close to fury. She looked at Mower, who had perched himself on a neighbouring desk and was watching her with a sardonic look in his eyes.

'I've waited with that kid for a week for this, sarge,' Val said in a furious whisper. 'And look where it gets me. The DCI's buggered off and the super's not even remotely interested in what she's saying. What the hell's going on?'

Mower did not answer directly.

'How reliable is what she's saying, do you reckon?' he asked instead.

Val pulled out her notebook and flicked over a few pages before she replied.

'She began to talk coherently yesterday,' she said. 'Only a few words at first, asking for her mother, asking where she was, asking what happened. The doctors advised not telling her anything yet. It would be too much of a shock on top of her physical problems, so I just answered vaguely. I promise you I didn't put any ideas into her head. I was very, very careful not to, sarge. Believe me.'

'I believe you,' Mower said. 'And then?'

'Then, when I went in this morning, she really seemed properly awake for the first time. And she seemed to recognise me. She knew she'd seen me before, at least. Even managed a faint smile.' Val worked hard to keep her voice neutral. There was no way she could let anyone in CID know just how close she felt to the pale, semi-conscious child she had been watching over with a devotion far beyond the call of duty for more than a week now, or how desperately she wanted her to recover.

'And she could remember the day of the shooting? It's unusual for traumatic memories to return like that. It very often gets blotted out.'

'She asked for her mummy again. And then she asked if her mummy got hurt, and I didn't know what to answer, so I just said mummy and daddy would be in to see her soon. But that seemed to really upset her. She looked straight at me and began to cry. She said she didn't want her daddy to come. Or the other man. So I asked her who the other man was. And she said the man who banged on the door and had a fight with her daddy.'

'Did she know who he was?'

'No,' Val said. 'He seems to have been a

261

stranger, at least to her. Which doesn't mean her father didn't know him, of course. But it rules out Gerry Foster from the pub, at any rate. The Christie children knew him.'

And you think this was the morning of the murders?' Mower asked. 'Can you be sure?'

'Not a hundred per cent. As I told the super. But the thing she seemed most frightened about was a gun. I asked her who had a gun and she said the man who came to the door.'

'Does she remember the shootings? Does she remember who shot her?'

Val shook her head. 'She seems to have blanked that out. When I pressed her just a little she got distressed so I didn't push it. She just said she tried to run away and everything went black, which of course it would have done when she was shot. And we have no idea if she was injured first, in which case she wouldn't have seen the others killed.'

'You can't blame the super for thinking it's a bit vague, Val,' Mower said.

'That's why I want to keep going with her,' Val said fiercely. 'The doctor says that if she's remembering something it may indicate that she'll gradually remember more. I want to stay with her, Kevin. I'm sure Emma's got the key to all this locked away in her head.'

Mower shrugged. 'Well, you heard what

the super said. Maybe the forensics will come up with something. But there's nothing to stop you visiting Emma in your own time. You seem to have done that already often enough. See if you can get any sort of description of this visitor. She may never be a very reliable witness but if we can match up what she says with some forensic evidence we may have something serious to go on.'

'The DCI wouldn't be so dismissive,' Val muttered angrily. 'Where the hell's he gone anyway, in the middle of a murder case?

'I don't know,' Mower said. 'But he looked as though he needed a holiday, that's for sure.'

'Something odd's going on with this case,' Val said.

'Maybe,' Mower said, cautiously. But he knew she was right, and half an hour later, when he was sure no one was taking any interest in his movements, he left the main CID office and went into Michael Thackeray's room, closing and locking the door behind him. He stood for a moment looking round at the desk – relatively tidy; the filing cabinets – tightly closed and, when he tried them, tightly locked; and the computer – switched off and unplugged. Wherever Thackeray had gone, he thought, he had tidied up before he went, almost as if he expected to be away a long time, if not for good. Anxiety growing in the pit of his stomach, he crossed the room and pulled out the desk drawers methodically, one after the other. But, to his relief, he did not find the bottle he feared might be there.

He sat down suddenly at the desk, letting out the breath he realised he had been holding for too long in a low sigh. Mower was not a man who offered respect easily, but he had watched Thackeray fight his demons as he handled a case that came far to close to his own experience, and had been impressed. Why should he have bottled out now, he wondered. It did not make sense. Stressed out he might have been, but that came with the job. Emotionally involved in the deaths of two children he had un-doubtedly been, but he had concealed it well. Only those who knew him as well as Mower thought he did could have guessed at the turmoil those small bodies had caused Thackeray. So if he had not cracked and asked for time away there had to be another reason, and it had to come from above. Val Ridley was right. There was something odd going on with this case and no one at police HQ was going to tell him what it was. He would, Mower concluded, getting to his feet and letting himself out of the DCI's aban-doned office, have to find out for himself.

Laura Ackroyd had rolled out of bed long

before first light that morning. She had slept only fitfully, her mouth was dry and her eyes felt swollen in their sockets. She did not dare look at herself in the mirror. As she padded across the chilly kitchen floor to override the central heating timer and put the kettle on, she wondered bleakly if this was the first day of the rest of her life. As she sipped her coffee, strong and black, she went over the previous evening's events in her mind for about the hundredth time since Thackeray had walked away, and wondered yet again if she could have said anything that would have changed his plans.

With only half her mind on what she was doing, Laura eventually found herself in the office, working like an automaton on some routine changes to the feature pages which formed a major part of the next day's Saturday edition. When the phone on her desk rang towards lunchtime she grabbed it with a dry mouth and thumping heart, in the certain conviction that it must be Thackeray, only to be flung into despair again by a voice that she only half recognised.

'Who?' she asked, more sharply than she intended and was conscious of the crime reporter, Bob Baker, watching her curiously from a couple of desks along. Val Ridley identified herself again and a glimmer of an interested response swam to the front of

Laura's consciousness as the detective suggested a quick drink.

'Fine,' Laura said, intrigued at last, in spite of a thumping headache and an increasingly sick stomach. 'I'll see you there.' She finished off her editing chores with more urgency than she had managed to summon up in the last three hours and put on her coat, and wrapped a scarf up to her eyes. If she could have covered herself entirely like a strict Muslim she would have felt more comfortable. Fortunately, it was only a short walk to the bar Val had suggested and she could easily fit her trip into her lunch hour.

Val was already sitting at a table with a fruit cocktail in front of her when Laura arrived, unwrapped herself carefully, and ordered a vodka and tonic from the attentive waitress. Her fragility, she thought, might best be cured by a kick in the teeth than by pussy-footing around with soft drinks. Laura took a sip of her drink and looked at the pale, self-contained police officer, in her black trouser suit and white shirt, with a curiosity she had never really felt before. She hardly knew Val Ridley, she thought, and wondered again at her apparent devotion to the sick child in the infirmary. Val fiddled with her own glass for a moment, as if working up the courage to tell Laura what she had implied she wanted to tell her.

'I really need to speak to the DCI,' she said

at last. Laura glanced away for a moment.

'So do I,' she said wryly at length, hoping that Val would not read desperation into her tone. 'But he said he needed some time and space on his own. I don't even know where he is.'

'I tried his mobile. He's not answering.'

'No, I don't suppose he is,' Laura said. Val made a figure of eight pattern on the table top with her glass, obviously considering her next move.

'If I tell you what I want to tell Mr Thackeray, will you promise not to use it in the *Gazette* until I think it's the only option?' she asked eventually. 'It's what you'd call a "good story", but I want to get some official movement on it if I possibly can. I need the DCI's advice, I really do. And his clout with the superintendent. He's bound to contact you before anyone else and you can pass the message on.'

Laura thought that she would not bank on that, with Thackeray in his present mood, but she did not want Val Ridley to know anything about the desperate state of their relationship, so she nodded as positively as she could manage.

'If you give me a message in confidence for Michael, of course I'll pass it on, if I can,' Laura said. 'And I don't usually offer private communications to my boss, whatever Superintendent Longley may imagine.

We do try to keep our professional lives separate.' Laura knew that Val Ridley probably didn't believe her but she reckoned it was up to her to decide how far she could trust a journalist. And that maybe depended on how urgent her message was.

In the end Val nodded and reached into her bag and handed Laura a single sheet of photocopied typescript.

'Emma Christie's coming round and beginning to remember the morning of the shooting,' Val said in a low voice. 'It's all a bit garbled, doesn't make a lot of sense, but if it's anything close to the truth it throws the whole case open again. The DCI will see the implications. I really need to talk to him about it because the superintendent is effectively closing the case down, concentrating on the hunt for Gordon Christie and not much else. He doesn't even seem very bothered about keeping an eye on Emma and listening to what she says.'

Laura thought of Michael Thackeray's complaints along similar lines and wondered just how big and smelly the can of worms was that someone was working so hard to keep the lid on.

She took the sheet of paper slightly gingerly and glanced at it.

'There was someone else there,' she said wonderingly.

'She seems to think so, though how

reliable anything she says is, I don't know. The doctors are very vague.'

'Right,' Laura said. 'And if we can't get hold of Michael...?'

'I don't know,' Val said. 'Maybe if the *Gazette* got involved... But you'd have to keep my name out of it. There's been information leaking out of the hospital anyway so it wouldn't be that odd if something else got out. Most of the nurses seemed to be desperate for Emma to wake up. We're all desperate, really. And if it wasn't her father with the gun, she deserves to know that, doesn't she? And for the truth to be known. It will be bad enough for her to have lost the rest of her family without believing that it was her own father who killed them if it wasn't.'

Laura could see how desperate Val was herself, and shivered slightly. She doubted very much whether anything she could do would help Val Ridley or Emma Christie. She could not even see any way of helping herself.

'I'll tell Michael when he contacts me,' she said. 'But I've no idea when that will be. Don't bank on me, please. I really don't think you should do that.'

Laura went back to the office reluctantly, with Val Ridley's piece of paper feeling like an unexploded bomb in her bag. By the end of the afternoon she had tidied her desk, deleted the clutter on her computer, spent half an hour in the loo trying to repair the ravages of the previous night with make-up, and was left at five thirty wondering how she could fill the rest of the evening on her own. She rang her friend Vicky's home number several times but got no reply, and she did not seem to be picking up her mobile. Vicky must still be away with her mother, she thought desolately, and there was no one else she felt even remotely able to unburden herself to.

Eventually, as she sat staring at her blank computer screen trying to summon up the resolve to go home to the empty flat, she felt a hand on her shoulder.

'Some of us are going to the pub for a quickie. Do you want to come?' asked Jane Archer, one of the younger reporters in the newsroom to whom Laura had dispensed good advice and an occasional shoulder to cry on after Ted Grant's fiercer assaults over the years.

Laura shrugged. 'Why not?'

The group in the Lamb started off in its usual large and convivial, end-of-the-week mode and, as an irregular participant, Laura found herself provided with drinks at regular intervals. She bought herself a sandwich in an attempt to mitigate the effects of the succession of vodka and tonics, but by mid-evening she knew very well she was not in any fit state to drive home. She also realised with something of a shock that Vince Newsom had joined the party and was watching her from the other side of the now thinning group.

'All right, babe?' he asked, as he caught her eye, and when Jane got up from her stool next to Laura to go home herself, Vince moved closer and was quickly joined by the *Gazette*'s crime reporter, Bob Baker.

'On your own tonight, sweetie?' Bob asked. 'I heard your copper was away. Funny that, in the middle of a murder case. He's okay, is he? Or are you sitting on a story there?'

'He's fine,' Laura mumbled, knowing she would not be believed and how quickly Thackeray's 'holiday' would become public knowledge and the sort of speculation that would spark. 'He just needed a break.' Even in her fuzzy state Laura could see that neither man believed her. She picked up her glass, which she thought she had emptied, but which now seemed unaccountably full again, and took another swig. The merest reference to Thackeray filled her with an irrational dread, which only the alcohol seemed to deaden. She was aware of Vince and Bob, one on each side of her, continuing a long and involved conversation about the murder case, which she was only hazily able to grasp and to which, as far as she was aware, she contributed little.

'D'you fancy a curry, darling?'Vince asked, so insistently that the question penetrated Laura's fuddled brain. But she shook her head fiercely.

'I must get home,' she said. 'I want to go home.' She missed the quick glance between Vince Newsom and Bob but took on board the fact that it was Vince who had volunteered to drive her back to the flat. She recalled later being in a car and someone searching in her bag for her front door keys, but that was all she remembered of the rest of that evening until she woke up next morning under the duvet wearing only her bra and pants and with a crashing hangover that had her rushing to the bathroom to be sick as soon as she found the strength to stand on her feet.

'Oh, damn, damn, damn,' she cursed as she splashed water on her face and inspected her reddened eyes and furred tongue in the bathroom mirror. 'Oh, how could I be such a fool.'

Chapter Seventeen

DS Kevin Mower was out and about early that Saturday morning. His first port of call was a utilitarian block of flats a mile and a half out of the centre of Bradfield, halfway up one of the town's seven hills. He found the main entrance unlocked and hurried up the stairs to a flat on the second floor, where he leaned on the doorbell for some time without arousing any response. Glancing over his shoulder to make sure he was alone on the narrow landing, which gave access to four front doors, he pulled a credit card out of his pocket and slipped it between the lock and the door jamb and, to his relief, felt the door give under the pressure of his hand very quickly. He slipped inside and closed the door behind him.

The flat smelt musty and cold, and even without opening any of the doors he knew that there was no one there, and had not been for some time. Even so he checked carefully in every room, glanced in the fridge and kitchen cupboards and ran an eye along largely empty shelves in the living room, without finding any evidence of what he feared. He stood at the window for a moment feeling frustrated and even more anxious than when he had started. He was not concerned so much about where Michael Thackeray had gone as about what he might be doing when he got there. But so far he had found no evidence that his boss might be drinking again, and for that at least he was grateful.

He left the flat as he had found it, made his way to police HQ, cautiously using Michael Thackeray's empty office to make some phone calls that he did not want anyone else to hear. It took half an hour to dredge up the information he wanted, although when he had got it he wondered what he could do with it. Discovering where Thackeray had flown to two nights earlier narrowed the search to one country, but offered no easy route to pinning down his quarry more clearly. He sat thinking about his next move, until his mobile shrilled and made him jump. He looked at the display and felt a shiver of anxiety. Superintendent Longley calling him when they were both off-duty did not bode well.

'Sir?' he said.

'Mower? That you? Have you seen that wretched rag this morning? The *Globe*? Have you seen what that bastard Newsom's got hold of now?'

'No, sir, I've not seen any papers...'

'He's only got hold of chapter and verse

about what the Christie child has been saying, everything Val Ridley told us yesterday. What the hell is going on here? Has Val gone bleating to the newspapers? And if not her, then who? Whoever this leak's come from, I'll string them up, and if it's a member of the force, they'll be out on their ear, I promise you. The division'll have no credibility left if it goes on like this. Can you start looking into it right away? There's no time to lose on this.'

'I'll talk to Val, sir,' Mower said. 'I can't imagine this is her fault, though. There've been leaks from the hospital already. It's much more likely to be Newsom suborning someone on the hospital staff...'

'Find out, Sergeant,' Longley said. 'Just find out. Do some bloody detecting and call me back the moment you've got a name.'

'Sir,' Mower said as Longley cut off the call. 'Three bags full, sir,' he muttered angrily, putting his phone away and making his way quickly downstairs and out into the busy town centre, where he bought a copy of the *Globe* at the first newsagent's shop he came to.

'Jesus wept,' he eventually said to himself, as he sat in a coffee shop with a latte taking in the full magnitude of Vince Newsom's scoop, which repeated, almost word for word, what Val Ridley had reported back on the day before. Then another thought struck him and he pulled out his phone again, and calling the infirmary and asking to be put through to security.

'You need to keep an extra close eye on Emma Christie,' he said sharply to the officer who picked up the call. 'The fact that she's awake and talking is all over the front page of the *Globe* this morning.'

'Oh, aye, I saw that,' the officer said. 'I didn't think...'

'Don't think. Just watch her,' Mower snapped. 'And put me through to the ward.' But when he was finally transferred, he discovered to his horror that he and security were both already too late.

'We've had to transfer her back to intensive care,' the ward sister said. 'She's had a relapse. She's very ill.'

'Natural causes?' Mower asked. The nurse was silent for a moment.

'Oh, my God,' she said at last. 'I think we'd better check.' But Mower thought he knew the answer already.

Laura Ackroyd might not have seen the front page of the *Globe* that Saturday morning at all if it had not been for Vince Newsom. Even after several cups of coffee she still felt limp and muddle-headed and by mid-morning was seriously considering crawling back under her duvet to see if more sleep would dispel the consequences of the pre-

276

vious night's indulgence. Still in her dressing gown, she had almost decided to ignore the insistent ring on the doorbell when a faint sense of panic convinced her that it heralded bad news about Michael Thackeray. She pressed the intercom and was not pleased to hear Newsom asking to be let in.

'Go away, Vince,' she said, her voice thick. 'I'm not feeling good.'

'I'm not surprised,' Vince said. 'But I've got something of yours here. You really wouldn't want to lose it.'

Confused, she opened the main door for him and unlatched her own front door. When he came in he glanced at her and smiled broadly.

'You didn't need to undress,' he said.

'Shut up, Vince,' Laura snarled. 'I feel like death this morning. So what do you want?'

'Well, I thought you'd want your notes back to do a follow-up on Monday. Ted Grant'll be pretty miffed to be scooped again, but that's the way it goes.' He handed her a folded sheet of paper which she immediately recognised as Val Ridley's notes.

'Where the hell did you get this?' Laura asked, her brain clearing suddenly.

'You could say it just fell into my lap, sweetheart. You did tell me to look in your bag for your keys when we got back here last night.'

'You didn't use it, did you?' Laura asked,

knowing how stupid a question that was. Vince Newsom would sell his own grandmother for a story.

'Da-da-a-a!' Vince said in triumph, waving the *Globe*'s front page, where the photograph of Emma in her hospital bed took pride of place, in front of her. 'Good stuff, though I can't imagine where you got all those quotes, you naughty girl. My little nurse got cold feet after the police warned her off. You must have been very persuasive.'

'You stole those notes,' Laura said, her face flushed. 'You'd no right to do that. I'll have you for that, Vince. Your editor, the Press complaints people, the police – I don't know, but I'll have you. I promise.'

'There's no harm done, sweetie, except to your pride. You can still follow it up in Monday's *Gazette*. You got pissed last night and you told me all about it. You showed me your precious notes. Don't you remember?'

'You're a liar,' Laura said. 'What you've done could put that child at risk, and there's no way I would have told you anything about it however drunk I was. No one will believe that. I'll hang you out to dry.'

Newsom's eyes suddenly went very chilly and his mouth hardened into something approaching a sneer.

'Well, honey, I really wouldn't get into any sort of slanging match with me about it, if I were you. Just put it down to experience, hey? You were too pissed to really know what was going on when we got back here last night, weren't you? Pissed and surprisingly friendly, as it turned out.'

'What's that supposed to mean?' Laura asked, suddenly feeling very cold.

'You really don't remember?' Newsom came back, his voice full of an incredulity which Laura knew was as false as all the promises he had once made her. 'Let's just say your tight-arsed boyfriend might not be too pleased to hear the full unexpurgated details of how I put you to bed and kept his place warm, darling. Know what I mean?'

'You're joking,' Laura whispered, her mouth dry, but she knew he wasn't. And she could dredge up nothing from the haze that the previous evening had become with which she could contradict him.

'You're a bastard, Vince,' she said.

'That's not what you said last night,' Newsom said complacently. 'So let's call it quits shall we? I got my scoop, you got your notes back, and the rest, as they say, is a blank slate. Best thing all round, I'd say.'

'Get out,' Laura said. 'You're disgusting.'

Newsom shrugged, put the page of notes and that morning's *Globe* on the coffee table and turned to the door.

'*Ciao*, baby,' he said. 'You wouldn't last five minutes on a London paper, you know that? Best settle down up here in the third world and have babies. It's the only thing you're good for.'

When the front door finally slammed Laura rushed to the bathroom, tears streaming down her face, and tried vainly to be sick over the basin. When the nausea eventually passed she turned the shower full on and stood under the stream of hot water for a long time, her mind blank. When she had dried herself and slipped into jeans and a sweatshirt she sat gazing at herself in the dressing table mirror, as if searching her own pale face for a truth she could not find, before summoning up the energy to dry her cloud of copper hair, and tie it back severely. She felt drained and empty inside as she contemplated the full extent of Vince Newsom's betrayal, what she knew he had done to her and, worse, what he might have done. She had no way of knowing, and that, she thought, was perhaps even more devastating than knowing for sure. She could not imagine how she could face Michael Thackeray again.

It was an hour or more before she was disturbed again and she let Kevin Mower into the flat without question. He glanced at her, his eyes full of anxiety, his usually impassive features slightly haggard in the grey light of a wet and windy day.

'You look rough,' he said, taking in her still red-rimmed eyes and ashen pallor.

'Not enough sleep,' Laura lied. Her problem, she thought, had been too much oblivion, not too little. 'What can I do for you?'

'I need to contact the boss,' Mower said. 'All hell's breaking loose with this case and he needs to know about it, whatever the super says. I see you've seen the bloody *Globe*.'

Laura nodded dumbly, not wanting to go down that road.

'Is Emma Christie all right?' she asked.

'No, not really,' Mower said. 'That's another thing the boss needs to know. She's back in intensive care. The doctors say they can't explain what's happened. Privately, I reckon someone's seen the *Globe*, is scared that she's talking and has tried to shut her up. We'll have to see what the medics say when they've checked her out to be sure. But at the moment, that's much too close to a conspiracy theory to impress Jack Longley in his present mood. And of course he's the one who decided to leave her security to the hospital instead of keeping our own people in there. I knew that would be a disaster.'

'Oh God,' Laura said.

'Laura?' Mower was sharp enough to realise that Laura's stricken expression was more than an outsider's token response. 'You don't know where that bastard Newsom got his facts from, do you?'

'He got them from me,' Laura said. 'He

wasn't intended to, but he did. We were all out drinking together after work last night and things got a bit out of hand...'

'And you got them from?'

'You know I can't tell you that,' Laura said, her expression tragic and her voice dull.

'You mean you won't tell me that,' Mower said angrily. 'Are you and that snake Newsom in this thing together? I can't believe that. What were you thinking about?'

'We go back a long way,' Laura said. 'Michael knows all about me and Vince Newsom.'

'Does he know all about you and Vince Newsom yesterday?' Mower flung back and was astonished when Laura sank onto the sofa and buried her face in her hands. He sat beside her and put a tentative arm around her shoulder.

'I'm sorry,' he said. 'I shouldn't have said that. I wasn't implying anything.'

'The trouble is, Kevin, I don't even know whether there's anything to imply. I was so drunk I can't even dispute what he says about last night. Someone put me to bed...' She shrugged helplessly. He looked at her, horrified.

'Are you saying he raped you?' he asked.

'I can't remember anything,' Laura said, feeling as helpless as she had ever felt in her life.

'But he says he slept with you?'

'I think he was just winding me up. He wanted to shut me up, stop me making a fuss about the notes. He says I showed them to him but I'm sure he just helped himself. They were in my handbag and he must have opened it to get my keys. I was out of it but I'm sure I wouldn't have shared those notes with him however drunk I was. Or let him into my bed.'

'I'll kill him, the bastard,' Mower said. 'And if I don't get him, you can be damn sure Michael will.'

'No!' Laura said. 'I don't want Michael to know any of this. It was my fault. I was drinking on an empty stomach. I was off my head when Vince brought me back here. I don't want Michael to know anything about it, nothing at all. Please, Kevin. It would wreck him, us, everything.'

Mower groaned.

'What a mess,' he said. 'But I still need to talk to him. He flew to Dublin, I did track him that far, but no one I've spoken to has the faintest idea where he might be staying. Do you have a clue?'

Laura shook her head helplessly.

'He has relatives in Ireland. His mother was Irish and he used to go and visit family over there before she got sick, I know that much. But I don't think he's had any contact with them for years.'

'It's a lead,' Mower said doubtfully. 'I can't raise him on his mobile. Would his father know where these relatives are, do you think? It's a long shot, but the mood he was in he might just go back somewhere he spent time on holiday as a child. Do you think?'

'I don't know, Kevin. I really don't.'

'Would you ask Joe Thackeray? It's more than my job's worth to use official channels.'

'I could try,' Laura said reluctantly.

'Please, Laura,' Mower said. 'And there's one more thing I need to ask you.' He hesitated for a moment knowing she would not like the question and he might not like the answer.

'Was he drinking again before he went away?'

Laura's eyes filled with tears but she shook her head.

'Not to my knowledge,' she said. 'He was very down, and I was worried sick, but I don't think he'd had a drink. I know him well enough now to know. At least I think I do.' And there was all the uncertainty in the world in her voice.

At more or less the same time that Saturday morning, Michael Thackeray was standing in borrowed wellington boots up to his ankles in muddy brown water in a boggy field in the west of Ireland. As a damp wind blew his hair, he glanced at the stocky, grey-haired man beside him and smiled a rare uncomplicated smile.

'Times have certainly changed,' he said. In front of them, on slightly higher ground, stood a ruin of whitewashed walls, green now with damp, and the remnants of collapsed thatch. It was thirty years since Thackeray had stayed with his mother in this traditional single-storey cottage, and twenty, his companion assured him, since it had been abandoned by his mother's elderly aunt in favour of one of the modern bungalows which had sprouted like mushrooms all round the village of Ballymalone in County Sligo.

'It was so different from our farm in the hills,' Thackeray said. 'Our problem was getting enough water to the animals, yours was too much water everywhere.' He squelched through the boggy grass and on to the drier ground, and peered inside what had been the cottage door. The chimney breast was the only structure still standing above head height, and he recalled the peat fires that used to burn day and night in the blackened fireplace and the soda bread his aunt had baked there. It was a way of life barely surviving then and long gone now.

'Sure, it's not easy land to farm here, either,' said his mother's older brother Sean O'Donnell. 'When we were growing up the young folk were still leaving in droves. Like your mother did.'

Thackeray nodded. His mother had gone to England to work as a nurse, met his father and stayed for the rest of her too short life. Visits to Ballymalone had ceased when his mother became increasingly sick with MS, and he had not seen his uncle since his mother's funeral several years before.

'Is your father still farming, then?' O'Donnell asked.

'No, he's retired,' Thackeray said. 'There's no money in those hill farms any more. It's a hand to mouth existence.'

'He didn't keep in touch after Molly died,' O'Donnell said non-committally. 'And not much before that. It was I myself who always had to make the calls to find out how she was.'

'He's still devastated,' Thackeray said, realising clearly for the first time how true that was. His father, he thought, must have given up his farm after his mother's death because he could see no reason to continue without her. The light had gone out of his life and there was no way it would ever be rekindled. And all Thackeray had given his parents was bitter disappointment. He shivered slightly and turned back to his uncle, who touched the same raw nerve.

'Life hasn't been easy for him,' O'Donnell said. 'At least I have my grandchildren.' Thackeray had played with his Irish cousins in these damp fields for a couple of weeks every summer until his mother became unable to make the journey 'home' any longer, and wished now his life had followed the smooth path theirs had into marriage and parenthood. He had long ago stopped expecting life to be fair as he had learned to live with his mother's increasing disabilities, but there were times when the old wounds still had the power stop him in his tracks. He turned away quickly and began plodding through the bog towards the lane and the road back into Ballymalone where his uncle had parked his car. Sean, he thought, was venturing down roads he did not wish to follow. The old man should know better, he thought bitterly. Or maybe he should not have come to Ireland.

That evening, the two men returned to Sean O'Donnell's bungalow after a hearty meal at the local hotel, still geared much more to the needs of the local farmers than to Ireland's ubiquitous tourists, Thackeray noticed, and sufficiently unreconstructed to still carry the huge painted advertisement in faded colours on its gable end for passages to New York and Boston, which he had gazed at uncomprehendingly as a boy. His uncle offered him a whisky, raised an eyebrow when it was refused, and watched him in silence for a moment, puffing on his pipe and sipping a Jamesons, from his favourite armchair beside a gas log fire.

'So why are you really here, Michael?' he asked at last. 'I'm not for flattering myself that it's just for old time's sake.'

'I was told to take a holiday,' Thackeray said, truthfully enough.

'And Ballymalone suddenly became a top holiday destination, did it? And the Pope's a Protestant?' the old man said.

Thackeray smiled faintly. 'I'm looking for someone,' he said.

'In this country?' his uncle asked sharply.

'He may have been in this country, but more likely in the north. But not now.'

'And what makes you think I could help?'

'Come on, Sean,' Thackeray said quietly. 'I used to come here summer after summer when the north was in flames. You never made much secret of where your loyalties lay.'

'My father was a volunteer,' O'Donnell said. 'I saw enough of all that when I was a boy. A civil war's a vicious thing. I never got involved, then or later, although there were some who tried to persuade me, including my own da.'

'Exactly,' Thackeray said. 'You must know someone who could help me. I only want a name, an identification. I don't even know which side this man was on. I'm not even certain he was here at all. But someone you know may recognise him. That's all I want.'

'That's all, is it? D'you not realise how

dangerous it is for you here, asking questions like that? You're a British police officer.' O'Donnell's fleshy face looked rigid and pale, and Thackeray realised perhaps fully for the first time that this visit might be a serious mistake.

'I thought, with things so peaceful now...' He hesitated.

'Peace is a relative thing in Ireland. You should know that,' O'Donnell said, his voice low and harsh. 'Memories are longer than you can possibly imagine.'

'We're twenty miles from the border,' Thackeray said. 'I can be in the UK in less than an hour.'

'And you think you'd be safe there? It shows how much you know. Was the man you're seeking safe in Yorkshire?'

Thackeray did not reply. He was suddenly overwhelmed by the feeling that this trip was a wild goose chase and, worse than that, a very dangerous one.

'I'll go back tomorrow,' he said. 'I'm sorry. I shouldn't have involved you in any way. It was a stupid idea. Forget it.'

His uncle sighed and gazed at the fire.

'What happened in the north in the Seventies raised all the ghosts again,' he said. 'Here, so close to the border especially, they rise up from the graves fully armed. Go to Dublin, or Kerry or the east coast and you'd know nothing about it. They're watching their house prices rise, fleecing the tourists, building their ranch-style bungalows, stuffing their faces at classy restaurants where a meal costs more than I used to earn in a month. But here everyone knows the men of violence and who's got away with what. And what they might get away with again.'

'I'll go tomorrow,' Thackeray said again. 'Leave you in peace.'

'Stay a while,' Sean said. 'You look as if you really need that holiday. Go fishing with your cousin Patrick. You used to get along well enough with him when you were a boy, didn't you? Relax. But don't talk about your job. You'll be fine if you keep a low profile, just another emigrant's child visiting. It's not unusual. And I've never mentioned what you do for a living. Have you got a photograph of this man you're seeking?'

Thackeray nodded cautiously.'

'I'll see what I can do,' Sean said. 'But carefully. And you keep out of it. Right out. And if I tell you to drive to the border, then you drive to the border and ask no questions. D'you understand?'

'I understand,' Thackeray said. He reached into the inside pocket of his jacket and handed his uncle a copy of the photograph of Gordon Christie taken at the school fête. 'That's him,' he said. 'He may be Irish. Or he may have been British army, SAS even, security services of some sort. I don't know and no one will tell me. But he was running from something or someone, and there may be an Irish connection. It's a long shot. A very long shot.'

'But there are people here who never forget a face,' O'Donnell said.

Chapter Eighteen

In spite of Kevin Mower's request, Laura did not attempt to trace Michael Thackeray that morning. Kevin might want to talk to him, she thought miserably, but she was not at all sure that she did. Let Sergeant Mower use the official resources at his disposal if it was that urgent, she thought. She was sure Michael could not be that difficult to find if someone tried hard enough.

In an attempt to subdue her own demons, she worked herself into a frenzy cleaning the flat from top to bottom, and when she had reduced herself to exhaustion with that, she showered, dressed and drove into Bradfield's new out-of-town mall. But as she hunted frantically through the shops for new clothes she did not need, she knew that what she was doing was merely distracting herself from problems she did not want to face up to. It did not work, and by mid-afternoon she had gone home, hurled her purchases on the bed without even opening the glossy bags, and flung herself into a chair with a vodka and tonic.

Before she had taken more than a sip she was interrupted by the phone.

'It's Janine,' a voice she vaguely knew said. 'Janine Foster, at the Fox and Hounds?'

'Of course,' Laura said, her brain grinding very slowly into gear as she placed Janine behind the bar of Gerry Foster's pub in Staveley. 'What can I do for you?'

'I've been trying to get you all day,' Janine said. 'I couldn't think who else to contact. Gerry didn't come home last night.'

Laura recalled the speed at which she had seen Gerry Foster drive out of the village the previous day and did not feel greatly surprised by Janine's news.

'Hasn't he contacted you at all?' she asked, with as much sympathy as she could muster, which was not a lot.

'Not a peep,' Janine said. 'I've been trying to keep this place open right through Friday night and Saturday lunchtime, our busiest times. He's gone off on his own before, if we've had rows, but he's never stayed out all night. His mobile's switched off. I'm worried sick.'

'Have you told the police?' Laura asked.

Janine seemed to hesitate for a moment before she answered.

'I don't know whether he'd want me to do that,' she said. It was Laura who hesitated then.

'What do you mean,' she asked at length.

'I don't know what the hell he's been up to, if you must know,' Janine said. 'There's a man I've never seen before sitting outside the pub in a car. He's been there all day, just sitting and watching, talking on his phone occasionally. When we opened at midday he came in and asked for Gerry, so I just told him he wasn't there. He had a pint, on his own in the corner, and then went out again, back to the car. He's still there.'

'You think he's waiting for Gerry?'

'What else could he be doing? It's obviously not me he wants.'

'You must tell the police,' Laura said.

'But what if he is the police?' Janine objected. 'I told you I was scared. I told you about the odd phone calls. I'm wondering now if Gerry was mixed up in something dodgy and he's trying to get away from the police. He's been behaving very strangely lately, long before the murders.'

Laura hesitated again.

'I might be able to find out if the police want to talk to him,' she said cautiously. 'But if the man outside's a policeman I can't see why he wouldn't identify himself. I don't think he can be.'

'Could you do that?' Janine asked, and

Laura could hear the desperation in her voice.

'I'll call you back if I get an answer. In the meantime, keep trying Gerry's mobile. He's bound to switch it on eventually.' Laura put as much confidence as she could into her reassurances, but she did not wholly believe them herself. Gerry Foster had been scared, she thought, when they had realised some-one might be hiding near Moor Edge cottage. And he had driven out of Staveley very much like a frightened man. She did not think he would be back any time soon.

Her mind fully engaged at last, Laura called Kevin Mower on his mobile and asked him if CID were watching out for Gerry Foster, but he denied all knowledge of any surveillance.

'Have you found out where the guv'nor is?' Mower asked, slightly impatiently.

'Not yet, but I will call his father,' Laura promised. 'I'll let you know.' But she was more interested now in finding Thackeray for her own reasons than in helping the police. She suddenly felt an overwhelming need to talk to him. After last night's debacle, some-thing had to be resolved between them. And this seemed as good a time as any.

Sergeant Kevin Mower mooched around the CID office that afternoon, unable to concen-trate and yet sure that there was something he had missed at the heart of the Christie case. He had checked with the hospital as soon as he had arrived in the office that morning: Emma, it appeared, was still fighting for her life. There was still no one available to tell him why she had relapsed so dramatically, and unlikely to be before Monday. He was left with his worst fears unconfirmed but no less real for that. Uniformed were fully occupied with a Bradfield United match, a local derby with trouble expected, and Superintendent Longley seemed to have stood most of his detectives down for the weekend, no doubt anxious about his overtime budget, and had retired to the golf course once he had passed on his fury about Vince Newsom's story in the *Globe*. The lack of urgency spooked Mower. It seemed unreal.

After a pie and pint lunch in the nearest pub, he had found himself drawn back to the office again and had been only mildly surprised to find DC Val Ridley sitting at her desk looking pale and drawn.

'Don't you have a home to go to?' he asked.

'Ditto?' she replied, her voice sharp. They were both single and their more-or-less happily married colleagues would have said unhappily so, although they would both have denied it vigorously. There had even been a time when the cool and rather distant Ridley had set her cap at Mower, only to be hurt-fully rebuffed. They had kept each other at a distance since.

'Have you been in to see Emma?' Mower asked. Val nodded, as he knew she would.

'She's unconscious, poor little devil,' Val said. 'I don't believe it's just bad luck. It can't be.'

'What are you saying? Someone got to her? You need some evidence for that,' Mower said, half agreeing with her but knowing they would have to wait for that until the medics concluded their tests.

'After this morning's little effort in the *Globe* anyone would know she's beginning to remember what happened. I talked to the staff on the ward and no one saw anything unusual before she collapsed. Not that that means much, the nurses are always so busy. And it really wouldn't be hard to get into that children's ward. In spite of the super's faith in them, I think the so-called security officers are useless. The place is seriously under-staffed, especially at weekends. If you had a white coat on, or a nurse's uniform, you could pull the curtains around the bed and do what you liked. No one would notice.'

'What do the staff say? They wouldn't tell me anything much on the phone.'

'She's no physical injuries that anyone can see but one of the nurses said they'd been looking for puncture marks. The trouble is the poor kid's so full of puncture marks they can't be sure if there's a fresh one there or not. But it gives an indication of what they suspect. She seemed to be on the mend when I said goodnight to her yesterday. They're testing her blood for absolutely anything that shouldn't be there, but that could take forever.'

'And is she going to wake up again?' Mower asked, his eyes bleak. Michael Thackeray would take the death of another child very hard, he knew, and Val Ridley did not look much more robust than their boss at this moment, although she hid her feelings well behind her cool, ice-maiden mask. What, he wondered, was she doing saying goodnight to this sick child anyway, as if she were a relative. It would be Auntie Val next and where could that possibly lead?

'They don't know what will happen,' Val said, looking steadfastly out of the window as she spoke. 'It's touch and go.'

'It can't be her father,' Mower said. 'There's no way a man on the run could plan an operation like that, get the right kit so as not to be noticed, sneak in and out without arousing attention. It's not feasible.'

'So who else wants her kept quiet?' Val said. 'Someone else who was there and was seen to be there when the family was shot? Someone else who was involved in the shooting? A different murderer, not her father at all? The man Emma said she saw and we're not investigating in any way at all? If she dies it'll be Longley's fault. He's lost the plot and I just don't understand why.'

The two officers looked at each other for a moment, both evidently deep in thought, but the train was lost as the phone shrilled. Mower picked it up and found himself talking to one of the officers at the regional forensics lab who sounded pleased to have made contact.

'Peter?' Mower said. 'Have you got something for us?'

'I was doing a bit of overtime,' the officer said. 'I hoped I might find someone in. Of course, I'll give you a full report on Monday but I thought this was a titbit which might intrigue you.'

'Go on,' Mower said, his spine tingling now, his brain kicking into gear.

'You know we found unidentified DNA at the Christies' place? Which is not unusual in anyone's house, of course. Folk come and folk go – friends, visitors, delivery people, and he had clients, didn't he?'

And?' Mower prompted, not wanting to be sidetracked into a discussion of the Christies' lifestyle.

'Well, I checked all the unknown samples against the national database and came up with nothing at all. Clean as a whistle, all the family visitors, apparently, which must be pretty unusual in the greater scheme of things. But then I remembered we'd been looking at the body in Christie's Land Rover. That didn't come up on the database either, as it goes, but you know that already...'

'Go on,' Mower broke in. 'Get to the bloody point, Peter.'

'One of the samples matches.'

Mower drew a sharp breath. 'Just let me get this straight,' he said, and realised that he had Val Ridley's full attention too. 'The man in the Land Rover, at present unidentified, had been in the Christies' house as well?'

'No doubt about it, mate.'

'But you've no way of telling when, I suppose?' Mower asked, feeling caution was called for here.

'No, but one of the hairs we picked up from this person was found on Mrs Christie's sweater. On top, not underneath, so unlikely just to have been picked up from the floor, where it could have been lying for days or weeks.'

'Recent then? Very recent?'

'We're going through all the other samples to see whether we've got more traces that could tell us where he went in the house and workshop, and possibly some indication of when. But if you've got anyone else in the frame for this I'd certainly be wanting to find an ID for this character. I reckon someone else was there around about the time of the murders, and now he's in Manchester, burnt to a crisp. All you've got to do is find out who he was.'

And that, Mower thought, as he thanked his caller and hung up, might be easier said than done, especially with a superintendent in charge who seemed to have already made up his mind who the killer was in this case. He knew that the Manchester police had so far drawn a blank in their efforts to identify the body in the Land Rover. Lists of missing persons had turned up no likely possibilities, criminal intelligence had provided no intelligence and forensic science had been no help so far. But Superintendent Longley had effectively stalled similar investigations on his side of the Pennines, for reasons he could not understand, and seemed to have put another child's life at risk in the process. Find Christie, Longley had said, that's all that matters. Well, maybe the answer was to take Longley at his word, Mower decided, and organise an inch by inch search of the moors around Staveley for Monday morning – dogs, armed officers, helicopters, the lot. If an assault on his budget of that magnitude didn't shake the super out of his complacency he didn't know what would.

'Come on, Val, cheer up,' Mower said. 'We're getting somewhere at last. There's a link with the Manchester body that nobody can ignore. First I'll push Jack Longley's blood pressure through the roof by organising a full scale search over the moors for Christie on Monday, on the basis that someone saw a prowler up at the cottage yesterday. Then I'll give him a get-out by dropping the forensic report on his desk. And in the meantime I'll see if we can persuade the boss to come back off leave and make sure this thing is investigated properly. It's the least we can do.'

Val shivered suddenly.

'Are you all right?' Mower asked.

'Someone walked over my grave,' she said. 'And how are we going to get Mr Thackeray back, d'you suppose?'

'We'll ask the lovely Laura Ackroyd if she's tracked him down, of course,' Mower said confidently. 'What I want you to do is take Sunday off, get some rest. You look like death warmed up.'

'Thanks, sarge,' Val said.

'I mean it,' Mower said, and in the end Val agreed that perhaps she needed a break.

'If anything happens at the hospital, I'll call you,' Mower promised as she shrugged herself into her coat, picked up her bag and walked slowly out of the office to face the Saturday afternoon shopping crowds with her shoulders sagging. This case is wreaking havoc round here, Mower thought as he flicked on his mobile again. But for all his confidence, when he called Laura Ackroyd on her mobile he found it switched off, and as the afternoon wore on he became more worried. It was not until after seven, when Mower was back in the pub with a bottle of lager in front of him, that she finally picked up.

'Where are you?' Mower asked, trying hard to keep the irritation out of his voice. Mobile phones, he thought, were supposed to be an aid to communication but today they were proving a barrier.

'Dublin airport,' Laura said, to his surprise. 'Don't worry, Kevin, I know where Michael is. I'll let you know when we're coming back. Isn't that what you wanted?'

'I need to speak to him. Urgently,' Mower said. 'He's still got his mobile switched off.'

'His father told me there's no reception to speak of where he's staying. Don't worry. I'll ask him to call you. Okay?'

'I suppose so,' Mower said reluctantly.

'I must go or I won't get a hire car. We'll be in touch, Kevin, I promise.' And with that Mower had to be content.

It was pitch dark when Laura drove into Ballymalone and for a queasy second she wondered if Joe Thackeray had been right in directing her here to seek out Michael Thackeray's uncle Sean O'Donnell. Joe admitted that the address he had was an old one, and he had had no contact with Molly Thackeray's family since she died. But Laura had checked the address with international telephone inquiries. There had been no reply to her calls but she felt confident enough then to book a flight and hire a car and drive the long winding road to County Sligo. She had nothing to do with her weekend and suddenly sorting out her relationship with Michael Thackeray seemed like an urgent priority. Now, parked at the kerb and gazing down the almost deserted village street, she wondered what sort of a fool she had been.

The village was long and straggly, the main street lit by only a handful of orange street lamps and the glow which filtered onto the damp pavements from the four or five bars that were scattered amongst the rows of cottages fronting onto the road. Close to what she assumed was the centre, where a couple of tightly closed up shops nestled together, there was a single taller building, of three or four stories, with the single word 'Hotel' painted on the gable end above some sort of faded advertisement she could not make out in the dark. She parked outside, zipped up her jacket against the soft but persistent rain, and went up a couple of steps into a deserted foyer. From some-where at the back there came the sound of conversation and laughter, but here all was quiet as the grave.

She banged a large brass bell on the reception desk and eventually a slight young woman dressed in a black miniskirt and red sweater, with her dark hair tied back from a creamy, oval face emerged from a door at the end of the hall.

'Will you be wanting a room?' she asked, with a look of sympathy for the rain-soaked traveller.

'I'm not sure yet,' Laura said. 'I'm looking for someone called Sean O'Donnell and I can't find any street names here in the dark. Do you know him by any chance?'

'Sure, everyone knows Sean. Didn't he used to be the postmaster? But he's retired now. You've only just missed him. He was in the bar just a moment ago now with his son Patrick and his nephew. He'll be home by now if he went straight there. You'll have a car?'

Laura nodded. So at least Michael was here, she thought. Joe had been right when he had said that if he had gone to Ireland at all he would be sure to call on the O'Donnells where he had spent his childhood summers. He had sounded almost jealous of a relationship with his wife's family that he had never been able to share. His sheep had kept him tied to the farm, twelve months out of twelve, he had muttered down the phone somewhat bitterly. But then Laura already knew that Joe's resentments were deep and wide ranging and included her own and Michael's lack of his all-consuming religious faith.

'Then drive through the village that way,' the receptionist went on cheerfully, pointing Laura's way. And when you come to the new bungalows on the left set back a bit from the road, Sean's is the second one.'

Laura followed the receptionist's instructions and found herself parked outside a low white bungalow surrounded by an extensive patch of garden and lit by a bright light on the porch. She gazed at the house for a moment feeling slightly sick. She was far from sure that Michael would welcome this intrusion and had no idea what his uncle would make of the unexpected arrival of another visitor from over the water. With some trepidation, she locked the car, left her overnight bag in the boot, and, taking a deep gulp of soft, damp air to steady her nerve, walked up the gravelled path to the front door to find out.

Her ring was answered by a tall, burly figure whom Laura thought for a disorientated second was Thackeray himself, before realising that it was someone else who looked uncannily like him.

'Is Michael Thackeray here?' she asked, uncertainly.

'Who wants him?' the stranger asked, but even before she could reply Thackeray himself appeared in the hallway, his astonishment tinged with anxiety.

'It's all right, Patrick,' he said. 'I don't know how she got here but this is my girlfriend, Laura. My cousin, Patrick.' Thackeray's introduction was cursory and he took Laura's arm firmly and hustled her into the house, closing the door quickly behind her.

'What the hell are you doing here?' he asked. Patrick O'Donnell, and his father, who had also appeared in the hall holding a glass of whisky in his hand, gazed at her in open curiosity.

'I thought you might be pleased to see me,' Laura said tartly. Thackeray glanced at his relatives and offered Laura a tentative kiss on one cheek.

'I am,' he said quietly in her ear. 'Believe me, I am. But coming here was not a very good idea.'

Sean O'Donnell took her wet coat and led the way into the warm and comfortable living room, where thick curtains were drawn against the wet and increasingly windy weather outside. She took the glass of whisky he offered her gratefully and sank onto the sofa beside Thackeray.

'I'm sorry. I couldn't contact Michael any other way and I really needed to see him,' she explained to the two O'Donnells.

'I'm very pleased to meet you, Laura,' the older man said, although his eyes were full of anxiety.

Later, after sandwiches and some strained conversation, Patrick left for his own home and Sean, obviously reluctantly, conceded that Laura should stay the night, watching the two of them sombrely as they moved into Thackeray's bedroom. Laura sat on the edge of the bed, only too conscious that her arrival might have caused friction which she really did not understand. Thackeray stood with his back to the door, his face in shadow and his eyes unreadable and when he explained the real purpose of his visit to Ireland, she shivered slightly.

'You think Christie was in the IRA?' she asked incredulously.

'No, I didn't say that,' Thackeray said wearily. 'I think Christie was in hiding, and if it was just some gangland thing, we'd have found out about it by now. He'd have turned up on some database somewhere, finger-prints, DNA, a known associate of someone or other. But with the spooks involved, trying to keep his picture under wraps, and knowing he was probably an ex-soldier, all the rest of it, I think it's more likely to originate here. It's a long shot, a wild hunch, the super would say, but it's all I've got to go on. I'm getting nowhere at home. In fact everything anyone can do to close the investigation down is being done, which only confirms my suspicions. If Gordon Christie and his family were executed I want to know why. My uncle has contacts, I knew that before I came. He'll test my theory, no more than that, hopefully get me an ID, and then I'll come home. But it's not safe for you to stay here. It's offering a hostage to fortune. As Sean has told me somewhat forcefully, a British policeman asking questions about terrorists could annoy people. I was foolish to come. And you must go home, Laura, you really must.'

'Did Kevin Mower contact you?' she asked. Thackeray shook his head impatiently, but listened, increasingly grimly, as Laura told him about the sudden deterioration in Emma Christie's condition.

'I don't know what the hell Jack Longley is playing at. But I'll talk to Kevin tomorrow,' he said. 'I switched my mobile off because I didn't want to be traced here. In any case, the reception's poor.'

'You know it wasn't just because of this wretched case that I came to find you,' she said quietly.

'I know,' he said.

'I need to know where we're going, Michael, if anywhere. We can't go on as we are. It's killing me.'

Thackeray crossed the room and sat down on the bed beside her, and put his arm around her. He sat in silence for a long time as if unable to put his thoughts into words.

And when he finally spoke it was slowly, as if each word was wrung from him against his will.

'I don't know where I'm going, or what I'm doing half the time,' he said. 'It's been like that since Aileen died. You'd think it would be a liberation after all that time but it doesn't feel like that. I want to move on but all the anger and grief from what happened keeps dragging me back. Can you understand that?'

Laura shook her head, her eyes full of tears. 'You can't let it wreck your whole life,' she said. 'I love you. I thought I was your future.'

'You are,' he said, and took her in his arms fiercely. 'Believe me, you are,' he said. After a few moments he pulled away and began to help her undress. The sexual chemistry that had always been there between them suddenly overwhelmed everything else.

'We must be very quiet,' he said, a flicker of laughter in his eyes as he dropped his own clothes in a heap on the floor. 'We've already shocked old uncle Sean's Catholic soul to its roots. He'll be off to confession in the morning to beg absolution for letting you stay overnight.'

'Well, I hope it gives the priest a thrill,' Laura whispered as she pulled him towards her. 'Because I've every intention of making love to you until morning.' But in her heart she knew that the reconciliation was only half achieved. There were things she needed to tell Michael Thackeray and, at that moment, she could not bear even to begin.

Chapter Nineteen

Michael Thackeray's mood the next morning, as his uncle drove him north from Ballymalone, was as uncertain as the Irish weather, which was still hurling dark clouds across the sky from the west, and occasionally sheeting the coast road with squalls of rain. To the left the Atlantic could occasionally be glimpsed lashing rocky cliffs and outcrops, and rolling in a tumult of foam up broad sandy beaches. To the right, through the mist, there were occasional glimpses of the Dartry mountains, where they tumbled down towards the sea.

He and Laura had been wakened by Sean O'Donnell soon after seven, emerging bleary-eyed and reluctant from their bed to be fed a generous breakfast of bacon and eggs in Sean's spacious kitchen. But Thackeray's uncle was obviously not in a totally hospitable mood, and as soon as they had finished eating he waved Thackeray into the sitting room, with a warning glance at

Laura which left her brooding over her tea feeling angry and excluded.

'I made some inquiries, and I can take you to someone who may be able to help you,' O'Donnell had said quietly. 'But just you, not your young woman. And after, you're to leave Ireland immediately. Those are the terms. You can take them or leave them.'

'I'll take them,' Thackeray said, without hesitation. 'But what about Laura?'

'She can stay here,' O'Donnell said. 'Then you can both go back to Dublin together when we get back.'

'Are we going far?'

'Up the coast beyond Sligo. A place called Bundoran, a holiday place, just over into Donegal. Did I not take you and your mother there with your cousins when you were a wee lad? We went right up to Tullan strand?'

'I think you did,' Thackeray said, recalling a chilly wind on a long golden beach and abundant tacky amusement arcades in Main Street where five over-excited little boys had taken shelter from the showers. 'Not too far, then?'

'Not too far. We'll be back by mid-afternoon, tell your young woman, and then you must go.'

His 'young woman' had been less than enchanted by the arrangement, Thackeray recalled grimly, but he had persuaded her in the end that he would be safe with O'Donnell and that she should remain indoors until they returned. By nine they had been on the road, skirting the centre of Sligo itself in driving rain and then heading up the coast towards Donegal, with the Atlantic on their left and the border with Northern Ireland only a few miles to their right. It was the point where the Republic of Ireland was most nearly cut in two by the British state.

They drove largely in silence, each absorbed with their own thoughts as O'Donnell took the quiet, winter rain-lashed road quickly and skilfully. In less than two hours they were driving slowly down the long main street of Bundoran, lined on each side with bars, amusements and souvenir shops, many of them closed at this time of year. At length O'Donnell pulled up outside the Crazy Horse bar, an American saloon where the decorative lights swung and glittered through the rain, as if trying to persuade any intrepid passers-by that the Irish winter did not exist.

'This is it,' he said, without enthusiasm. Are you sure about this, Michael? These are not people to trust.'

'You don't need to be involved,' Thackeray said. 'I'll go in by myself.'

'No,' O'Donnell said. 'I made the arrangement. They'll expect me to be with you. If you like, I'm the hostage. They'll know where to find me afterwards – if they need to.'

Thackeray looked at his uncle for a moment, appalled at the implications of what he had said, but O'Donnell just shrugged and got out of the car.

'Come on,' he said. 'Let's get it over with.'

At first they thought the place was deserted. It was huge space, and appeared completely empty, the tables bare and no one in sight behind the great circular mahogany bar. But at one end of the room, where the lights had been switched off, no doubt deliberately, they saw three men seated at a table, two facing them and one with his back turned. As they approached the two men who had their back to the wall stood up and approached them, barring their way.

'O'Donnell?' one asked, and Thackeray's uncle nodded.

'Lift your arms, the both of you,' the second man instructed, and they ran expert hands over their visitors to check, Thackeray assumed, for weapons or recorders. His mouth felt dry as, evidently satisfied, the men waved the two of them into the seats against the wall that they had just vacated, facing the third man who had so far not even glanced in their direction. The searchers took up a position behind the seated man, arms loose at their sides but still full of menace.

Thackeray found himself facing a hunched,

313

cadaverous figure, elderly but quite how elderly it was almost impossible to guess. His face was grey and lined, his mouth thin and unsmiling, and his eyes intensely blue and totally without warmth.

'So you're an English policeman bold enough to come asking questions here,' he said in a voice so low that it was difficult to hear. His accent was unequivocally Belfast born-and-bred. 'Do the Garda know what you're about?'

'No,' Thackeray said. He could see no point in lying. He was sure this man would know the answer to his question already. 'I came to see my uncle.' He nodded at O'Donnell who gave him the most tentative of nods in return. 'I also hoped I might be able to identify someone I'm looking for, as it's been suggested he has – or had – Irish connections. No one official knows I'm here, in Dublin or at home.'

The man nodded and was silent for a moment, as if considering these answers carefully. The silence was oppressive and the man's two minders tensed, as if ready for action. Thackeray tried to control his breathing, knowing exactly how nasty the situation he had put himself and Sean O'Donnell into could turn.

'And this man you're looking for, whoever he is, what has he done?' his interrogator asked at last.

'His family were found shot and he's disappeared,' Thackeray said. 'We think the father shot them but we're not sure. It's possible they were executed. All the evidence points to the family being in hiding for some reason. We think the reason may lie this side of the water.'

'Show me your photograph.' Thackeray handed it over and the man on the other side of the table gazed at it for some time without comment before handing it back. Thackeray would not have thought it possible that those blank eyes could become colder but they had.

'His name is Gordon Robertson,' he said. 'And you're right to think that you're not the only ones seeking him out. We thought he'd gone to Spain. He was the one who got away from an atrocity of our own.'

'Meaning?' Thackeray asked, unable to keep the tiny surge of excitement out of his voice.

'Six years ago in Derry, before the latest cessation, one of our volunteers was eating his evening meal at home with his family. There was a knock on the front door and before his father could prevent him one of the children opened it without checking who was there. Four men burst in and shot our man and the entire family, the wife, three children, no survivors. The killers were members of a Protestant splinter group,

315

people who reckoned the UDA wasn't tough enough. Three of them were later arrested and sentenced to life imprisonment. Gordon Robertson was never picked up.'

'The whole family was killed?' Thackeray said softly.

'The whole family.'

'And now his whole family has been shot.'

'If you're thinking what I imagine you're thinking, Mr Thackeray, I'd put the idea out of your head completely. To my knowledge no one from my organisation had found Gordon Robertson or offered him any harm, although you may be sure that there are some in Derry who would dearly like to. But there's more to this story. It's just as likely that his own associates would gun him down if they ever came across him again. And maybe kill his family as well. There was plenty of talk in Derry after the shootings about the reason Robertson got away. The arrests were too quick, the evidence against the three others too readily forthcoming. It was widely believed that Robertson was working for the British security forces – before the shootings, maybe, and certainly afterwards. It's my belief that you should be asking your questions much closer to home. I'd wager Gerry Adams' peace agreement that your own security people, and ours in Dublin, know all about Gordon Robertson and where he's been holed up for the last six years. If they don't they're not as good at what they do as they pretend to be.'

'I'll ask them,' Thackeray said. He took the photograph from the table and put it away in his pocket. 'I'm grateful for your information,' he said.

'We have never deliberately waged war on children,' the old man said. Thackeray took a sharp breath at the hypocrisy of that, but said nothing. The old man was evidently not finished.

'I want you to go as quickly as you came, Mr Thackeray. It was a very foolish thing you did, coming here. Go home now, and your family in Ballymalone will be safe enough. Talk to no one on the way. I don't want to hear from you or your colleagues again.' There were no overt threats but the menace in his voice was palpable. Thackeray doubted that he had ever been so close to the total ruthlessness of the fanatic, and hoped he never would be again.

The two looming figures behind the old man made clear that the interview was over and Thackeray and O'Donnell made their way quickly back to their car, turned around, and headed back the way they had come. A little way out of Bundoran Sean O'Donnell pulled into the side of the road and switched off the engine. He was trembling.

'I'd not be doing that again, Michael, if I were you,' he said. 'I take it you learned

317

what you wanted to know?'

'Oh yes,' Thackeray said. 'I know what to do now. All I can say is thank you. Will it put you in any danger?'

'Not if you do as you're told and leave the country,' O'Donnell said.

'I won't ask you how you arranged it.'

'Best not,' O'Donnell said. 'Take it from me, you only need to know one man of violence, and this close to the Border we all think we know one at least. With a family history like ours, it's enough.'

'Evidently,' Thackeray said. 'Do you want me to drive? You look shattered.'

O'Donnell nodded, his face creased with tiredness.

'Shattered is an understatement, Michael,' he said. 'And we shouldn't hang about. You can be sure you'll be watched all the way home.'

Sergeant Kevin Mower was slumped in an armchair in Laura Ackroyd's living room, designer jeaned legs stretched out, hands behind his head, but his dark eyes looked anything but relaxed. Thackeray had called him from Manchester airport and the returning travellers had found him sitting outside the tall Victorian house in his car, the faint thump of dance music disturbing the late night peace. As Thackeray had gone ahead to open the doors and switch off the alarm, Mower had touched Laura's arm briefly to hold her back.

'Did you tell him about Newsom?' he asked. Laura shook her head briefly and put a finger to her lips.

'I will, I will,' she murmured, although she did not entirely believe it herself. Mower said nothing, walking into the flat ahead of her and flinging himself into the armchair with a faint shrug, although he could not hide the anger in his eyes. Laura went into the kitchen to make coffee and hide her own distress. After a night and a day when her relationship with Thackeray had regained some semblance of normality she had pushed the memory of her disastrous evening with Vince Newsom to the back of her mind and passionately wished to keep it there. But she guessed that in the end she could not.

'I don't believe you two,' Mower said, after listening to a brief description of their trip. 'You actually talked to the IRA?'

'Provisionals,' Thackeray said.

'Just like that?'

'Not quite, just like that,' Thackeray said carefully. 'Not with my family's history. I always suspected my grandfather had been involved, on the fringes at least.'

'Jesus wept,' Mower said. 'And your uncle?'

'No, not my uncle. I used to go over there

in the Seventies when the recent troubles were at their height. He was quite obviously appalled by what was happening. But he's a fierce republican, for all that. My mother was too.'

Laura watched Mower's reaction with a faint smile. She had heard parts of Thackeray's family history which she had never heard before, the Irish parts, on the long journey home, but she knew that many people in England found it hard to distinguish between a political republican and a terrorist.

'Don't worry about it, Kevin,' she said. 'Nothing illegal happened, and Michael found out what he wanted to know about Christie.'

'So he's not Christie, which we suspected anyway, and which confirms something I've been told,' Mower said. 'I'll fill you in on that in a minute. So you reckon he was hiding from the Provos?'

'I don't think it's as simple as that,' Thackeray said. 'I'm sure the Provos would think nothing of shooting him if they stumbled across him again, but I didn't get the impression they were looking very hard. My man may have been lying, of course. But he also said that his own side wanted him as well, so that's another possibility. I don't think the unionists want to congratulate him on what he did. It's very nasty, very

Irish.' He shrugged.

'They think he gave evidence against them?' Mower asked.

'Something like that. He was never charged, never appeared in court, but the rest of them are serving life and he vanished,' Thackeray said. 'Or they were serving life. It's possible they've been released now under the terms of the Good Friday Agreement. We need to check that out tomorrow. If they're out of gaol it may explain why Christie's cover seems to have been blown now, and not earlier. And maybe why he and the family were attacked.'

'So we're looking for a bunch of Ulster Protestant thugs out for revenge?' Mower asked incredulously. 'Or the Provisional IRA? Terrific. The super's really going to love you for this.'

Thackeray smiled thinly.

'I doubt very much we'll be invited to Derry to pursue our inquiries,' he said. 'This is way over our heads.'

'No wonder the spooks were getting their knickers in a twist,' Mower said. 'But as it happens, I'm one step ahead of you on this. I put out feelers of my own with a man I know – ex-Met, but more importantly, ex-army. He gave me a slightly different ID.'

'Our fell-walking major reckoned Christie had been in the army,' Thackeray said.

'My man says he's not Gordon Robertson,

Ulster terrorist, but Gordon Roberts, British Army undercover operator, discharged after the shootings in Derry and, as far as anyone knew, resident in Portugal with his family ever since, well out of harm's way. Only he wasn't. Not for the last three years anyway. For some reason no one understands, he came back and the people who should have known didn't know until very recently. Hence the panic and obstruction when they realised just who we were looking for and why.'

'If they can't keep track of their own people, how the hell can they keep track of terrorists?' Laura asked angrily.

'I dare say what happened in Derry was an embarrassment to them if one of their own people was involved,' Mower said. 'I guess they'd be terrified of being accused of collusion in a massacre. There've been enough suggestions like that over the years. The security people must be paranoid about Northern Ireland by now.'

'What happened in Ireland is incidental,' Thackeray said. 'What it does do is give us even more grounds for thinking that maybe Christie – or Roberts as I suppose we should call him – didn't kill his family at all. Someone else did.'

'Well, do you want the good news or the bad news, guv?' Mower asked. 'There's a lot more been happening since you went away.

And I reckon the whole case is beginning to stack up quite differently.'

When he had finished running through the latest developments – Emma Christie's suggestion that there had been someone else in the house the day of the shootings, the new forensic evidence and Emma's sudden collapse – Thackeray seemed to have shaken off his tiredness and come back to life and even Laura, who had looked even more pale and drained than he had when they had got home, was sitting up in her chair again and taking notice. Thackeray glanced at her.

'You're not hearing any of this,' he said, and she grinned.

'Deaf as a post,' she said. 'But how's Emma, Kevin? Is she okay?'

'Last time I checked she was,' Mower said. 'But I can't say they're brimming over with confidence. They don't even know what happened to her.'

'But if this was all some Irish revenge attack why hang about to try to murder a sick child? Surely the killer would get away, back to Derry or wherever, where he'd be relatively safe,' Laura said.

'Assuming he's not already dead,' Mower said. 'If the man in the Land Rover had been to the cottage he may well be our man. No one in Manchester seems to be claiming any knowledge of him. And Christie may also be dead, or else he's got himself well away from Yorkshire by now.'

'In which case why would someone still be trying to kill Emma? If that's really what's happened at the hospital? A dead man doesn't worry about being identified,' Thackeray said. 'I don't think this is as simple as that. I still want to know more about Christie himself. I want to know exactly where he's been and what he's been doing for the last six years. He's had plenty of time to make other enemies and we now know that at least one of his friends or enemies, who visited the cottage, had a gun in the Land Rover with him when he died. A gun which has been used in serious crime in this country, according to Manchester CID. It may be the Irish thing which sent Christie into hiding but it may not be that which sparked this tragedy. He may have quite different enemies in this country who wanted him dead for reasons we don't know anything about yet.'

'There's the unexplained money,' Mower said. 'Where did that come from? And what did he do to earn it?'

'Quite,' Thackeray said. 'Tomorrow we see the super. And we tell him about the Irish connection, and we tell him there's more leads in this case than roads to Rome.'

'And we need the spooks to come clean about what they know,' Mower added. 'So far they've been a hindrance, not a help.'

Just then his phone rang and Laura and Thackeray watched as he listened, his face appearing to freeze as he took in what he was being told.

'Thanks,' he said curtly as he switched off. He looked at the other two and shook his head, evidently horrified.

'Emma Christie just died,' he said quietly. 'They couldn't save her.'

'Oh shit,' Laura said, letting her hair fall forward across her face to hide her eyes full of tears. Thackeray just nodded, stony-faced, struggling to control a rage that threatened to overwhelm him.

'So we may have ourselves another murder,' Mower said.

'They still don't know what killed her?' Thackeray asked.

'They'll have test results tomorrow, they said. Personally I'd put money on them finding something, which means that either Christie's managed to finish the job off himself or we're one step further away from nailing a serial killer. She'll never tell us anything useful now, poor little beggar. What a mess we've made of protecting her. Val Ridley will never forgive us.'

Chapter Twenty

Major Donald Wright took off his small backpack and wriggled his shoulders to ease their stiffness, before sitting down on the step of the stile which took the footpath over the last drystone wall and onto the open moorland beyond. For a few moments he took regular, deep breaths, feeling his heart rate slow after the steep climb from Staveley. It was one of those rare winter days of blue skies, soft westerly winds and sunshine bright enough to bring the dun-coloured winter landscape of the high hills briefly back to life. Overhead a hawk circled, a black crescent spinning against the sun, and Wright felt high enough here, on a spur that gave an unimpeded view of Bradfield and its neighbouring villages spread out in the river valley below and the land rising again in blue hills to the east, to be a bird of prey himself.

He was finding these climbs harder than he used to, he had to admit, and much harder than when he and his wife had walked for miles over the hills together. He used to make it up as far as this viewpoint most days, but had not achieved it for a week or more.

Today he had determined to make the effort, even though the climb made his heart race. It still filled his lungs with pure air and that sense of exhilaration he had always found in high country. He seldom met anyone on these winter walks, although in the summer the moorland paths were popular with ramblers who often came great distances to walk the Pennines. And today was no different. He felt alone in the vast landscape, but liberated, rather than overwhelmed by it. This was a place he loved.

Breath regained, he climbed over the stile, determined to make it to the summit of Brough Top, half a mile and a steep gradient in front of him, but as he set off briskly his attention was attracted by a raucous flurry of crows, evidently disturbed by his approach. The object of their attentions was concealed by a clump of gorse bushes, and Wright would have ignored it if it had not been for one particularly persistent bird which flew in frantic circles round his head as if trying to drive this human intruder away. Cautiously Wright left the rough track and scrambled across dead moor grasses made slippery by the recent snow until he could see the object of the crows' attention more clearly. He had expected to be faced with the rotting corpse of a dead sheep, although he knew that it was too early for the flocks to be let out up here to graze. But what he found was far worse and set his heart pounding again.

The body lay half concealed under the gorse, the spines snagging on a torn dark anorak and badly stained trousers, although whether with mud or blood Wright could not decide. The old soldier was not unused to death but this find sickened him because as far as he could see, without approaching so close that he would obliterate anything that he guessed the police would find valuable, the corpse had no face and only bloodied stumps for hands. He guessed the crows were to some extent to blame, but knew enough of battle injuries to know that the man's exposed flesh had been badly burned, so badly that parts of the mouth had disappeared, leaving a skeletal grin on the remnants of the face. He hoped devoutly that the victim had been dead before that happened.

Shaken, he backed away and regained the footpath, scrambling as quickly as he could now back down the track to the village below. He had never grown accustomed to carrying a mobile phone and he had to retrace his steps back to his own house to make his emergency call to the police. Meanwhile, on the hillside above, the crows fell silent and resumed their grisly feast under the wide blue sky.

By four that afternoon, with the sun

fading in a welter of gathering pink and orange cloud over the looming hills to the west, the pathologist Amos Atherton was peremptorily demanding that the police lights be focused more directly on the mutilated body he was examining *in situ*. DCI Thackeray and Sergeant Kevin Mower watched his endeavours from a slight distance, standing close to the gorse bushes that had hidden the body for an indeterminate length of time from anyone passing by on the footpath twenty yards away. Eventually Atherton hauled his heavy form upright and struggled back up the slight incline towards the police officers.

'There's nowt more I can do here,' he said. 'The light's too poor. I need him on the table to be able to judge what the hell happened to him.'

'Has he been there long?' Thackeray asked.

'I don't think so,' Atherton said. 'There's no decomposition to speak of beneath his clothing. The bloody birds have gone for his hands and face, which were severely burned anyway, so they've made a bad job worse. I've never seen anything like it, Michael, if you want the honest truth. There's no damage to speak of to his jacket, just a bit of singeing at the collar and cuffs. No signs of fire that I can see in the immediate vicinity. Just severe burns to the face and hands in a sort of overlapping circular pattern. It's bizarre. The poor beggar must have been in agony.'

'The burns killed him, then?' Mower asked.

'Well, I wouldn't have said so normally. They're severe but not that extensive. Quite survivable, I'd have said, though he'd have been in hospital for months and not have much of a face left at the end of it. But I've not found any other signs of injury so maybe his heart gave out. It happens. Or his throat and lungs were damaged. Can't tell you much about that till I open him up.'

'Identification?' Thackeray asked.

'Nothing in his pockets,' Atherton said. 'You can have a look at him if you like, but it's not a pretty sight.' Thackeray nodded and dropped down the slight incline Atherton had just scrambled up and gazed down for a moment at the ruined face of what had once been a human being and was now a red and black grimacing caricature of a man. He shuddered slightly and climbed back up to where Mower was silently watching him. Thackeray shrugged, his mouth dry.

'It could be Christie, I suppose. Or Roberts, whatever we're supposed to call him. What's left of his hair is dark, he's about the right build. Apart from that it's impossible to tell. But I don't reckon those burns were accidental. I think he was deliberately burned to death.'

Mower said nothing as the stretcher bearers moved down into the hollow to remove the body, but drew a sharp breath as the horror of what Thackeray had said sank in.

'Cordon the immediate area off, Kevin,' the DCI said. 'We'll give it a thorough search at first light. Whether we've found Gordon Christie or not makes no difference, really, does it? It's odds on there's some connection so close to the cottage, and we're still going to be looking for a psycho with a blowtorch in the morning. That's the only weapon I can think of that would leave a man looking like that.'

Atherton gave Thackeray a sharp look.

'I reckon you're right,' he said. 'I didn't think of that. You could do a hell of a lot of damage very quickly with a blowtorch. With a steady hand and a strong nerve.'

'As strong a nerve as you need to shoot children in the back, do you think?' Thackeray asked.

Laura Ackroyd had gone into work that morning with a sense of foreboding. The death of Emma Christie and speculation about her fate was about to make the front page headline in the *Gazette*'s first edition, and there was that subdued hum of excitement in the newsroom which always emerged when a big story broke. Laura was grateful that the task of attending the police press conference fell to the crime reporter, Bob Baker. She was furious to see that he returned to the office in the company of Vince Newsom and organised herself an early lunch so that she could avoid both men. She had still not told Michael Thackeray what had happened the night he went away and the knowledge that sooner or later she would have to confess to an episode which filled her with shame almost overwhelmed her. As she left the office the two of them had their heads close to Baker's computer screen, but she knew that they had watched as she put her coat on and heard them break into muted conversation as she left the newsroom.

Out in the bustling streets of the town she used her mobile to try to contact Thackeray only to be told he was not available, and she still got no reply from the home of her friend Vicky Mendelson. She bought herself a sandwich and a coffee and sat glumly over her lunch for ten minutes, gazing at the scurrying town centre shoppers, before joining them in an unenthusiastic trawl of the fashion shops in search of clothes she didn't really need. How could she have allowed Vince Newsom to wheedle his way back into her life so disruptively, she wondered, as she tried on a chiffon top in a shade of apricot that she knew she would never wear. As she sat in the changing room trying to extricate herself from the clingy fabric which she reckoned was a size too small anyway, her mobile rang and when she recognised Val Ridley's voice her stomach clenched.

'I've been trying to get you all weekend,' Val said, her voice harsh with suppressed anger.

'Sorry, I was away till last night,' Laura countered quickly, knowing all too well what was coming next.

'How the hell did the *Globe* get hold of that story? It wasn't from the stuff I gave you was it? I couldn't believe it when I saw it.'

'Where are you?' Laura asked. 'We need to talk.'

'I think we do,' Val agreed, her voice low now. 'Ten minutes in the Lamb?'

Laura pulled on her own clothes quickly, dumped her unwanted bargain with the indifferent shop-girl outside the changing room, and hurried away through the lunch-time crowds to meet Val standing by the door of the pub.

'Let's walk,' Laura said. 'We don't want to be overheard in there.' The police officer nodded grimly and they hurried in silence across the town centre until they found an empty bench in the windswept square in front of the gothic town hall. Val had a crumpled copy of Saturday's *Globe* in her bag, and she pulled it out angrily as they sat down.

'You know Emma's dead?' she asked. Laura nodded.

'The *Gazette* will be out soon,' she said, glancing at her watch. 'It's the front page lead. I'm sorry Val. I really am. I thought she was recovering.'

'So did everyone,' Val said. 'I don't believe it's natural causes. I think someone killed her, though no one's found any evidence yet.' For a moment she seemed about to disintegrate, making a noise in her throat that was half moan, half scream, and grabbing Laura's arm for a moment with such force that her companion winced and pulled away. With an effort, she pulled herself together again and spread Saturday morning's *Globe* across her lap with trembling fingers and stabbed her finger at the picture of Emma in her hospital bed, which had been repeated for a second time on the front page.

'This bastard Vince Newsom,' she said, 'where did he get this from, for God's sake? It's word for word what Emma said to me. No one's going to believe I didn't tell him. Was it you? You promised you wouldn't do anything with what I gave you, for God's sake. It was for the boss's eyes only. You promised. Did you give him the details? Or did you *sell* this bastard the story?'

'Val, you've got to believe me,' Laura said, frantic herself now at the implications of Val's suspicions. 'I didn't tell him anything. I promise you. But you're right, it was from your notes. He stole them out of my bag and I was too drunk to notice. It was unforgivably stupid of me, but I never suspected he would do anything so awful. You have to believe that. Please.'

Val Ridley got to her feet and stood in front of Laura for a moment, her hand poised, almost as if she was going to hit her across the face. But then she crumpled again, her face drawn and her eyes full of tears.

'I should never have trusted you,' she said. 'She died because I trusted you. I killed her.'

'You don't know that,' Laura said desperately. 'She was seriously ill. Anything could have happened.'

'You're all the same, you journalists,' Val said, systematically ripping the newspaper into bits and throwing it into a waste bin. 'Conniving, cheating, lying – anything for a story. I must have been mad to think you'd be any different. And now a child is dead.'

'It wasn't like that,' Laura said desperately but Val was already turning away, her face contorted with anger and grief.

'I'll see you in hell,' she flung back over her shoulder.

Reluctantly, Laura walked back to the

office just after one, only to meet Baker and Newsom coming down the stairs from the newsroom as she went up.

'Hi, babe,' Newsom greeted her with an expansive smile as they met. 'Not still smarting, are we? Get over it, sweetie. Stuff happens.' She did not respond, conscious of their laughter as they swept out of the building in obviously high spirits, the tragedy they had been writing about having as little effect on them as any lingering memories of Friday night's betrayal. Maybe I'm too bloody sensitive for this job, she thought. Maybe Vince is right. But as she settled back at her desk she knew that the job was not the problem. She knew that the only way to break the hold Newsom now had over her was to tell Michael Thackeray the truth, and she shuddered to think what the consequences of that would be.

The lights in Superintendent Jack Longley's office burned late that evening as he presided over the crisis meeting he had insisted on after Janine Foster had identified the body of her husband from his clothing and his wedding ring, all carefully removed from the mutilated body now lying in the morgue, awaiting the ministrations of Amos Atherton. Facing him across the conference table were DCI Michael Thackeray, whose unscheduled return from holiday Longley had greeted

336

with apparent relief, Assistant Chief Constable (crime) Percy Rhodes from county HQ, and a representative of the security services whom Rhodes had apparently summoned urgently from Manchester and who admitted only to the name of Smith. But Smith, Thackeray was delighted to see, was at last beginning to look uncomfortably flustered by the ACC's staccato enumeration of the facts they had so far established since the shooting of Gordon Christie's family just over a week earlier. Rhodes glanced at Thackeray and indicated that he should carry on.

'We've established that Christie was in fact Gordon Roberts, an SAS soldier who worked undercover in Northern Ireland some years ago,' Thackeray said.

Smith shook his head. 'You know we can't confirm or deny that,' he said.

'Well, let's just say I've confirmed it to my own satisfaction from two separate sources,' Thackeray snapped. 'So the next question is, what are the connections between Roberts, and an unidentified body in a burnt out car in Manchester, a brutally tortured pub landlord, also dead, and Roberts' own family, the last member of which died in suspicious circumstances in hospital yesterday. Can you throw any light on any of that, Mr Smith, or are you under orders to continue to obstruct my inquiries?'

'We now have six deaths being investigated

here, Mr Smith, all connected to Christie or Roberts or whatever you choose to call him,' ACC Rhodes said explosively. 'I think the least we are entitled to expect from you people is some cooperation.'

Smith swallowed hard and gazed at the ceiling for a moment.

'I am authorised to tell you that we had recruited Foster, the publican, on an informal basis. He was ex-army himself and well placed to help us, as he'd been in the village some time.'

'Well placed to help you with what?' Thackeray asked.

'We wanted Christie watched. We wanted to know who his contacts were. It has to be admitted that we were taken by surprise when he turned up in this country again. Our information was that he and his family were settled in Portugal and we had no further information on him until quite recently. At that point we felt we ought to keep an informal eye on what he was up to here. He had enemies in Ireland and a lot of information which could be embarrassing to the British Government. We also had some evidence that he still had access to weapons. We instituted surveillance some months ago. Foster was willing and able to help us with that. Foster's mistake was to get too close, to get involved with Linda Roberts. If Roberts himself is still alive, that may be why Foster is now dead.'

'Roberts had been involved in at least one sectarian assassination in Derry which ended in the massacre of an entire family. In other words, he was a killer. Is that right?' Thackeray asked.

Smith did not reply but Thackeray took his silence as assent.

'And you suspected he might have access to weapons? Did you not think that information might have been relevant to my investigation when his own family was shot? You knew he was at risk living in Staveley, in spite of his attempts at an alias, and even worse that his wife and children could also be at risk. Didn't the similarities between what happened in Derry and what happened in Staveley strike you as significant?'

The eyes of the three Yorkshire officers were fixed on Smith for a long moment, but he looked only slightly uncomfortable.

'Roberts' activities in Northern Ireland are still classified. Nothing I could have told you would have helped you find him. Your failure to do that is entirely your own, I'm afraid, Chief Inspector.'

'But our failure to look for anyone else in connection with these deaths is at least partly because we knew nothing about his background,' ACC Rhodes broke in.

'I was not authorised to comment on his background,' Smith insisted. 'Any inquiries related to that would have been within our jurisdiction anyway, and anything which might have helped you would have been passed to you on a need-to-know basis. We had, indeed have, no evidence of a Northern Ireland connection to recent events, no evidence of anyone coming to the mainland from either faction over there. Nothing from our sources in Derry or Belfast which could have put us, or you, on red alert. We made the same assumption you did: that Christie had killed his family.'

'You'll forgive us if we take that with a certain amount of scepticism,' Rhodes said. Smith merely shrugged.

'Did your people help the family move abroad?' Thackeray asked.

'No. We offered help with a new identity here but in the end Roberts made his own arrangements because he wanted to keep his family together and went to Portugal. That suited us fine.'

'Protecting women and children wasn't on offer if they stayed here?' Thackeray said sharply.

'It's difficult,' Smith said, looking uncomfortable again. 'Children are almost impossible to control. They chatter too much. Going abroad is much the best solution in these cases. Unfortunately Roberts, for reasons we've not been able to ascertain, decided to come back.'

'He's been in Staveley for almost three years,' Thackeray said. 'How long is it since you became aware of that?'

'No more than six months ago,' Smith conceded. 'And then purely by chance. He was recognised by one of our officers based in Manchester who used his initiative and followed him home. We immediately offered again to arrange a safe haven abroad for them all. Roberts turned us down. He said his wife wouldn't go away again.'

'So for years he was living relatively openly in Staveley with his entire family at risk from reprisals from two terrorist groups?'

'By his own choice, chief inspector. Entirely by his own choice. And under an assumed name. And as I've said, we have absolutely no evidence of Irish involvement in this case. We would have picked up some chatter, I think, if anyone from over there had tracked him down. I suspect that your first theory was in fact the correct one. For some reason Gordon Roberts flipped and murdered his family. It's by no means uncommon, as I'm sure you know as well as I do.'

'Especially amongst ex-soldiers?'

'Some have difficulty in settling to civilian life,' Smith said.

'Did he have any sort of counselling after what happened in Derry?' Thackeray asked.

'I don't know. I can check. It's not compulsory.'

'We take post-traumatic stress very seriously now,' ACC Rhodes said magisterially. 'We insist on counselling.'

'You say you've had Roberts under surveillance...' Superintendent Jack Longley began.

'Very informally. We simply asked Gerry Foster to keep an eye...' Smith broke in.

'The same Gerry Foster who was horrifically killed,' Longley said. 'I can buy your theory that Roberts suffered some sort of breakdown as a result of his own experiences, but in ninety-nine cases out of a hundred like that the killer turns his gun on himself. But not this time. We've not found his body and we have three other related deaths. Those are not the actions of someone who has flipped, as you put it. Did Gerry Foster, or anyone else for that matter, come up with any evidence that Roberts had other enemies, maybe not Irish, but anyone else who might want to get rid of him and his family? Not forgetting that the child who died yesterday indicated that there had been someone else in the house when the shootings occurred.'

'Gerry Foster came up with very little of value,' Smith said dismissively. 'If Roberts had other enemies we never heard about them.'

'But someone hated or feared Gerry Foster enough to kill him in the most agonising way imaginable,' Thackeray said, his face grim. 'Whoever the psychopath is out there, and it may well be Roberts, he's very dangerous indeed. I hope you sleep easily at night, Mr Smith. I'm not sure I would, in your position.'

The meeting over, Thackeray lingered for a moment in Longley's office after the visitors had left. Longley looked at him warily.

'We failed pretty miserably with the little girl,' Thackeray said.

Longley glanced away. 'I didn't think she was at risk. We still don't know she was at risk. Perhaps we made a mistake.'

'I'd put money on it,' Thackeray said, knowing he would get nothing approaching an apology for what he considered to be Longley's massive error of judgement. 'Her parents aren't going to be in a position to complain, are they?' He did not give the superintendent time to reply, turning on his heel and thundering downstairs to his own office where he found Kevin Mower waiting for him.

'Don't you ever sleep?' he asked wearily, glancing at his watch.

'I thought you'd want to know about Emma Christie,' Mower said. 'The hospital reckon it was a massive dose of insulin that killed her. It's very unlikely to have been administered by accident.'

'Murder then?' Thackeray said, sounding

as unsurprised as he felt. He looked at his desk where a white envelope lay on top of a pile of waiting files. He opened it slowly, anticipating more bad news, and was not disappointed. Mower watched his face darken.

'Guv?'

'It's Val Ridley's resignation,' Thackeray said. 'She reckons she was responsible for the leak to the *Globe*. She's obviously blaming herself for Emma's death.' Mower nodded, recalling how distraught Val had seemed after Vince Newsom's story had appeared.

'She's too good an officer to lose,' he suggested. 'Hang on to the letter until I've talked to her.'

'Maybe,' Thackeray said distractedly. He folded the letter up and put it in his pocket. He said nothing to Mower but he was even more concerned by Val's concise explanation of how information had reached the tabloid reporter than at the prospect of losing a good detective. In fact the panic which threatened him had nothing at all to do with Val Ridley's guilty conscience and everything to do with why Laura Ackroyd had failed to tell him over the couple of days they had enjoyed together in Ireland that she too might have been implicated in providing Vince Newsom with his latest scoop. Following Mower down the stairs and out into the rainswept town centre, he knew that this was a night which might end very badly indeed if he let it.

Chapter Twenty-One

PC Gavin Hewitt was not best pleased. Up on the moors behind the village the forensic teams and uniformed officers were doing a fingertip search of the area where Gerry Foster's mutilated body had been found. Down at the infirmary in Bradfield, Amos Atherton was meticulously dissecting Foster's body to attempt to discover the cause of his death, while in other parts of the hospital a major investigative team was interrogating anyone who had been on the premises at the time Emma Christie suffered a catastrophic relapse in the children's ward where, according to her nurses, she had last been seen sleeping peacefully. Meanwhile, Hewitt had been sent on what he regarded as the unforgivably routine assignment of taking a statement from the old boy who had stumbled across Foster's body the previous afternoon.

Hewitt set off for the village early, in the hope of something more interesting coming in his direction later, and not even Major Wright's warm welcome, which included a cup of tea and a plate of chocolate digestives, had completely mollified him as he had settled in the comfortable armchair offered and begun to record the major's precise recollections of his horrifically curtailed afternoon walk. The proceedings did not take long, although it was obvious that Wright was happy enough to spin them out.

'If you'll just sign here, Mr Wright,' Hewitt insisted at last, growing weary of the old man's increasingly futile efforts to recall anything further that might be of significance. Wright glanced at the overtly impatient policeman, and did as he was requested.

'Of course, you've saved me a phone call anyway, young man,' he said, as he put his fountain pen carefully back on his small desk. 'I was going to ring your station to report the gunshots.' Hewitt was closing his folder and half on his feet when the full significance of what Wright had said hit him.

'Gunshots?' he said. 'What do you mean?'

'I mean gunshots, Constable,' Wright came back with some asperity. At about 0900, heard them quite distinctly, four shots from, I would guess, a high powered rifle. And later, more shots from some weapon I couldn't identify. An automatic pistol maybe.'

Hewitt looked at Wright incredulously

until the major became impatient.

'I've heard countless snipers in my time, young man,' he said. 'This sounded exactly like another.'

'Were they close?' Hewitt asked, recalling that he had been told to interview a major, though the rank had slipped his mind.

'Close enough,' Wright said. 'Definitely in or around the village, I would say. And in a southerly direction. Difficult to place exactly, of course. I was in the bathroom at the time. But I would put the direction as south, further down the Bradfield road.'

'I'll get onto it straight away,' he said.

But ten minutes later, after he had used his car radio to report exactly what Wright had told him, he decided that in the circumstances a little initiative might win him brownie points back at the station. He started the car and rolled slowly down the hill through the meandering village street and pulled up again outside the gates of the Old Hall. Bruce Weldon, he knew, had denied all knowledge of gunshots to CID, and what evidence of them he had seen with his own eyes had apparently been very quickly obliterated. But just maybe, he thought, a second episode might have changed Weldon's mind about reporting his problems.

As soon as he got out of the car and approached the wrought iron gates to seek admittance, Hewitt knew that he had struck gold. Across the neatly raked gravel of the drive he could see two burly men in jeans working clearing glass at the front of the house where two of the small paned windows had been shattered. Hewitt did not think that he was being over-imaginative to suppose that in the sitting room beyond there would be further evidence of damage caused by gunfire. But when he pressed the intercom, one of the workmen crunched across the gravel towards him with a surly expression.

'Nah then?' he asked.

'We've had a complaint about shooting in the area,' Hewitt said. 'Is Mr Weldon at home.'

'Out all day,' the man said and began to turn away.

'Did you hear...?' Hewitt began.

'I reckon if Mr Weldon needs you lot he'll call you,' the man said over his shoulder. 'In t'meantime, I should bog off, if I were you. We don't need you here.'

Hewitt took a sharp breath and turned back to his car. It was about time CID took some notice of his work in Staveley, he thought, and he reckoned he had something now which would make them sit up and take notice.

Laura Ackroyd was finding it difficult to concentrate on work that morning. She had not seen Michael Thackeray for more than twenty-four hours, or heard from him since a brief phone call to tell her that he would be at a late meeting the previous evening. He had not come back to the flat nor attempted to contact her since, and she had wondered over her snatched breakfast why their relationship seemed to have plunged back to the same level of chilly non-communication which had dogged it for months now. The fear, which kept her mind switching away from her computer screen all morning, was that he had somehow discovered what had happened with Vince Newsom the previous week.

Whatever she did, she did not seem to be able to escape from the ubiquitous presence of Newsom, whom Ted Grant appeared to be allowing to work closely with Bob Baker. The two of them glanced occasionally in her direction, their smiles smug and their whispered conversation jovial, but she had no idea in what direction their inquiries were taking them.

Halfway through the morning her own phone rang and she immediately recognised the voice of Janine Foster, the now widowed landlady of the Fox and Hounds in Staveley.

'Could you come up? There's something I need to talk to you about,' Janine said, her voice husky with emotion.

'Are you sure?' Laura asked, full of

uncertainty. 'Shouldn't you be talking to the police?'

'No,' Janine said sharply. 'I don't want them just now. It's you I want to speak to. I need some help.' Laura hesitated and glanced across the office to where she could see Bob Baker and Vince Newsom listening shamelessly to her conversation. There might be a story in this, she thought, and with a flash of dislike for both men she thought of a way of disarming the pair of them, at least temporarily.

'Okay,' she said to Janine. 'Give me half an hour. I'll see what I can do.' But when Janine hung up, Laura did not. She kept the receiver at her ear as she pulled a local map out of her desk drawer and spread it out in front of her, pen in hand. For a minute she made affirmative noises into her phone and notes on the map. Finally saying goodbye to her now non-existent caller she drew a ring around a site on the map and hung up. She sat for a moment as if thinking about her next move, and then made her way over to Ted Grant's office, to check that he had no objection to her taking an early lunch break. She was fully aware, glancing out of the corner of her eye, that either Bob or Vince was taking a close interest in the map and other notes she had left on her desk, although when she strolled back across the newsroom to pick up her coat the two men were head-to-head again at Bob Baker's workstation.

She picked up the map and notes on her way out, not looking back but knowing very well she was being watched, but when she got to her car she stuffed the bundle carelessly into the glove box. As bait they had served their purpose. As she drove out of the car park and headed across the town centre she glanced in her mirror before committing herself to the Staveley road. Just as she had suspected, she was not being followed and she relaxed, with a maliciously self-satisfied smile. After all, she thought, they did not need to take the risk of following her, as they thought they knew exactly where she was heading. The only trouble was that the goal she had set for them was thirty miles into the hills in the wrong direction, and the weather forecast was for more snow. She sincerely hoped there would be a blizzard.

Janine Foster was waiting for her by the front entrance of the pub, to which she had attached a large notice announcing its closure until further notice. As Laura got out of her car Janine grabbed her arm.

'I think I'm going mad,' she said. 'Either that or some beggar's playing tricks on me.' She pulled a mobile phone out of her pocket and thumbed it for a second before handing it to Laura.

'It's a text message from Gerry,' Janine said. 'Only it can't be, because he's lying dead in the morgue in Bradfield, the police said. I identified all his stuff last night, didn't I? But then this arrives. They wouldn't let me see his body yesterday. Said it was unrecognisable and would be too upsetting for me. So what's this about? D'you think they've got the wrong man? Could he still be alive?' There were tears running down Janine's face now, smearing the carelessly applied mascara, and Laura handed her a tissue as she stared at the message on the phone. It was very brief, simply asking Janine to meet the caller at the back of Moor Edge cottage. It was signed simply with the letter G.

'Did he always sign himself G?' she asked. Janine glanced at the phone distractedly.

'Yes, yes, he did, and I signed J. Saves time, dunnit?'

'How many people would know that?' Laura asked. Janine shook her head.

'No one. How could they?' Laura flicked to the menu and brought up the number that had transmitted the call.

'Is that Gerry's phone?' she asked. Janine looked at the tiny screen again and nodded.

'Yes,' she said. 'His phone wasn't amongst the other stuff they showed me last night. He must be alive, mustn't he? The body must be someone else. It's all a horrible mistake and he's not dead at all.' Laura looked at the distraught woman and knew that her hopes were very unlikely to be realised. It was far more likely that someone else had acquired Gerry Foster's mobile phone than that the police had misidentified the body of a murder victim who just happened to be wearing Foster's clothes. But she knew that it might be impossible to convince Janine of that.

'Are you sure you're up to this?' she said cautiously. 'So soon...?'

'I want to know what the hell's going on,' Janine came back fiercely. 'I know Gerry were no angel. I wasn't surprised he was having an affair, though what he saw in that pale little bitch I don't know. But to be killed for that? And the way he was killed? It makes no sense. I can't get my head round it. There has to be more to it than that.' Laura nodded, thinking that however distraught Janine might be, there could possibly be an element of truth in what she was saying, and that in any case she was not going to be convinced otherwise without some sort of proof.

'So let's do what he wants you to do,' she said. 'Let's go up to the cottage and see if he's there.' At least this time there was no possibility of going inside the house, as she had so reluctantly done with Gerry himself two days ago. She shuddered when she recalled how he had come away with Linda Christie's scarf and wondered what had happened to that. Today at least a quick look round the outside of the house should soon establish that there was no one there and the phone message was the cruel hoax she was sure it would turn out to be.

She drove Janine to the cottage and parked outside. The police tape was hanging in shreds now, most of it whipped away by the wind, and the cottage windows were still curtained and in darkness. The two women got out of the car and Laura pushed open the wooden five-barred gate which gave access to the side of the building and the yard and outbuildings at the back. There, too, there was nothing to be seen or heard except the faint soughing of the wind over the bracken and gorse behind the buildings, and the sudden flap of a bird disturbed by their arrival.

'There's no one here, Janine,' Laura said. 'I'm sorry. It really is just a hoax.' But Janine picked her way on high heels through the mud and peered into the back windows of the cottage, which gave onto the kitchen and dining room, and then stepped carefully across the rutted yard and did the same at the grimy glass of Gordon Christie's workshops. Laura saw her stiffen suddenly and draw back, to stand rigidly against the wooden wall where no one inside could see her. She seemed to take a couple of deep breaths and then waved at Laura urgently to approach. Nervously, Laura picked her own way across the muddy concrete and stood beside Janine, her heart thumping.

'What is it?'

'There's someone in there,' Janine said, grabbing Laura's arm fiercely. 'It's not Gerry but there is someone, lying behind the sort of workbench thing on the far side of the room.'

'Lying?' Laura hissed. 'D'you think he's dead? D'you think we've found another body?' Janine shook her head fiercely.

'He's moving,' she said. 'I could see his head. That's how I know it's not Gerry. No beard.'

'Right,' Laura said. 'So who...?'

'Gordon Christie maybe,' Janine suggested. 'I don't know, do I?'

Laura twisted herself away and cautiously peered through the window herself. The light inside the workshop was dim but as her eyes became accustomed to the gloom she could make out the huddled shape that Janine had spotted in the far corner of the room. It was a man, curled on what looked like a couple of sacks, but what horrified her most was that there appeared to be a pool of dark liquid – which at first she assumed must be oil but then realised with a shudder was probably blood – around the upper part of his body. And when she looked more closely there were more dark stains between the corner where the man was lying and the door. She turned away again and glanced across the yard and was not surprised to see more red splashes, almost indistinguishable from the mud, all round them.

'He's hurt,' she said. 'We'll have to get help. Does the mobile really not work up here?'

'It's dodgy all round the village,' Janine said. She flicked the phone on but quickly shook her head. 'No signal,' she said.

'Go back down to your place and call the police and an ambulance from there,' Laura said. She reached in her pocket. 'Here, take my car.'

Janine nodded distractedly.

'Don't go in there,' she said.

'Of course not,' Laura came back quickly. 'I'll just keep an eye on him.' She watched as Janine picked her way back across the muddy yard and disappeared round the corner of the house. A few moments later she heard the car start and caught a glimpse of it as it reversed down the bumpy track. Laura took a deep breath and glanced through the window again. The man seemed to have curled up on himself, with his back to the door, and Laura wondered again if he was dead. Cautiously, she reached over and lifted the old-fashioned latch on the workshop door and inched it open. The response, to what could only have been a slight increase in the intensity of the light inside, was immediate.

'Is that you, Janine? I need some help here. Those bastards hit me.'

Laura opened the door more widely.

'It's not Janine,' she said. 'I'm Laura. She sent me instead.'

'Jesus,' the voice said, and then lapsed into a groan, which was followed by nothing more than heavy breathing from the far side of the room. Laura could see the bloodstains on the floor more clearly now and realised that Christie, if it was Christie, must be seriously hurt. Leaving the door open, she stepped into the workshop and walked slowly over to the corner. She recognised the man the police had been hunting for so long from his photograph, even though he was unshaven and pale-faced, and slumped with his eyes closed in the corner of the room behind his own workbench. A mobile phone lay on the floor beside him. The blood which had formed a pool by his left side had soaked his shirt and jacket and his left arm lay limp at his side.

Laura knelt down beside the injured man.

'I'll see if I can stop the bleeding,' she said, but Christie moved with surprising speed with his other arm and she found herself facing the muzzle of a pistol held in a surprisingly steady hand.

'Who the hell are you?' Christie asked.

Chapter Twenty-Two

The report of Janine Foster's call to the police took time to filter through to CID before landing like a detonating grenade on Michael Thackeray's desk. He flung open his office door and went into the main incident room, where not much appeared to be happening, with the piece of paper crumpled in his fist and a look of fury on his face.

'Kevin,' he said. 'Have you seen this?' Kevin Mower looked up from his computer screen and shook his head.

'A problem, guv?' he asked. Thackeray smoothed out the paper as best he could and let Mower read it. The implications of what Janine Foster had reported hit him, too, like a blow in the stomach.

'Laura's there,' Thackeray said, unable to disguise the note of panic in his voice. And according to our enterprising PC Hewitt, it's like the Wild West up there.'

'I was working on that, guv,' Mower said quickly.

'Move. Now,' Thackeray said. 'Get an

armed response unit organised, the chopper, the lot. I'm going up there to see what Mrs Foster has to say for herself. This whole thing's running out of control and Laura seems to have walked right into the middle of it.' He spun on his heel and hurried out of the room without leaving Mower any time to object. But Mower hardly needed the urgency of the situation reinforced. If there had been a panic button to press he would have pressed it.

Thackeray drove to Staveley faster than the law allowed but more slowly than his fear demanded. He flung his car into the pub car park, noticed Laura's car parked close to the gate and banged loudly on the locked pub door, hoping against hope that she would be safely inside. But Janine Foster opened the door quickly, looking terrified, and only glanced at the warrant card he waved in her direction.

'You took your time,' she said. 'It's more than half an hour since I dialled 999.'

'Tell me what happened? Is Laura Ackroyd here?' He waved at her car as if to explain the question. Janine shook her head.

'She's still at the cottage keeping an eye on things,' she said. 'I brought the car down. We thought it was urgent.'

'You're damn right it's urgent,' Thackeray said. 'Tell me exactly what happened.' So Janine did.

359

'Could you see whether Gordon Christie was armed or not?' he asked when she had finished, but Janine shook her head.

'And how do you think he got hold of your husband's mobile?'

'I've no idea,' Janine said. 'He certainly had me fooled.' She stood on the pub doorstep looking desolate as the first flakes of snow began to fall from the darkening sky.

'I'm sorry,' Thackeray said. 'It was a cruel hoax.' He touched her arm lightly. 'Stay here,' he said. 'I'm going up there to get the lie of the land and get Ms Ackroyd out of harm's way. The heavy mob won't be far behind me. If you could make sure they find the right lane to the cottage when they arrive, I'd be grateful.'

'They'd best be quick before we're snowed up again,' Janine said glumly as Thackeray turned back to his car. He drove the last quarter of a mile to the turning to Moor Edge and parked his car on the verge. It would be safer, he thought, to walk the rest of the way and give Christie no hint of his approach. With luck Laura could walk back down to the hill and sit out the rest of what might turn into a long siege in the warmth of the pub. But as he approached the cottage and made his way round the side of the building to the yard, his heart began thumping uncomfortably again. He could see no sign of Laura and the windows of the house and the outbuildings were all in darkness, a gloom made more intense by the rapidly darkening sky and increasingly fierce flurries of sleety snow.

Cautiously he made his way across the yard and, as Janine and Laura had done earlier, flattened himself against the wall and peered through the grimy glass into the interior of the workshop. He could see very little but even as he watched, his ears told him what he wanted to know and filled him with a cold fear that almost froze his brain. Someone inside the workshop spoke and another voice responded. There were two people inside and Thackeray guessed that for whatever reason, and he could not imagine a good one, Laura had gone inside and become, if Christie had a weapon, a hostage.

Thackeray took a deep breath and threw away in a split second years of training in risk assessment, hostage negotiation, not to mention his own natural caution. He reached out an arm and pushed the door open a couple of inches, knowing that whoever was inside could not fail to notice the slight increase in light.

'Thackeray,' he said loudly. 'CID. I'm not armed and I'm coming in.'

For a second as he stepped inside there was silence, then two urgent voices at once.

'Stay where you are,' Christie said.

'He's got a gun, Michael, be careful,' Laura added, her voice full of fear.

Thackeray stood very still, not least to accustom his eyes to the almost complete absence of light. Gradually he was able to make out the two figures on the other side of the cluttered room, both on the floor, Christie half lying with most of his body hidden by the workbench, and Laura seated close by him with her back to the wall beneath a shelf piled high with what looked like cans of paint, her knees drawn up beneath her chin.

'You! Put the light on and close the door,' Christie said unexpectedly. 'The switch is on the right.' Thackeray turned slowly and did as he was told, and then turned back. He could see Christie's gun then, pointed directly at Laura's head.

'Take your jacket off,' Christie said. 'Shirt sleeve order. Drop your coat on the floor.' Again Thackeray did as he was told with a shrug. He guessed the man wanted to be sure he was not carrying a weapon or a recorder.

'Right,' Christie said, the gun never wavering. 'Light out. We're like sitting ducks here with it on. Then walk slowly over this way and sit down beside little miss reporter here, where I can keep an eye on both of you.'

Thackeray took his time making his way

across the room, not wanting to startle Christie by tripping over any of the clutter that he had glimpsed in his brief survey of the workshop. As his eyes grew used to the gloom again he was able to drop down beside Laura and quickly slip an arm round her. He could feel her trembling and knew it was with fear, not cold, although he could already feel the damp chill of the workshop through his own cotton shirt.

'What is it you want, Christie?' he asked quietly. 'This isn't going to get you any-where. Janine Foster tells me you've been hurt. Let's get you to a doctor and take it from there.'

'He's been shot,' Laura said. 'I tried to stop the bleeding but I don't think I did much good.'

'Shut up,' Christie said sharply. 'I need to think.'

'You've not got much time,' Thackeray said. 'There'll be a couple of dozen armed police outside within ten minutes. We know your real name is Roberts and you were in the SAS. You know as well as I do that hostage-taking never ends well.'

Christie grunted, as if startled at that, and tried to push himself upright, groaning slightly with the effort.

'You found out that much did you?' he said. 'Well, your lads may get here and finish me off, or it may be someone Weldon sends.

His goons don't know where I am but it won't take them long to work it out. If you're so clever, how come you didn't know what that beggar and his son were up to right under your noses? Tell me that. How come it wasn't until my wife and kids got caught in the crossfire that you took an interest in Staveley's very own Mr Big.'

'Drugs was it?' Thackeray asked softly, not surprised. The horrific death of Gerry Foster had convinced him, as nothing else had, that there were serious criminals involved in what had been happening in Staveley, and that Christie himself was not likely to be in that league.

'Guns,' Christie said, his voice full of contempt. 'Weldon's the armourer for half the gangs in the north of England. And when he sussed out my background he couldn't believe his luck, could he? Untraceable weapons, untraceable killer with the best possible training, special terms for bulk orders.' The voice was strained but oozed with bitterness.

'Contract killing?'

'Either Weldon's very clever or you lot are very stupid,' Christie said. 'And I needed the money. Working as a bloody mechanic's a dogsbody job. Killing people's the only valuable skill I ever got. It could have gone on for ever if my wife hadn't put two and two together and decided we'd better move on again. Spain, she thought, this time. Silly cow thought it would be that easy.'

'Did you kill your family?' It was, Laura thought, the question Thackeray needed an answer to more than any other. She felt for his hand and held it tightly.

Christie groaned again.

'You're not listening, Mr CID,' he said. 'Stuart Weldon killed my family and he would have killed me too if I hadn't shot him first. What he didn't know was that since we fell out over me refusing to do the next job they had in mind I hadn't gone anywhere without a pistol.'

'That was when you had a row with the two of them in the lane?' Thackeray suggested. 'We found a witness to that.'

'Well, good for you,' Christie said. 'I wanted out. I'd had enough. Two days later Stuart comes round to the house at breakfast time waving a gun about and shouting the odds. The kids were terrified and Linda starts screaming...'

Christie stopped, as if he was re-running the scene again in his head.

'He lost it and shot Linda, the kids ran and he got them as well. I tried to get his gun but he bashed me across the head with it and I was stunned for a bit. Then he asked where Scott was and said we'd have to catch up with him. I knew he was going to finish the pair of us off but he made me drive and had the gun pointed at the boy the whole way. In the end, when Scott had the sense to jump out of the Land Rover, Weldon fired off a couple of rounds into the snow to try and stop him, and I managed to get my own gun out.'

'And then you drove him to Manchester and torched the vehicle?'

Christie grunted what his listeners took to be assent.

'What about the weapon?' Thackeray asked, not wanting Christie to stray too far from the point. 'The one in the Land Rover wasn't the one which killed your family?' Thackeray pressed him.

'I swapped weapons. I wanted you to think Weldon was me and I might have killed myself so he had to be found with my gun, the gun and the bullet had to match. And anyway I was running out of ammo. He had plenty in his pockets, so I took that.'

'And what happened with your son back on the moors?' Thackeray's voice was gentle now.

'I looked for Scott,' Christie whispered. 'Couldn't find him...' He groaned again. 'I hunted for him until it turned into a total white-out. I just hoped he'd found somewhere to shelter by then.' Christie stopped and Thackeray knew that he was trying to imagine what he himself had actually seen, a small body wrapped round

366

itself in a vain search for warmth under the blanket of snow. 'He didn't make it, did he? I kept tuning into the radio when I could but I never heard...'

'I'm sorry,' Thackeray said, the words forced out of him. 'He would go to sleep, they said, feel nothing.'

'But those of us left don't feel nothing, do we?' Christie said vehemently, although the effort forced him into a spasm of coughing and Thackeray wondered for a second whether the gun had wandered off target. He did not feel inclined to risk finding out.

'We feel everything,' Christie went on. 'The ones who are left behind. We feel it all. We blame ourselves even if we didn't pull the trigger.' Laura felt Thackeray take a sharp breath. Laura knew that this was a line of questioning he should not be pursuing for a multitude of reasons.

'Did you pull the trigger that time in Derry?' Thackeray asked eventually, but Christie did not react as angrily as she feared he might.

'I did not,' he said softly. 'And I should have finished that off properly too. Prison was too good for those bastards. I told the brass that the people I was with were mad dogs, they might go too far. But they wouldn't listen.'

'Who did you tell, exactly?' Thackeray whispered.

'You can work that out, Mr CID,' Christie said. 'You can work out who put me there, in that house, with those kids, and those lunatics with an Uzi. You might say there was some justice in the same thing happening to me.'

And after all that, getting as far as Manchester, you came back here?' Thackeray said. 'Why didn't you get out of the country when you had the chance? You could have been long gone before the bodies were found.'

'And leave that bastard alive? And Emma all alone? Stuart's might have been the hand that pulled the trigger but the brain was his father's. I wanted Bruce Weldon dead as well. I think he knew about Derry. He'd found out somehow. There must have been feelers out in Manchester from Ireland, maybe. There's a lot of links between crime there and crime here, and enough people wanted to see me dead. And I think he just wanted to punish me for defying him, for refusing the next job, and the one after that, for wanting to get out. I think he wanted to punish me in the way he knew would hurt me most. Perhaps Stuart wasn't intended to kill me at all, just make sure that they were all dead and it was my fault they were all dead.'

'He's a sadist? Psychotic?'

'Oh, he's that all right,' Christie said. 'The

368

son's a pale shadow of the father, believe me.'

'So you came back, and you shot at Weldon's house? More than once?'

'I've got a sniper's rifle. There's a spot on the moor where you can see right into the windows. I thought I had him today but I must have missed and he had his goons waiting. He's a sharp beggar, is Weldon. He wouldn't have survived so long if he wasn't. Sharp and ruthless. And, as you say, a psychopath. One of the bastard's hit me and I only just made it back here. They won't give up. They'll still be out there looking. The cavalry had better look sharp or we'll all get it.'

And Gerry Foster? Did you kill Gerry Foster?' Thackeray asked, wondering where Christie's disregard for life stopped. He might call Weldon a psychopath but he suspected the former soldier came close to that himself. But Christie had fallen silent again, and his breathing seemed to be growing more laboured.

'You need a doctor,' Laura said. 'Let us get you to the hospital.'

Christie ignored her and eventually found the breath to speak again.

'Gerry's dead?' he asked, and Thackeray found it hard to believe he was dissembling. Somehow it seemed too late now for Gordon Christie to bother avoiding the truth.

'Why would I want to kill Gerry? He was all right, was Gerry.'

Thackeray did not think this was the moment to inform Christie of his wife's relationship with Gerry Foster, if Christie really did not know about it. Some vague memory about keeping hostage-takers calm rose to the surface of his mind.

'Where did you get his mobile phone?' he asked. Christie snorted, or it could have been a laugh.

'It was in the house,' he said. 'I didn't want to sleep in there. Couldn't, as it goes, you know? But I went in to get some blankets and tinned food. Linda's emergency rations from the kitchen cupboard. I found the phone in the bedroom, on the floor. God knows how it got there, and I didn't know whose it was at first, but the battery was charged so I just hung onto it, switched it off to conserve it, in case it came in useful. Today, when I crawled back here, it came in very useful. And for once I got a signal, sent Janine a text. Could see from the stored messages that Gerry signed off with a G. She'd have driven me out of here if she'd seen the gun, no problem.'

It might have worked, Thackeray thought, if someone hadn't already tortured Gerry Foster to death and brought the police back in force to the village. Christie's voice was beginning to fade now, and each sentence ended with a slight gurgle in his throat. Thackeray was beginning to doubt that he would be able to pull the trigger if he made a move to take the gun from him, but the decision was taken away from him anyway when a shot rang out outside the building and the window behind them shattered, scattering glass towards them in sharp shards. Laura screamed and another shot hit the wall above them, followed by a confusion of noise and intensely bright light suddenly illuminating the inside of the workshop from the yard outside.

'Stop firing,' Thackeray shouted, but was unable to gain any coherent message in return from outside, although another couple of sharp reports did not seem to be aimed in their direction.

'You asked me what I wanted,' Thackeray and Laura heard Christie say urgently. 'I only want one thing. I want to see Emma, and then you can do what the hell you like. I don't care any more. But I do want to see my Emma again.'

'You knew she was in hospital?'

'I heard it on the radio.' Christie said. 'I was listening out for Scott's name but it was hers I heard.'

'I'll see what I can do,' Thackeray lied. But even as Laura drew a sharp breath the lights went out again and more shots came through the broken window. Christie pulled himself upright and fired several times across the room into the darkness outside. Laura, who had flung herself face down when the shooting began, heard something heavy fall beside her. For a long moment there was silence, and then the lights came on again and she saw the door open and several burly figures in uniform holding guns at the ready move cautiously into the room.

Gordon Christie lay where she had first seen him, a fresh bullet wound in his head, the weapon he had eventually used still clasped in one limp hand, sightless eyes gazing at the ceiling. But more horrifying still was the sight of Michael Thackeray sprawled face down on the dusty floor, eyes closed, blood spreading slowly across his white shirt from the wound in his back. As the armed police officers fanned out through the room she moved closer and bent her head to his, but try as she might she could not hear him breathing.

Laura stood by the tall window in her living room gazing out at the snow-covered garden and trying to control the shaking which had overtaken her since she had arrived home. She knew she was still in shock, and that now there was nothing more to do it might overwhelm her completely. Kevin Mower had bundled her into his own car and driven behind the ambulance carrying Thackeray to the infirmary, neither of them of them knowing whether he was dead or alive. At A and E they had found he had been taken straight to theatre in the hope that the doctors could successfully remove the bullet which lay dangerously close to his heart. Mower had led Laura to a quiet corner, as white faced as she was herself, sat her down, brought her a cup of sweet tea and held her hand.

'I'll have to get back,' he said quietly. 'There'll be all hell let loose. But I need you to tell me what Christie said while you were in there. Anything you think might be significant.' Somehow she pushed her fear to the back of her mind and repeated as much as she could remember of what Gordon Christie had willingly enough confessed while she and Thackeray had been shut in the workshop with him. Mower listened quietly until she had finished and then got to his feet.

'I'll need to go back,' he said. 'They need to know all this stuff about Weldon. The gunman we arrested at Moor Edge has apparently refused to say anything about where he came from or who sent him. This is all hearsay and Christie's dead, but it should give us enough to organise a raid on Weldon's place. I need to let the super know. Will you be all right?'

Laura had glanced at her watch. It was still only five-thirty, only four hours since she had gone up the hill to Staveley to see Janine Foster, starting the whole horrific chain of events.

'They said he would be in theatre for at least two hours,' she said. 'I'll go into the office and write something for tomorrow. I'll get them to call me if there's any news.'

Are you sure?' Mower said, doubtfully. 'Can you cope with that?'

'I'll go mad if I sit here with nothing to do,' Laura said helplessly. 'I went up to Staveley looking for a story, didn't I? And I got one. I'll be better if I keep my mind occupied.'

Kevin Mower looked at her anxiously, taking in the flushed cheeks and too bright eyes, and knew she was close to hysteria.

Are you sure?' he asked again, but she insisted and he saw her across the town centre to the *Gazette* office before walking through the slushy streets to police headquarters.

The revelation that the body in the burnt out Land Rover in Manchester was Stuart Weldon's was niggling him as he took the stairs up to Jack Longley's office two at a time, but it was not until he knocked and was asked to go in that the stray fact he sought came back to him. Longley, flanked by Smith from the security services and the ACC all looked up from the conference table as he came in.

'Which bastards opened fire?' he asked the senior officers without preamble.

'Weldon's men, just as the armed response unit arrived,' Longley said. 'They were obviously determined to finish Christie off.'

'Well, they did that all right,' Mower said bitterly. 'And it looks as if they may have finished the DCI off too.'

'What's the latest?' Longley asked, his voice barely audible.

'He's in theatre,' Mower snapped. 'It's not looking good.'

The three men nodded but said nothing.

'I've got a note of everything Christie said from Laura Ackroyd, but I remembered something else important,' Mower said, wrenching his mind back to the still on-going investigation. 'Insulin. It's not just guns we need to look for at Weldon's place. It's insulin, as well. That's what killed Emma Christie, and Weldon's son was a diabetic. Old Major Wright knew that. Somewhere in that house there'll be a supply of insulin. Presumably he arranged for someone to give her an overdose. I just hope it was one of his goons and not a member of the hospital staff.'

In the familiar surroundings of the office, Laura immersed herself in an adrenaline fuelled assault on her keyboard, tapping out a vivid version of the events she had just recounted more soberly to Kevin Mower, and trying to drive out the fear which threatened to overwhelm her. Within half an hour she had finished, and still there had been no call from the hospital. She glanced behind her and noticed to her surprise the light in Ted Grant's office was still on and the door ajar.

'First person, exclusive,' she said, her voice dull now as the adrenaline rush subsided, dropping a printout of what she had written onto his desk. 'And where was your crime reporter when all that was going on?'

'Stuck in a bloody snowdrift up beyond Arnedale, apparently,' Grant said angrily. 'I've just had Vince Newsom's newsdesk on asking if I've any idea where he is, an' all. He's not answering his mobile. I don't suppose you know the answer to that do you?'

'I saw them go out together at lunchtime,' Laura said, with a ghastly attempt at a smile. 'But I've no idea where they were going.'

Aye, well, it was a good thing you were in the right place at the right time.' He picked up her printout. 'This'll take the smile of the *Globe*'s front-page tomorrow, won't it.'

'I hope so,' Laura said. 'And off Vince Newsom's too.' But her satisfaction at that prospect had turned to ashes and reality quickly closed in again as she closed down her computer and she was seized by a sudden terrible panic as she hurried back to the hospital. Thankfully, she quickly found the A and E nurse who had attended Thackeray, and who already knew that he had survived his surgery and was now in intensive care. She walked up to the top floor ward feeling sick with anxiety, to be met by the nurse who had expelled her from that very ward when she had first tried to see Emma Christie what seemed like a lifetime ago.

'You again?' the nurse said sharply.

'Michael Thackeray,' Laura whispered. 'He's my ... partner.' The woman's face softened slightly and she waved her towards a bed at the far end of the ward.

'He's comfortable,' she said. 'But critical. He's not conscious yet but if you want to see him, do.'

Laura had no idea how long she sat beside Thackeray's immobile form before someone put a hand on her shoulder and she turned round to find Kevin Mower behind her again.

'You need to go home,' Mower said. 'We'll ask them to call you if there's any change. You must get some sleep.'

'How will I sleep?' Laura asked, helplessly. But she let herself be led downstairs to Mower's car.

'Did you arrest Weldon?' she asked half-heartedly on the drive out to her flat.

'We did,' Mower said. 'His cellar was stuffed full of armaments of one sort and another, and his son's room had enough phials of insulin to kill an entire ward of patients. One of his goons admitted that they'd made two attempts to get to Emma in case she could identify Stuart. The second one succeeded. I don't think Bruce Weldon will be troubling anyone again for a very long time.'

'Christie said the only skill he had was killing people,' Laura said. 'Is that what the army does to people?'

'Yes, to some people,' Mower said. 'He was pretty efficient as a killer and was never taught how to stop. But Weldon was the real psycho. One of his gunmen has decided it's in his interests to tell us everything, including how Weldon personally tortured Gerry Foster to death because he thought he knew where Christie was hiding.'

'Poor Gerry,' Laura said. 'I got to quite like him in the end. He was really in love with Linda Christie, you know. He went back to the cottage to find something to remember her by.'

Mower looked at her for a moment.

'I won't ask how you know that,' he said dryly. 'But I guess that's how he dropped his phone.' He parked the car gingerly in deep snow that would not be cleared before morning and saw her into the flat.

'Will you be okay by yourself?' he asked. 'I have to get back to HQ. We'll be at it all night down there. I just took five to find out how the boss was doing.'

'I'll be all right,' Laura had said with far more confidence than she felt. And she let him go. But she did not sleep that night, sitting in the chair by the fireplace watching the hands of the clock snail around the dial until at seven the first glimmer of daylight stole through the curtains. She showered quickly and persuaded a taxi to pick her up on the main road to avoid the treacherous packed snow in the street outside. By seven-thirty she was back in intensive care where, to her indescribably relief, she saw that Michael Thackeray's eyes, sunk in dark sockets, were open.

Her knees almost gave way as she sank into the chair beside the bed to be greeted by the glimmer of a smile.

'You weren't hurt?' he whispered.

'No,' she said. 'How do you feel?'

'Very tired,' he said. She took his hand and bent her head over it to hide her tears.

'There are things I need to tell you,' she said.

'I know, but not now,' Thackeray said faintly and closed his eyes. She stayed beside him for a long time, clasping his hand in hers as if her life and his depended on it.

The publishers hope that this book has given you enjoyable reading. Large Print Books are especially designed to be as easy to see and hold as possible. If you wish a complete list of our books please ask at your local library or write directly to:

Magna Large Print Books
Magna House, Long Preston,
Skipton, North Yorkshire.
BD23 4ND

This Large Print Book, for people
who cannot read normal print,
is published under the auspices of

THE ULVERSCROFT FOUNDATION